The Package

Glenn Crabtree

The Package by Glenn Crabtree
Copyright ©2008 by Glenn Crabtree

All rights reserved. This book is protected under the copyright laws of the United States of America. This book may not be copied or reprinted for commercial gain or profit. Unless otherwise identified,

Scripture taken from the HOLY BIBLE, NEW INTERNATIONAL VERSION®, Copyright ©1973, 1978, 1984 by International Bible Society. Used by permission of Zondervan Publishing House. All rights reserved.

ISBN 978-1-58169-304-1
For Worldwide Distribution
Printed in the U.S.A.

Axiom Press
P.O. Box 191540 • Mobile, AL 36619
800-367-8203

Dedication

To my partner in all things,
my wife, Jenny,

To my children,
Amy, Carrie, Heather, Kellie, Krissy, and Tim,

And to my grandchildren,
Austin, Chase, Christine, Madison, Malachi, Natalie,
Olivia, Trinity, and Whitney,
and others yet known only to Him.

May the message of hope herein
be an inspiration to you all.

Table of Contents

Prologue   1

1. Beginnings   5
2. The Accident   15
3. The Phone Calls   29
4. Emergency Room   40
5. The Promise   47
6. Preparation   65
7. First Night   73
8. Fourth of July   82
9. Memories   87
10. The Nightmare   97
11. Mystery Note   105
12. Sunday Morning   112
13. Revelation   120
14. Counseling   129
15. The Prayer   138
16. The Post Office   145
17. The Package   151
18. The Keys   159
19. Questions Answered   165
20. The Visit   181
21. The Next Spring   189
22. Final Notes   195

Epilogue   204

Foreword

To read *The Package* is to take a trip through the history of a family who, like most in America, wanted a good, safe, and happy life. Instead, they found that life is filled with unexpected twists and turns. I think we are all dreamers to one extent or another. We see the "happily ever after" messages of life and long to find some sense of that experience for ourselves.

The Mullins family wanted to do no less. Our author takes us on a journey with them through beautiful beginnings, the loss of their dreams, and finally their struggle to find their way in an altered world.

One trip to the family cabin changes Jim's life and that of his family forever. A second trip alters eternity for him. *Could it do the same for those he loves?*

Jim's daughter, Stephanie, has secrets that have made her who she is. *Can we hope to have a full and meaningful life when we harbor dark secrets?* Daughter Cassie is a driving force, a perfectionist, who demands much of others and, tragically, even more of herself. *Could we ever know even a measure of joy when we are busy drawing strict lines of behavior for ourselves and others?* And then there is sweet Anna, whose love for her Lord gave her a burning desire to help her sisters find their way to a father who loved them, and to a God who longed to draw them to His heart.

The Package allows us to walk with Jim and those he loved through years of growth, change, and ultimately the greatest gifts a father ever gives his children. What a glorious picture of God, our heavenly Father! What a beautiful story that parallels the walk so many of us are taking as we move toward heaven and home!

Join the author as he opens to us the wondrous story of Jim, Denise, Stephanie, Cassie, and Anna. This is a family that will capture your interest and, through their struggles, will lead you right to the heart of God.

Don't miss this book, for I believe it comes straight to you from a Father who wants you to find freedom from your woundedness, release from your fears, and peaceful resolution in your relationships. *The Package* will give you a beautiful blueprint to help you find each of these gifts of mercy for your life.

As you discover yourself relating on many levels to what is written about this family, I pray, by God's grace, you will discover yourself on the same amazing journey of healing and restoration. It is a gift from your Father, and it will change your life!

Lana Bateman
President of Philippian Ministries, Inc.

Preface

The Package is the culmination of two and a half years of effort, which began when a simple message was delivered to me by a close friend: "God has a gift for you, and he wants you to get out your pencil and paper and wait on him."

In early 2006, after some coaxing, I took that advice and literally set a pencil and some paper in front of me. As I waited with my heart tuned to the voice of the Holy Spirit, the idea for this story came to me. I found myself frantically scribbling down a story line, biographies of characters, and finally the words they spoke—all of which resulted in a play entitled, *The Package*—a process that took a mere ten days.

Over the fifteen years I have been producing Christian theater, numerous people have handed me scripts they believe are—by their own assessment—"great." Yet, upon reading them, I discovered a truth—most of us are misled by our own self-assessments. Possessing that knowledge, I promised myself I would avoid falling into that same trap—I would never write a play—but with this script I had violated my own determined sensibility.

Continuing to set my insecurities aside and stepping out in faith, believing that the story was truly a "gift," the Christian Art Players of Cincinnati, Ohio, brought *The Package* to life in October, 2006. The audience reaction was as we had all hoped—they were enthusiastic about the production. Yet, far beyond what we imagined, the story moved them in a direction toward Christ and caused them to look at their life in a new light.

After viewing the theatrical version, many people encouraged me to further develop the story and characters into a book, believing it would provide many more people the opportunity to receive the story's message of hope. With that encouragement, I proceeded to undertake something that, without God's intervention, I would never have thought to attempt, namely, to write a novel. This task has taken nearly a year and a half to complete, but it has happened with ease, making it seem as though this book was simply meant to be.

It has taken the influence of many people throughout my life to enable this project to come to fruition, some laying foundations that have endured with me for many years. I wish to acknowledge the spiritual mentoring of my lifelong friend, Jerry Morgan, who preached a sermon in a Grange hall when I was eleven that began my journey in a relationship with Christ; the late Dr. Steve Judah, who taught me so much about who I am, and helped me find the ability to emerge whole from personal crisis; Judy Vineyard, whose encouragement to "get my pencil out" brought about this story; Jeff Gordon, whose faithful support of my imagination made the stage version of *The Package* possible; the cast and crew of Christian Art Players production of *The Package* that brought this story alive for the first time (Linda Dew, Amber Browning, Sharon Alcorn, Bob McGuire, Charlie and Pia Rader, Chard Eshom, Wendy Gordon, and Alissa Ashworth); my wife, Jenny, who has walked this journey with me in times of both joy and sacrifice; and my parents, who have given me more blessings than I could count.

Therefore, with great humility of spirit, I pass on to you this "gift," a story given to me by a most gracious heavenly Father: One who *loves* you whether you are bloodied by failures or drowning in sorrow; who *seeks* to bind up your mortal wounds though you are undeserving of mercy; who *longs* for nothing more than a personal relationship with his children—with you—in his time.

–G.C.

PROLOGUE

The storm was finally over.

It began in the early morning hours, and waves of thunder and rain blew through the hollows for most of the night. The previous day was unusually warm for October in western Pennsylvania, and the ensuing cold front came through with a fury. The morning sun, now emerging above the edge of the hilltops, declared its intent to overthrow the mastery of the nighttime storm clouds. Sunlight pierced through the trees to the ground where the warm rainwater was steaming into the cool morning air.

Stephanie Mullins sat on the covered porch of her cabin in an old rocking chair with a wool blanket wrapped around her shoulders. Even without her usual make-up, the morning sun on her face testified of a youthful appearance that defied her thirty-nine years. Her beautiful blond hair usually flowed over her shoulders like a golden waterfall, but on this morning, it was tied up behind her head with a comb and a red ribbon.

A few minutes earlier, Stephanie had emerged from the cabin door dressed only in her pajamas. Once outside, she had found the morning air quite crisp and retreated back inside where she donned some thick socks to insulate her feet from the chilly planks of the porch. She had also pulled the large blanket that now enveloped her over her shoulders.

Stephanie felt refreshed from a good night's sleep. A sound sleep during a thunderstorm was unusual for her. In fact, she usually avoided the attempt altogether, often straining to remain awake. She considered the irony that a storm of such magnitude occurred on her last night at the cabin. *Perhaps,* she thought, *it wasn't simply an ironic coincidence but purposed symbolism.*

Sitting in her rocker and feeling protected from the cool morning air, she continued her usual morning routine. It was a pattern she knew ultimately would be altered, for this day would be unique compared with any she had experienced since she had first come to the cabin nearly fifteen months ago. The smile on her face was evidence of her expectancy.

Stephanie rocked forward and backward in her chair, and with each motion, she heard the rat-a-tat of the rocker bottom hitting against the

The Package

wood planks in the floor. It was a soothing sound she had grown accustomed to hearing. However, on this morning, a quiet melody was underlying the rhythm from the rocker. She pushed her foot against the floor to stop its motion and closed her eyes to listen.

In her self-imposed stillness, the sounds that follow a long, steady rain in the Appalachian forest filled her ears. The nearby brook with its many rocks and tiny waterfalls sang a familiar but indiscernible melody. Droplets barely clinging to the tips of the lofty sycamore leaves were finally yielding, cascading down onto lower leaves and ultimately falling with a gentle but resonant plop onto the leaves that autumn had already brought to the ground. The residual water still draining from the roof quietly gurgled in the downspouts. It seemed as if the water separated from the singing stream were declaring its yearning to join the chorus.

A gentle breeze rustling the leaves on the treetops captured her attention. As she turned her face toward the sound, the passing rays of the sun danced on Stephanie's closed eyelids. She felt its warmth on her cheeks and after a moment, opened her eyes to a shimmering show of light. The sunlight flickered through the ever-changing pattern of leaves and glistened within the raindrops still dangling on their edges.

Stephanie then shifted her gaze back to the grounds around her cabin. As her eyes adjusted from gazing into direct sunlight, the treetop light show found its way through the canopy to the ground. The shimmer made the rising steam appear as though it were actually dancing in celebration. Stephanie's spirit leapt in response, bringing another smile to her face. *Maybe there are angels dancing in the morning mist*, she thought. For Stephanie, it was not unthinkable that angels might be within the mist. She had seen an angel before—at least once.

Suddenly, a chill in her fingers distracted her. In response, she wrapped both hands around her usual morning coffee and picked it up from the small table sitting beside her. In every season of the year, the aroma of a good cup of coffee added to the morning experience. Furthermore, on a cool fall day, it had the added benefit of being hot. Stephanie grasped her mug even more snugly and found the heat quite consoling to her fingers. *Oh, the unsung benefits of coffee in the morning*, she thought to herself. *Great taste, great smell, and a great hand warmer too!*

Stephanie laid her head back onto the rocker for a few minutes while her hands warmed and then again turned her attention to the small table next to her. Lying on the table were several items she had brought out of the cabin with her this morning; namely, two books, a pen, and some stationery.

Still clutching it with both hands, she gently returned her coffee cup to the table. Picking up the books, one in each hand, she laid them side-by-side on her lap, considering the similarities and yet notable differences between them. She had possessed one book for a long period of time; the other, while she was well acquainted with it, had arrived by shipment only yesterday. One she read briefly in bed the night before; the other, she intended to read ceremoniously on a hike this afternoon. She personally knew both authors—one her entire life, the other she had met only recently. Both books conveyed stories of injustice. One told the story of a life deserving punishment, yet received none; and the other depicted a righteous man who was brutally murdered. Both were narratives about a father and his love for his children. Each was a story of love, life, punishment, and death. *Strange bedfellows*, she thought. *Strange, indeed!*

Returning these books to the table, Stephanie picked up the pen and stationery. *One more letter to write*, she thought. On the previous morning, she had written letters to her two sisters, Cassie and Anna. This final letter was one she had planned to write but had deliberately put off until this particular morning. Stephanie wanted to capture what she was feeling at this moment. She had tried hard not to preplan her thoughts.

The fact that she had mixed feelings about what this day would bring was unquestioned. Bouncing the pen on her lip, she looked across the yard to see the real estate sign hanging from its frame. Occasionally, the breeze would rise up and push it just enough so its hooks would creak, as if to remind her it was still there. However, the SOLD placard now sitting above it signified that it would be quieted soon enough.

Stephanie knew that selling the cabin was the right thing to do; perhaps, it was even a necessary thing to do. Resting her head again against the rocker and closing her eyes, a smile appeared as she recalled memories of life in this cabin: summer days with her parents, the Fourth of July with her sisters, and the day that the package arrived—the package that changed her life forever. However, painful recollections suddenly punctuated her warm thoughts, causing her smile to subside. Dark memories of the accident, the nightmares, and the violation challenged her confidence.

Shaking that conflict aside, Stephanie had to acknowledge that this moment was one of the best of her life. On this, her 39th birthday, she would begin a new chapter. Putting the pain behind her once and for all,

The Package

her future would begin, and her past would die. Like a tree sheds its leaves, she would shed that which was used up; and like that same tree, she would give birth to new life like the coming of spring. She paused to pray and thank God for the day.

Stephanie reopened her eyes, put her pen to paper, and began to write. But only moments later, her mind again drifted back to the sunshine dancing on the ground. She sat back in her chair again and watched the dance of creation around her. It truly was a celebration, and she knew it.

1

BEGINNINGS

Stephanie Mullins was born on October 9, 1970 and grew up in the town of Whitaker, Pennsylvania. Her father, Jim, settled there with Denise, her mother, when they were first married in 1967. In those days, Whitaker was a small bedroom community that housed many of the workers from the large steel mill across the river in Braddock. It was a sleepy town sitting on a plateau overlooking the winding Monongahela River about ten miles southeast of Pittsburgh. Whitaker was many things to many people, but first and foremost, it was a steel town.

Jim and Denise were high school sweethearts, and Denise sacrificed much of her young adult life waiting for her love to complete his enlistment in the Army. Jim's father had served in the South Pacific in World War II, and Jim grew up listening to reports of the Korean War on the radio. James, as his mother called him, was a patriotic young fellow in whom his father had instilled a belief that every young man owed service to his country. While Jim's love for Denise caused his heart to challenge that conviction, he knew he could not thwart his sense of obligation. Denise prayed he would change his mind, but she knew that she could not demand it of him because for Jim, it was a matter of honor.

Four years later, the long wait was over. Jim's discharge followed two long years of duty in Vietnam. The elation of returning home to Denise's arms was enough to bring the young soldier to tears. But even after his return, he continued to do what he had done every day for four years. Each morning he replayed his memory of Denise standing in that bright yellow dress, waving good-bye with tears in her eyes and blowing kisses to him as he boarded the train for boot camp.

Jim was head-over-heels in love with Denise before he left. But after experiencing the dregs of humanity, which is a consequence of the ugliness of war, and returning home to a beautiful woman who had loved him faith-

The Package

fully throughout their separation, that made him love her with a depth that defied his description. This was not because he was unable to verbalize his feelings, but because they were deeper than his own understanding. He simply loved her beyond words.

If it had been possible, Jim would have gladly married Denise on his first day home. But Denise had dreamed of a beautiful, formal church wedding, and she asked that they wait. Jim was grateful that she had faithfully waited for him, so he determined in his heart to return that same gift to her. He would wait for her, and patiently.

But a mere two days after his return, an excited Denise suggested they forgo the formality and get married as soon as possible. She was impatient; she had endured four long years without him. Now, with him standing right there, near her, holding her, talking to her—she simply could wait no longer. He shouted agreement before she finished her first sentence.

So with that, Jim and Denise married that next weekend in a simple ceremony in a little church a few miles north of Pittsburgh. After a brief reception, they headed for a honeymoon in Atlantic City, New Jersey, and spent a romantic two weeks basking in the sun, laughing in the ocean surf, riding the giant Ferris wheel, and strolling on the boardwalk together. But on that first night, they didn't make it any further than the hotel three miles up the road toward the interstate. After all, they had both waited for more than four years. And, as the truth came out much later, they didn't exactly check out the next day either.

After returning from their honeymoon, Jim took a job at the Braddock Steel Mill and within a few weeks, they purchased their small home across the river in Whitaker. Without much surprise, slightly more than nine months later in June of 1968, the family had its first addition—Cassidy Ann Mullins. For Jim and Denise, it was an unparalleled day in their lives. In their arms, they held a child who was the manifestation of their love for one another. In Cassie, they saw the focus of their hopes and dreams for the future. Parenting was as natural as breathing for both of them, and Jim discovered that he now had another sweetheart. He was a steel man, but a smile and a giggle from his little girl melted any toughness inside him with ease.

As a mother, Denise was gentle and loving. Her warm, engaging smile had captured Jim's heart within a moment of their first meeting. She was passionate about everything; she loved to talk, sing, and laugh out loud; her energy brought life to every corner of their home. She was kind in her manner, compassionate in her correction, and comforting whenever a fall bruised an elbow. She was efficient in managing their home, somehow staying ahead of the laundry, cleaning, and cooking, while being frugal in every way she could. Jim would sometimes purposefully sit at the kitchen table or on the sofa and admire her routine at a distance; she seemed to glide through life with ease. He could not believe that he could be so fortunate.

In contrast to her gregarious temperament, Jim had a quiet nature. It was not the kind of quiet that exhibits uncertainty, but one which results from an inner strength—a tranquil self-confidence that requires no assurance. He was like a calm sea possessing the strength to bring calamity but exercising restraint to subsist in peace.

A mere nine months after Cassie was born, the second miracle in their married life occurred, when, in early 1970, Denise became pregnant again. Jim already had a daughter, and though he never voiced it, this time he hoped for a son. When October came and Denise delivered another baby girl, Jim's past hopes were forgotten. Holding little Stephanie Lynn, it took only a moment to rediscover his soft heart for little girls. "There is a special relationship between fathers and daughters," he would tell friends with a wide smile, and Jim cherished those special relationships every day.

Jim continued to support his young family by working at the mill, and his conscientiousness and diligence earned him a promotion to foreman. However, his career was not his passion. To say he had no great love for the steel business would be an understatement. Working steel was a hot, dirty, and sometimes dangerous business. But the work was steady in those days, it paid well, and it provided for his family. In fact, Jim had only three passions in his life—his wife, his little girls, and the Allegheny Mountains of Pennsylvania.

"You think those are mountains!" a man at church laughed. "You should see Colorado!"

Jim rolled his eyes and shook his head. He had heard that comparison too many times in his life. "I've seen Colorado," he answered, "big, bold, rocky crags. But my mountains are covered top to bottom with a blanket of green. The biggest and the brashest isn't always the best."

Jim had a way with words, which made him appear to be a contradiction. He was a tough and masculine steel foreman; however, he was also one who could sometimes speak effusively, rendering profound truths with sophistication. Friends and acquaintances knew that Jim had little to say most of the time. They also knew that when he did speak, even with very few words, he said a great deal.

With the arrival of the summer of 1972, the anxious family awaited the birth of their third child and a new sibling. Early in the pregnancy, Jim and Denise decided that if the baby were a girl, they would name her Sophia, which was Denise's mother's name. If it were a boy, they would name him Daniel. Twenty-month-old Stephanie, at her father's coaxing, wanted a little brother and would put her ear to her mommy's womb and talk to the baby in her own toddler language calling him, "An-nyl." So when Denise delivered another baby girl, she suggested they name her Anna because of the phonetic similarity to the name Stephanie had called the baby in the womb. Thus, Anna Sophia became the newest member of the Mullins family, and she was Grandma Sophie's pride and joy, for obvious reasons.

Six weeks after Anna was born, Grandma Sophie offered to watch the girls for the evening while Jim and Denise went out on a date to celebrate their fifth wedding anniversary. They dressed up and dined together by candlelight at the best restaurant in town. Jim could not help but notice how stunning Denise looked in the black dress she had purchased for this occasion. Her long brown hair had a natural waviness that reflected the various colors of light within the room. When she looked at him, he could see the candlelight dancing in her beautiful green eyes.

"So, Daddy," she asked, "what's it like to have three daughters?"

"It's wonderful," he said. "I couldn't be happier."

"I thought you might be disappointed about not having a son."

"Not really," he said, hesitating for a moment. "Well, maybe just a little. But I love the girls."

"I know you do," she said.

Jim remembered that when Denise was pregnant, she suggested that if the baby weren't a boy, perhaps they should try once more. He was curious as to whether her feelings had changed.

"Do you still want four children?" he asked.

"What about you?" asked Denise, gently tapping the edge of her lip with her napkin, being careful not to smudge her lipstick.

"I asked first," he said. "Don't make this my decision."

"Well, to be honest," she answered, "I thought I would want another child when I was pregnant. But I'm not so sure now."

"Why?" he asked.

"Well, thinking about the future, we need to be realistic. I want to be able to provide for them. I want them to have a good life, and not have to make constant sacrifices at every turn."

"I'm happy with our girls," he said, "and I want you to know I don't need a son to be happy. I was afraid I would hurt your feelings to say so. I simply want to fulfill your hopes and dreams."

Denise sensed his sincerity. "Do you know what one of my dreams is?" she asked.

"What?"

"I want the children to go to college."

"Don't you think they're a little young?" he said, laughing.

"You know what I mean, silly," she said, waving him off with her hand and smirking. "Seriously though, I always wanted to go but could never afford it. I want to make sure we set some money aside to make it possible for them; that is, if they want to go."

"Let's work on a financial plan to make that happen," he said, smiling. "That's a good dream. We need to get started." Jim's mood grew subdued as he continued dinner, and Denise sensed the change.

"What about your dreams, Jim?" she asked. "What do you want?"

"My dream sounds selfish after that," he said, embarrassed. "We need to do what you said. We need to plan for the girls' future. That's the right thing to do."

"Come on, Jim," she said. "Let's have it."

"It's silly, really. It's nonsense."

"James Mullins, I am not leaving here until you tell me." She shook her fork at him and said, "You got it?"

Jim was practical and realistic, and knew that Denise was careful with money. He couldn't imagine how his dream could be affordable. It went without saying. But he also knew he was backed into a corner—she would insist that he tell her. He decided to relent and put his fork down on his plate, freeing up his hands. He needed them to communicate passionately. It was his way.

"Denise," he began, "you know I grew up in a very rural area. No fire hydrants, sidewalks, or street lights." Jim struggled because he didn't want to disappoint Denise or make her feel insecure. "Please understand, sweetheart, Whitaker is a lovely town. And wherever we live is fine, as long as I'm sharing my life with you."

"Yes," she said as she licked the tip of her finger and playfully marked

9

The Package

an imaginary point for him in the air. It was a sweet thing for him to say. "But, go on," she encouraged.

"But my dream?" he said. "My dream would be to own a cabin in the woods. A place where our children can run and play freely, without the confines of a neighbor's yard, a fence, or the danger of a city street."

"Do you want to move?" she asked gently, trying to hide her concern.

"No, darling," he answered. "I know that's impossible. We need to live near the mill. I need the job. But, now and then, I dream about having a place away from the city where we could spend weekends and time off together."

At that moment, Jim realized that between his embarrassment and becoming lost in his imagination, he was not looking at Denise. He slowly directed his eyes back toward her. She sat with her elbows on the table, resting her chin on her hands, while still clutching her fork. She smiled as her compassionate eyes again glistened in the candlelight. "It's a crazy dream, I know," he admitted as he began eating energetically, trying to dismiss the topic. "We can't afford that, especially if we need a college fund for the girls. And we do." He quickly picked up his wine glass and took a drink.

Denise set down her fork and reached across the table with an open hand. He felt ashamed for what he perceived as a self-centered discussion. But he put down his glass and placed his hand in hers, although he was still not looking at her directly.

"Jim," she said gently, trying to attract his eyes. "Jim," she said again. He finally looked up toward her.

"It's not crazy at all," she said with passion. "You simply want your girls to feel some of what you felt growing up. That isn't something to be embarrassed or ashamed about, and spending time away together as a family would be precious." She gave him a loving, encouraging smile and squeezed his hand. "It's not crazy, Jim. It's your dream, and it's beautiful."

Jim shook his head in amazement as he looked at her and remembered why he loved her, as if it could be possible ever to forget.

"For now," she continued, still squeezing his hand, "I suggest we make one evening a week 'family night,' and we'll use that time to take the kids to dinner, a park, or a special event. And we'll find some places to visit on the weekends away from the city. Deal?"

"Deal," he said. "That would be great! It would be good for the kids, and I would enjoy some weekend getaways. That's a great plan!" Jim suddenly realized he might be a little over exuberant. "But it would be lot of work for you, though, with the baby and all, to even prepare for that."

"We can do it," she said, shaking his hand. He knew that she could too. Denise could do anything she determined to do. "Anna won't be a baby forever," she said as she resumed dinner. "We've got plenty of time. We'll keep saving, and who knows?" she said, giving him a wink coupled with a hopeful smile.

Jim smiled bashfully and looked away; Denise was flirting with him. But then he gazed at her intently as her focus turned to a waiter who was pouring her another glass of iced tea. It seemed that she just grew more beautiful every day.

They continued their meals quietly for a few minutes, each one considering what they had shared with the other. Finally, Denise introduced a new subject. "We probably should start taking the kids to church too," she said. "Don't you agree?"

"What brought that up?" he asked.

"It's something I've been thinking about. We both attended church when we started dating. But with the war and all, we got out of the habit. The kids should be going, though. If for no other reason, we should do it for them. Right?"

"Yes," he had to acknowledge. "You're right. We should do that."

Jim knew this was a responsibility of having kids; you took them to church. His parents took him; Denise's parents took her. Responsible parents started taking their children to church at some point. But Jim wasn't fanatical like some people. True, the Christian faith was the faith of his parents and had been passed down to become his faith. It should be the faith of his children. At his core, he believed taking his children to church was important, and he would do it. He would do it for them; he would do it for Denise.

In the autumn weeks and months that followed, Jim and Denise kept their promises to each other and spent considerable family time together. They visited a number of local churches, settled on one they liked, and began attending faithfully. College funds were started for the kids, and every week Denise would go to the bank and make deposits into each of their accounts. But she made another weekly deposit as well. Since she kept the checkbook and paid the bills, she was able to set up a secret fourth account—a "dream" account—that Jim knew nothing about.

Denise saved with discipline for nearly five years as they continued with their family nights and weekends away. In August of 1976, Jim and Denise attended a fundraiser where a man mentioned that his grandfather was selling an old cabin in the hills. With Denise by his side, Jim seemed dispassionate about it. But later, from across the room, Denise watched Jim latch on to that gentleman for the entire evening like an unrelenting toddler, gathering every single piece of information he could about the cabin. Continuing to observe him from a distance, she couldn't help but be hopeful and excited for him.

After they arrived home, as they prepared for bed, she asked him about the discussion. "I heard you talking about a cabin to that man at the party tonight," she said.

"Yes," he answered. "He mentioned it when you were standing there with me, didn't he?"

"He *mentioned* it?" she replied in a mock accusation.

"Well, *he* brought it up."

"And you talked about it for *two hours*," she said. "Did you talk to anyone else about anything else tonight?"

"I'm sorry, Denise," he said. "I guess I got carried away. I'm sorry if I upset you. I won't let it happen again." He gave her a hug and a kiss, feeling sorry that he had let his imagination get the best of him.

They both climbed into bed and lay there for a few moments without speaking. Denise seemed lost in thought and looked at the ceiling with a vacant stare. Jim knew he'd upset her, but her distant mood was uncharacteristic. Maybe she was pregnant and was afraid to tell him.

"Are you going to turn out the light?" he asked hesitantly.

"After you tell me how much," she answered.

He was pleased she was giving him a way out, and he rose up on his elbow and looked at her. "I love you more than you could possibly imagine," he said, smiling.

She grinned and popped her head off the pillow and gave him a gentle kiss. "You sweet man," she said. "That was a good answer. But I want you to tell me how much he wants for the cabin."

"Too much," he said. "Forty-five thousand. Might be able to get it for less than forty, though. I don't know. Why?"

"How much of a down payment would you need?"

"At least ten percent. Why?"

"Want to go look at it this weekend with the kids?" she asked, still feigning a bit of impatience.

"Denise, that's a wonderful and kind thought," he said with regret. "But we don't have four thousand dollars." He dropped his head back onto his pillow, realizing the futility of their conversation.

"You have no idea what you have," she said, without moving from her pillow.

"Oh yes I do," he said, easing back up onto his elbow and gently brushing her cheek with the back of his fingers.

"No, you don't," she said, giggling with delight. She excitedly reached under her pillow and flipped opened a savings account book in front of his face. She tried again to put on a sense of seriousness. "What about this? What do you know about this?" she asked.

Jim looked at the savings book and saw a balance of $3,718.40.

"What is this?" he said, looking confused. "I've never seen this before."

She hid her face behind the book and peered over its top edge with her eyes. "It's your dream, Jim," she said. She then lowered it to reveal her full face and repeated it again softly. "It's your dream."

"What are you talking about?" he said, still confused.

"I've been secretly saving this for five years, since our fifth anniversary when you told me about wanting a cabin." She placed the savings book in his hand and closed his fingers around it. "It's my gift to you. We can take a little money from each of the girls' college funds to make up the difference."

Jim was speechless.

"We can do this!" she said, giggling with excitement.

"You've been saving this for five years," asked Jim, with tears in his eyes, "for me?"

"I waited on my first dream for four years," she explained, stroking his face with her hand. "And here you are with me. I learned that good dreams require patience. A good dream is worth waiting for." He still could not speak. "So, do you want to go next weekend?" she asked.

To Jim, the next weekend seemed like it was a year away. He called off work the very next day, and he and Denise made a trip to the hills while the kids were in school. With Denise's secret piggy bank, Jim was able to close the deal on the cabin, and within a few weeks, he became its owner. The day Jim first held the keys to the cabin was one of the best days of his life. Only his wedding day and the days his children were born could top it. He felt like a teenager with his first crush.

That very next weekend, he and Denise took the children on a surprise trip to the cabin. As they walked through the front door, Denise wrapped her arms around his neck, looked in his eyes, and smiled. "Welcome to your

The Package

dream," she said, while kissing his lips. He responded by pulling her closer. "I brought my dream with me," he said, giving her a wink and another kiss.

As they went about the business of unpacking the car, Jim paused on the porch as he often did at home to simply watch her; again, he realized how much he loved her. With a little planning, she had changed his life. Twice she had shown extreme patience—once when she had waited four years to marry him and again when she surreptitiously saved money for this cabin for five long years.

It was a lesson he would never forget.

2

THE ACCIDENT

The Mullins family enjoyed eight years of summer weekends and holidays together at the cabin, swimming in the local creek, hiking in the woods, chasing crawdads and tiny fish in the nearby brook, and playing card or board games in the evenings. On cooler spring or fall days, they would sit next to a crackling fire in the fireplace and drink cups of cocoa while they played games together. The days at the cabin built a sense of family unity that couldn't be duplicated in the day-to-day bustle of life in Whitaker. Each of them found joy in their relationships with the others, and comfort in the solitude of the woods and meadows that surrounded the cabin.

As the years passed and the girls became teenagers, they would frequently bring friends with them for weekends away at the cabin. Jim and Denise had the wisdom to understand that inviting the girls' friends along brought benefits to the family. It helped ease one of the difficult challenges that every teenager faces—the choice to spend time with family at the expense of time with friends. For the girls, it was an opportunity to build friendships in a unique way—by sharing the place they found so special.

But time changes all things, be they good or bad, and in the fall of 1987, its relentless march ushered in a new era for the Mullins family—the first fledgling emerged from the nest. In early September, Jim and Denise stood with Cassie on the campus of Boston College, trying to muster the courage to say good-bye and then begin the long journey back home without her. Cassie, now 18, was beginning her freshman year, and while this parting was long-planned, the reality of it was creating anxiety. As they stood near the car, struggling to part ways, Denise beamed and said, "I'm so proud of you, sweetheart."

"Thanks, Mom," said Cassie. "I really like it here. But maybe I shouldn't have picked a college so far from home."

The Package

"Cassie, we've discussed this again and again, and every time you've concluded this is the right place for you. It's your heart's desire." Placing her hands on Cassie's shoulders at arm's length, Denise stared into her eyes and said, "I understand you're feeling a little scared and sad right now, but you'll be fine. I promise."

"I know I will," said Cassie, pulling her mother into an embrace. "But I'll miss you both so much."

Cassie gave her mother a kiss on the cheek, then stepped backwards and held both her hands for a moment, smiling at her with a tear in her eye. Releasing her mother's hands, she then gave her father an energetic hug. He responded warmly, planted a kiss on her cheek, and slowly backed away.

Jim got into the car and watched as Cassie embraced her mother one last time. Denise, with her eyes fixed on Cassie the entire time, worked her way to the car, opened her door, and then climbed inside. As Jim backed out of the parking space and they drove away, everyone waved to each other until the car rounded a curve and Cassie was out of sight.

Within a few quiet minutes, Jim saw that Denise was staring numbly out her window at nothing. "Are you okay?" he asked gently.

Denise turned toward him, and suddenly her face melted into a sob that she quickly hid behind a tissue from her purse. Jim understood that Denise had practiced restraint to bolster her own dream—a college education for her daughter. Therefore, she had disciplined her emotions for Cassie's sake; but now, freed from her self-imposed obligation, her feelings overwhelmed her. The dam that had restrained her tears had finally given way. He touched her hand but said nothing, understanding her need to release her emotions.

As Denise had predicted, Cassie adjusted well to the college environment, and they talked often on the phone, though she stayed on campus until the Thanksgiving holiday. At Christmas, she arrived home having excellent first semester grades, and her family was extremely proud and excited about her success.

When Cassie returned to school in early January, the weather along the Ohio Valley turned extremely cold, making for a long, bitter winter. Weekend trips to the cabin had diminished since the early fall, largely due to Stephanie and Anna's high school activities that dominated the family's schedule. But finally, early April brought with it the promise of a beautiful weekend, and the weather, coupled with the providence of a free schedule, presented the first opportunity of the year to return to the cabin.

The Accident

That first evening back at the cabin was as most other Friday evenings spent there. Friday was family night, a tradition that had carried over from when the girls were small. Once they had all settled into their rooms and finished dinner, they built a fire in the fireplace and played a game of Monopoly at the kitchen counter. Denise made hot chocolate—a family night tradition. They played and laughed together well past midnight.

As much as they all enjoyed that evening at the cabin, not everything had been fun and games. Over the years, Jim had learned that the deed to the cabin came with a free do-it-yourself maintenance plan. Earlier in the evening, Jim's usual inspection of the cabin had revealed that a previous storm removed several of the wood shingles from the roof. Realizing that the weather forecast called for thunderstorms on Saturday afternoon, Jim laid out a plan to replace the missing shingles the next morning before the wind and rain rolled in later that day.

Early that next morning, Jim began organizing his tools and made a trip to the hardware store to get the necessary supplies. Climbing up on the roof about mid-afternoon, he began making the necessary repairs. He initially thought he'd have no trouble finishing before the storm arrived, but the damage in a few places was more extensive than he had anticipated. Standing on the roof with additional work yet remaining, he observed that the sun was beginning to set, and thunderclouds on the horizon were causing the twilight to accelerate into darkness.

In this "neck of the woods," as Jim would say, losing electricity for several days following a big storm was commonplace, so the wise homeowner kept a stash of emergency supplies stocked and ready. Late that afternoon, consistent with her usual pre-storm routine, Denise checked the cupboard to assure that they had sufficient provisions. She inspected the flashlights, candles, and matches—all were adequate. However, they were nearly out of propane gas bottles, which were fuel for several lanterns and a cook stove, so she picked up her purse and a rain jacket, walked outside, and called out to Jim on the roof, "I need to run to the store to get some propane." Kneeling on the roof, Jim looked back over his shoulder and saw her standing near their car with her purse in hand. "I checked the cupboards, and we're out," she continued. "We have only part of one container."

"Okay," Jim shouted back, "I should be done in about half an hour. I'll take you when I finish."

"Honey," she answered, "it's getting dark, and I think we may need it. The radio says this storm is pretty big. There's already a severe thunderstorm warning fifteen miles west of here."

The Package

Jim knew she was right. The wind was already blowing hard enough to make it difficult to hear and challenging to stand on the roof. "All right, here are the keys to the car," shouted Jim as he threw the keys from the roof to the ground in front of Denise.

"Okay, I'll be back in a few," she answered. Denise blew him a kiss as she got into the car. She backed the car up to turn it around and pulled forward out of the driveway. Jim waved to her as she headed down the road and reengaged in his effort to finish the roof ahead of the storm.

Denise drove toward a small general store with several gas pumps outside called the Puddle Stop, which was located about five miles north of the cabin next to a very small pond—hence the name. A stocky, red-haired fellow named Bart Ferris owned this local landmark. He was outgoing and friendly, which were necessary traits for anyone owning a successful business in this or most any rural area. Everyone knew Bart and liked him, and Bart treated everyone who entered the store as a friend. Bart stood at the front window of his store, peering upward at the ominous clouds overhead. While he watched, Denise pulled into the parking lot, exited her car, and then scurried into the store, mere seconds before the sky burst open.

"Hey, Bart! How ya feelin'?" she asked whimsically. Teasing Bart was Denise's standard procedure, and Bart likewise returned her banter.

"With my fingers!" he replied, laughing.

"Well, I haven't heard that one since . . . when was it? . . . The Stone Age?"

"Oh, that hurts," he said. "How about this rain? Big storm, looks like."

"Yep," said Denise, breaking away and heading for the rack where the propane cylinders were kept. "That's why I'm here!"

"Where's that husband of yours?" yelled Bart. "Has he done run off and left ya?"

From somewhere out of sight she yelled back, laughing, "Actually, I done run off and left him!" Her tone turned serious. "Bart, I don't see any propane cylinders back here. You have any?"

Bart walked back to the rack where Denise was standing and searched its contents. "Gee, Denise, it looks like I'm out," he said. "I think I got some coming in next week. You want me to set some back for ya?"

"No," she said. "I need some tonight, so I'll run over to the store in Hope."

"Hope's a pretty small town," he said. "Sure you remember how to get there?"

The Accident

This was an old joke Denise had heard at least a hundred times. She said the punch line with him as she moved toward the door. "Wouldn't want you to get hope-lessly lost!"

"Stone Age, Bart!" she smirked, scurrying out the door while pulling her jacket over her head. "Good-bye!"

"Bye!" said Bart, smiling and waving to her as she left. From the security of his front window, he watched her get into her car and drive off into the storm. Bart always enjoyed seeing Denise—she always brought a smile.

Back at the cabin, Jim had just finished the required shingling in a light drizzle when the storm finally arrived in full force. Raindrops as large as quarters pummeled Jim as he scurried down the ladder. Leaving it resting against the side of the roof, he rushed inside the cabin to avoid getting drenched. Once inside, he checked his watch and realized that his "half hour to finish" had turned into an hour—like most every task he did. He also noted that Denise hadn't returned, and knowing that her trip should have taken only a half hour, he became concerned.

Within a short period of time, darkness had fallen, and Denise was still not home. Amid the loud crashes of thunder and waves of rain, Jim frequented the front window watching for her arrival. Stephanie and Anna, both sitting on the sofa, were passing the time reading. Jim's pacing to and from the window so distracted and annoyed Stephanie that she suggested he call the Puddle Stop.

Jim took her advice and called Bart to see if Denise had been there. "Jim," he said, "we were completely sold out of propane, so I think Denise headed over to Hope to get some. Sorry." Jim felt a sense of relief, now having an explanation for the delay. "If I see her," said Bart, "I'll have her call you."

At that moment, a blazing white light was instantly accompanied by a gigantic, deafening thunderclap, causing both Stephanie and Anna to shriek. Simultaneously, the phone went dead, and the light in the room evaporated, as if the darkness breathed it in and it were no more.

Thinking that a lightning bolt might actually have hit the cabin, Jim became momentarily distracted from his worries about Denise. In the darkness, he and the girls searched the cupboard for the candles and matches stored there. After they found and lit several of them and placed them around the room, they heard the sound of a car arriving and saw passing headlights from the window flash across the room. Jim headed toward the door, relieved that Denise had finally returned. But before he got to the

The Package

door, he noticed that the room was filled with a modulating red light coming through the window. Jim, now frantic, flung the door open and stepped out on the porch to see a deputy sheriff's car with its emergency lights blazing. The deputy opened his door, and holding on to his hat in the wind and rain, he began moving toward the house. Jim, now oblivious to the rain, ran to meet him halfway.

"Are you Jim Mullins?" the deputy shouted over the pouring rain.

"Yes," he answered. There was a brief moment where the only noise was the splatter of the rain beating on the brim of the deputy's hat.

"I am very sorry, Mr. Mullins, but I have some bad news for you." The deputy pointed toward his car. "Can you come with me?"

Jim stood in the pouring rain, recognizing there was trouble yet feeling uncertain as to what he should do. He looked back toward the cabin and saw Stephanie and Anna with their faces pressed against the front window. Jim looked again at the deputy, who had begun moving toward his car. Wiping the rain from his eyes, he shifted his gaze back toward the faces in the window again. While Stephanie and Anna were now teenagers, as he stared at them in this crisis, they appeared as vulnerable young children. Returning to where Jim stood, the deputy shouted, "Are you coming, sir?"

"I need to go into the house," Jim shouted. "Can you come in please?"

The deputy hesitated for a moment, nodded yes, and together they made a run for the front door. Followed by the deputy, Jim went into the cabin. As they entered, both girls left the window and rushed to their father, saying nearly in unison, "What's wrong, Dad?"

"Something's happened, girls," he answered. He stood between them, placed an arm around each of them, and held them close. The deputy's flashlight combined with the flickering candles made the light dance eerily in the room. The deputy moved to stand in front of the three of them.

"Okay, what happened?" Jim asked nervously. The deputy paused and looked at the girls and back to Jim as if to warn him that the news was bad. "What's happened?" Jim demanded more urgently.

"There was an accident over on Route 8, a few miles west of the town of Hope. Lightning hit a tree and knocked it down across the road. It was on a blind curve, and a car came around the corner and crashed into it. We pulled the registration on the car. It says it's registered to you. Someone at the scene knew you; they told us you were probably here."

Jim weakened as fear overcame him. He eked out the question he knew he needed to ask, "Is my wife okay?"

The Accident

"There was a Denise Mullins driving the car," he continued, cautiously. "I assume she is your wife?"

As Jim nodded yes, he stared into the face of the deputy, whose demeanor betrayed him—he looked like a man who had told a sad story far too many times. He took off his hat with deliberation and said, "I'm very sorry, sir. I'm afraid your wife didn't make it. I'm really very, very sorry."

"Where is she?" cried Stephanie. "Can we see her?" The deputy didn't get a chance to answer before she latched onto his jacket at the shoulders. "*Where is she!*" she demanded, before finally collapsing to her knees in front of him, sobbing.

Anna broke away from her father's arms and melted onto the sofa. "Oh, my God," she said softly. "Oh, my God."

Using his sleeves, the deputy acted as though he were wiping rain off his face in order to hide the tears of compassion he was shedding. "I'm sorry. She was taken to the county hospital. But there's nothing they can do for her. I can take you, if you like."

Jim nodded yes. He and his daughters struggled to gather themselves while they labored to pull their raincoats on, went to the police car, and began the trip to the hospital. Jim buckled his seat belt, and as he sat quietly in the front seat of the police car for the next few minutes, he fought to maintain his composure, feeling so incredibly empty and helpless. The sights and sounds around them blended together into an unmanageable chaos: the girls whimpering in the back seat, the flashing red lights illuminating the passing trees, the pounding of the wipers, and an image of Denise blowing him that last kiss. Overwrought, Jim finally broke down and sobbed like a child.

While struggling through her own sorrow and tears, Anna heard her father crying in the front seat. He had always been so strong, and while he was sensitive, she had never seen him this distraught. She tried to console him by reaching up and touching his shoulder.

Jim turned toward Anna, reacting to her touch. Compassion was apparent in her face, and it strengthened him enough to regain his composure. Knowing he needed to be strong for his girls, his crying eased a little at her encouragement. Again, he sat silently for a few additional minutes, trying to corral his emotions. He looked across the car at the deputy, who had taken charge and was handling the situation. Jim guessed that he couldn't be more than twenty-five or thirty—only a few years older than his own children. *How much tragedy he has seen in his young life*, he thought.

The Package

The deputy caught him staring. "I'm sorry, sir," he said. "I wish I could give you some kind of hope."

"It's Jim," he said. "Please call me Jim."

"Yes, sir. I mean—Jim. I'm sorry."

It was quite late in the evening when Jim finished his business at the hospital. Having now confirmed that the truth he sought to deny was indeed reality, he picked up the phone and called Cassie in Boston.

"Hello?" she answered.

"Cassie?"

"Dad? Is that you?"

"Yes," he answered.

"It's pretty late," she said. "What's up?"

"Cassie, there's no easy way to say this, so I'll just come right out and say it."

"What's wrong?" she asked, concerned.

"There was a car accident tonight, and your mother—" His voice broke. "Your mother was in the car. She died, Cassie."

"*What!*"

"Cassie, I'm sorry," he said sadly. "I'm so sorry. I don't know what else to say." There was nothing but silence on the phone. "Cassie," he said worriedly.

"I'm here," she said, struggling. "How?"

"A storm blew a tree across the road. She was driving alone, came around a blind curve, and crashed into the tree. There was another driver following her, a young man with his girlfriend. They collided into the back of the car and crushed it farther into the tree."

"Oh, dear God," she responded.

"They think it happened when the second car hit her. She died before they got her to the hospital. I'm sorry, Cassie. I know this is a terrible way to find out."

"Dad, I'll call . . . I'll call the airline," she stammered, crying. "I'll be home as soon as . . . as soon as I can get there. Okay?" It was the extent of what she could express through her tears.

"I'll call you back to find out when you're arriving," he answered, "and I'll pick you up at the airport. I still need to find a car to get back home."

"Okay, Dad," she said. "You okay?"

The Accident

"I don't know what to say, Cassie. I'm still in shock."

They stayed on the line for a few more minutes while saying almost nothing. Neither one could bear to disconnect from each other. But, out of necessity, they each finally said goodnight.

That night, while the rain continued to fall and the wind howled, a grieving husband and three brokenhearted daughters shed tears on four different pillows. Many prayers were said, and while none of them realized it at the time, each of their prayers was heard.

A friend who lived near the cabin drove Jim, Stephanie, and Anna to Whitaker late the next day, and Jim picked up Cassie at the airport. Over the next several weeks, Jim's life became a swirl of frenzied emotions as he dealt with the funeral, his daughters, and his sense of loss and loneliness. He did all he could to fight through the pain, using every scrap of knowledge and experience he had. However, it rapidly became more than he was equipped to manage.

Cassie returned to Boston shortly after the funeral to resume her studies. In early May, about two weeks after the funeral, Jim made a move that surprised most of his friends. He decided to take a month off from work to spend some time "away from it all" in his cabin. Jim was usually a predictable man, and even he was aware that this move was somewhat unconventional.

"You're going back to the cabin?" asked one of Jim's close friends, feeling somewhat surprised.

"Yes, I am," he said. "My cabin is still a solace for me, still a place of beauty, and it is still the last place on earth I saw Denise alive."

"Don't you think it would be better for you and the girls to move on?" his friend asked.

"I am moving on," he replied. "This is what I need to do in order to move on."

Since it was May, Stephanie and Anna were still in school with about a month remaining before the summer break. Convinced that he needed the time away, Jim made arrangements with the school for the girls to complete their studies at the cabin. He thought the time away might also do the girls some good. The first major family conflict without Denise occurred when Jim discussed this plan with Stephanie.

"What about my friends?" she said. "My life is here."

The Package

"I think the time away as a family will be good for all of us," he answered.

"We aren't a family anymore! We can't *be* a family anymore!" she shouted as she began storming out of the room. "I am not going back to that stuffy old cabin. My life is here—in Whitaker!" Stephanie terminated the conversation with the slamming of her bedroom door.

Jim had to acknowledge that Stephanie was right; in some sense, they weren't a family anymore. Denise was the glue that held them all together. It wasn't because of any personal shortcoming on his part. He was a good father. His children loved him; he loved them. But, in truth, what *was* their family was now no more.

Jim had tried to resolve this issue with Stephanie more than a few times, and it was clear that neither of them was budging from their initial position. The discussions had escalated into serious arguments that were becoming vicious. But Jim also understood that the emotions after the funeral were running strong and deep, and in that understanding, he found a way to excuse the bad behavior for both of them. However, no matter how he tried, Jim could not shake what he felt was his need to go to the cabin— the need to get away. He finally told Stephanie that she simply *had* to go with him. To say her response was negative would be an extreme understatement.

On the morning of the day that Jim had planned to leave for the cabin, for some reason that he could not explain, Jim decided to take the girls to church in Whitaker. The service was pleasant, but he could not reconcile his feeling of loneliness. He had never been to church without Denise; they had always gone together.

Following the service, as he headed toward the exit, he heard a voice cry out, "Jim!" He turned and saw Theresa Allen, one of Denise's close friends, making her way through the crowd toward him.

"Jim," she said again more gently as she embraced him. "How are you doing?"

"I don't know, Theresa," he replied. "I've never been through anything like this before. How can I get my arms around it? I really can't explain it to you."

"Denise loved you and your girls with her whole heart," she said, trying to reassure him. "I know. She told me—often."

"I don't know how to go on without her, Theresa." He saw concern in her face. "I'm not trying to scare you. It's just that . . . well, I need to figure out how to do it . . . learn how to go on."

24

The Accident

"Focus on your girls, Jim," she said. "They need you."

"And I need them," he said. "Maybe more than they need me."

"I'll pray for you, Jim. If there is something more I can do, name it."

"All right," he said. "Since you offered, I plan to go to the cabin today and stay there for a while with the girls. Can you keep an eye on the house for me?"

"Are you sure that's a good idea?" she asked.

"Why would your keeping an eye on the house be a bad idea?" he answered.

"No," she said. "Going to the cabin. Are you sure that's a good idea?"

"I can't explain it, Theresa. It's just something I have to do. So can you keep an eye on the house? Maybe go every three or four days and take care of the cat?"

"Jim, what about the girls?" she asked with concern. "Are you sure?"

"It's no problem; I can find someone else to do it," he retorted as he began to walk away.

"I'll do it," she said in a reassuring tone. "I said I would, and I will. I just want to make sure you know what you're doing."

"I think we already established that I don't. I've never done this before," he said as he began to walk away. "Thanks!"

As she watched Jim walk away, Theresa knew she needed to make good on her promise—actually, on both promises. In addition to praying, she now had a cat to feed.

Stephanie, seeing that time was running out on her options, took the offense by taking the family "discussions" public; her actions caused quite a stir. She was loudly complaining to Ben and Maggie Davis about the whole situation as her father approached the group. Jim became embarrassed and tried to manage the predicament, but he knew it was more than he could handle. He resorted to searching for a respectable exit strategy.

"Stephanie," said Mr. Davis, "why don't you go and tell your friends good-bye while I speak to your father alone for a minute."

"I don't want to say good-bye to them!" she cried. "I don't want to go to that stupid old cabin!"

"Stephanie," said Mr. Davis, "for the sake of your mother, if for no one else, give me a minute alone with your father."

Stephanie finally relented and ran ahead to talk to her friends.

"Listen, Jim, if Stephanie doesn't want to go with you, and you need someone to watch out for her here, she can stay with us and remain in school."

25

The Package

"I don't know," said Jim. "That's not fair to you or your family. And I think she should be with her family. We need to get through this together."

"If you don't want to do that, I understand," he said, "but I thought I'd make the offer."

With Stephanie's emotional state, Jim knew he had more to deal with than he could manage, and while he felt she should go with him, the thought of taking this problem off his plate looked very attractive. "Are you sure you want to do that?" he said. "I wouldn't want to impose."

"It's not an imposition," said Ben. "We'd be happy to help out."

"Is Maggie okay with it?" he asked.

"Sure, we talked about it. She's fine."

"Well, if you're sure, I'll go home, have Stephanie get her things together, and I'll drop her off about two o'clock. Would that work for you?"

"Yes," said Ben. "We should be home all afternoon."

"All right then. I saw Maggie near the front door. I'll thank her on my way out, and I'll see you this afternoon." Jim headed for the exit but paused for a moment to thank Maggie. Once outside the building, he called out to Stephanie.

"Stephanie, could you please come here for a minute?"

She left her friends and crossed the lawn to him. "What do *you* want?" she asked snidely.

"I just talked to Ben Davis. He said that if you want to stay here in town, you could stay at their house while Anna and I are away. Do you want to do that?"

"Can I?" she asked hopefully.

"If that's what you want to do," he answered.

"Really?"

"I'd like you to come with me," he said, "but if you feel you need to stay in town, you can stay with the Davises. I'll take you over this afternoon before I leave."

Stephanie smiled and hugged him. She took off running to tell her friends the good news. "Thanks, Dad!" she yelled back as she ran.

Jim waved in acknowledgement and breathed a sigh of relief. Stephanie's frustration level was beginning to worry him. He felt a pressing need to go, and she was desperate to stay. He thought they had found a suitable compromise. At the very least, she seemed satisfied with it.

After they arrived home, Stephanie gathered her things together for her extended stay with the Davises. As they loaded her things into the

26

trunk, Jim considered making one last appeal to her. But he knew it would be fruitless and might even make the last few minutes together stressful, so he decided to keep the tone positive. He drove Stephanie to the Davis' home, gave her a hug, and said goodbye. "I love you, Stephanie," he said.

"You too, Dad," she said. "Come back soon. I'll miss you."

Anna and Stephanie traded embraces as well. Jim again thanked Ben and Maggie and then watched Stephanie wave good-bye as he drove away.

After they had gone a few miles down the road, Jim looked over at Anna, who was crunched into a pillow trying to sleep. He was glad she was going with him, but he was also glad for the quiet. The drive to the cabin gave him time to be alone with his thoughts.

If there was one thing that made Jim uncomfortable, it was change. He had been very secure with who he was, where he was, what he saw, and what he knew. But a flood of change had been thrust upon him like a hurricane battering upon a defenseless shoreline. It was overwhelming. His desperation demanded that somehow, somewhere, he'd find some sense of normal. He had convinced himself that some time away would help him make sense out of the chaos. It would help him find a way to get life back to normal for his family, even though he could not imagine what normal looked like without Denise.

Years later, Jim would look back and say that history had proven that the month away at the cabin was what he needed. It changed his life and his relationship with God. God spoke to him in ways he had never heard before. He wasn't sure if God were speaking to him differently, or if he had never taken the time to listen. However, during that time at the cabin, God did speak to him.

On his drive to the cabin after Denise died, he questioned whether he had the capacity within himself to go on without her. But God had worked a change inside of him. He had learned that he needed to embrace the suffering in his life if God were to accomplish what he desired. While that change took some time, he finally found healing for his loneliness. Though he would never stop loving his relationship with Denise, he now knew there was another relationship that had been lacking in his life—a relationship with God. The month at the cabin had changed that.

But Jim was acutely aware of other changes occurring around him. The girls were never the same after the accident—especially Stephanie. They

The Package

were teenagers at the time though, and Jim didn't know if the changes were related to the loss of their mother or something else. Maybe this behavior was normal for girls in their late teens. He laughed at himself as he thought, *If only you could experience what it was like to parent teenage girls before you actually had to do it—that would certainly make it an easier task.*

As the years passed, Jim had always wished he had been stronger in those days; he wished he could have been a better father and less of a grieving spouse. There was still some time left to fix some of that, but it was growing short. It was time for him to be the father that God intended. He prayed it wasn't too late.

He knew it would take a miracle.

3

THE PHONE CALLS

The winter weather was breaking in New York City, and Stephanie had the window over her desk ajar in order to enjoy a bit of the spring air. She and her business partner spent most of their time in the office working the phones, and the noise of the traffic outside was making work difficult. "Could you please shut that window?" asked Becky as she put her hand over the receiver. "I can't hear a thing."

Becky Friedman had met Stephanie nearly fifteen years earlier. At that time, Stephanie was working as an upscale hairdresser, and Becky worked at a hotel, planning large-scale weddings, fundraisers, and corporate gatherings. Both had outgoing personalities, similar interests, and shared many of the same ideas about life.

Stephanie and Becky had quickly become friends. For a short period of time, they were also roommates in the city, but eventually the comings and goings of other squatters in the apartment, particularly of the male gender, soon made the arrangement untenable. They talked about it, decided to put their friendship first, and Stephanie moved to her own place in Jersey.

Becky was extremely capable at her job. She was one of those lucky people who somehow managed to take up a profession that aligned perfectly with her talents. But Becky also had dreams. A few years after she and Stephanie met, Becky began talking about starting her own event planning business. She had developed a fair number of contacts with high profile clients and thought she could get many of them to pay her to plan their events. She encouraged Stephanie to join her in the enterprise, and within a few short months, they were in business.

The endeavor quickly became a success. Stephanie's skills complemented Becky's, and they developed a thriving business. In a short period of time, they found that the corporate arena was a bust. On the other hand, for a chic wedding or a blockbuster fundraising event, they had become the ladies about town.

Stephanie reached up and closed the window as Becky requested. The office was a half floor below street level, so with the window closed, only passing colorful shadows of men's slacks and women's dresses were visible in the frosted glass. The office was small but inexpensive—at least for New York. However, from the moment a client walked through the door, it was apparent that these two women knew what they were doing. The office was immaculately outfitted.

Stephanie had just returned from showing a client a twelve-room estate with a floral garden and a lake that she and Becky liked to promote for weddings. As she sat at her desk watching Becky wheel and deal with a caterer about truffles and crab cakes, Becky appeared to remember something, waving at Stephanie and pointing to her in-basket. Stephanie looked and found a telephone message from Anna. She had apparently called a few hours ago.

Of her two sisters, Stephanie was closest to Anna. She felt that Anna understood her, although she was also quite aware that Anna didn't like many things about her New York lifestyle. All in all, she believed that at least to some degree Anna had found a way to accept her as she was. Conversely, Stephanie's relationship with Cassie had been strained. When she spoke to Cassie, it seemed as if she was shouting across a chasm and her voice was never heard. She felt as if Cassie treated her like a child, as if Cassie were always trying to fix her like a broken toy.

Again, she looked at the message in her hand. Even considering the amity she had with Anna, it was rare that either of her sisters called her. Such events were usually prompted by bad news, like the death of an aunt, or a lost job, or a nephew in trouble. While she wondered what this news might be, she set the message aside for that moment, choosing to wait until she could formulate what she might say when she returned the call. A few minutes later, as Stephanie was working up a quote on her laptop, the office telephone rang. Becky answered it.

"Spectacular Events, this is Becky, how can I help you?" Becky listened to the voice on the phone. "Yes, she's here. Let me get her for you." Becky punched the hold button on the phone and hung up as she said, "It's for you. It's your sister again."

Stephanie picked up the phone and activated it.

"Hello, Anna."

The Phone Calls

"Hi, Stephanie. How are you?"

"I'm okay. What's up?" she answered.

"Stephanie, I'm calling to let you know that Dad's pretty sick. He went to the doctor a while back and had some tests. He got the results today, and I'm afraid the news isn't good."

If there were bad news Stephanie feared receiving, it was this news. Even after her father returned from his month away at the cabin, conflicts between them continued and escalated. A few weeks after her 18th birthday, Stephanie met a young man in Pittsburgh. Within a month, she had packed her bags and moved into an apartment in the city. The resulting tension between Stephanie and her father strained their relationship to the breaking point. They seldom communicated with each other beyond exchanging pleasantries at holiday gatherings. Jim did make numerous conciliatory efforts early on but finally conceded that he should give her space, believing that it was Stephanie who needed to find the desire to move their relationship forward.

If she were pressed on the issue, even Stephanie would have acknowledged that spite for her father had motivated her move to New York. She certainly did not fall in love. A roommate was needed to make ends meet. It was convenient, and it met a lot of needs.

Even in the present time, Stephanie had gotten to the point where mischief and misdeed were what she believed her family expected of her, and that was what she delivered. It had become a downward cycle of feeling that being nonconforming was who she was; and the more that others came to expect it, the more outrageous she would become. She was well aware that the behavior had no logical outcome that was good, but it was who she was. What could she do about it?

"What did the doctor say?" she asked, returning her attention to the telephone. Anna didn't answer. "*What did the doctor say?*" she repeated with urgency.

"Steph," said Anna, "I know you and Dad haven't been close for a long time, and I'm concerned about you."

Stephanie was annoyed by the deliberate change in subject. "Don't worry about me. I'm fine," she replied. "Just tell me what the doctor said."

"Dad is dying," said Anna.

"What's wrong with him?"

"He has a heart condition called restrictive cardiomyopathy," replied Anna. "He doesn't have much time left."

The Package

"How long?" The worry in Stephanie's voice was apparent. Stephanie heard nothing but Anna gently crying. "Anna, *how long?*"

"A few months maybe," replied Anna. "The doctor said they can't predict it that precisely. He just said 'soon.'"

Stephanie placed her hand on her forehead and rested her elbow on the desk. She had expected the time might be measured in years. She became introspective and overwrought with questions. *What did I do to deserve this?* she asked herself. *Can I ever tell Dad the truth?* Twenty years had provided no answers to these questions. She feared that another twenty could do no more.

"Months?" asked Stephanie. "Are they sure of the diagnosis?"

"Yes," replied Anna, "Dad said they ran two series of tests. He says they are sure."

For a moment, Stephanie felt empathy for her father. This emotion unsettled her however, because she was experienced in shutting out his feelings. But she knew this situation would force her to face some issues—issues she was still not prepared to face. *What should I do?* she thought. *If I reach out now, will he resent me?* Stephanie hadn't spoken to her father in nearly two years. "Should I call him?" she asked Anna. Again, there was silence on the phone, and Stephanie became annoyed. Surely, Anna could provide this guidance. It was a simple question. It seemed that everything involving her family always became so complicated.

"I think you know the answer to that question, Stephanie," she finally answered. "It's up to you to decide whether you want to accept it."

Why does everyone feel so compelled to challenge me all the time? she thought, having heard this kind of oblique answer before. "Anna, if you have something to say, *just say it!*" she snapped. "It's like everyone in this family always has to beat around the bush. I only asked if I should call him. Can't you just give me a straight answer?"

Anna replied without hesitation. "I think you should call him, but that's only what *I* think."

"Okay, I *will* then," she retorted.

Her sharp reply fit a familiar pattern, and Anna knew time was growing short for Stephanie and her father to resolve their conflicts. It was time for some frank talk, and Stephanie had just insisted that she stop beating around the bush. So Anna decided to give her what she demanded. "The question is not whether you should call him," said Anna, "but whether you have the determination to say what you need to say to him. No beating around the bush, right?"

The Phone Calls

Stephanie found herself silenced by the truth of Anna's statement. She had indeed given the direct answer Stephanie demanded of her. Even Stephanie knew that there were things that needed said, hidden truths that yearned to be revealed—she couldn't escape it. Yet she still had no tolerance for Anna, or anyone else for that matter, telling her what she needed to do.

"I've got to go," said Stephanie. "I'll call you later."

Anna understood the limit. "Okay, let's stay in touch," she said. "I love you."

Stephanie felt the characteristic lump in her throat. It happened every time someone uttered those words. She always felt as though she had nothing real to say in response. "I know you do," she answered. It was the best reply she could utter.

"Bye," said Anna.

"See you."

The line went silent, and a million thoughts spun through Stephanie's head. Issues she had put off for years now stared her in the face and were unavoidable. Stephanie sat gazing into the receiver in her hand that now had no voice at the other end.

Becky saw her blank stare and asked, "You okay?" When Stephanie didn't answer, she whispered, "Are you still on the phone?"

"No, and I'm fine," she said, leaning back in her chair while still clutching the phone. She wondered if the lack of honesty was apparent in her voice, but a quick glance at Becky revealed that she had accepted her answer, as she was already reengaged in her work. Stephanie looked toward the window and watched the ongoing endless bustle as she tapped the telephone receiver on the palm of her other hand. *Am I still on the phone?* she thought, reflecting on what Becky had asked. In a sad revelation, Stephanie saw how this pitiful scene mimicked her life. She had all the appearances of being connected to the world around her, but despite her facade, she always found a way to disconnect from everyone. The reality of her life was that she was talking to emptiness and listening to no one. In a city of more than ten million people, Stephanie was alone.

It was about three o'clock in the afternoon on that same March day when Cassie Carlisle's cell phone rang in the high school guidance office where she worked. Usually, she turned her phone off at work, but for some reason she had forgotten to do it that morning. Cassie was counseling a fe-

The Package

male student at the time, and she reached into her drawer, pulled out her purse, extracted her phone, and turned it off. Before it powered down, she noticed the number on the caller ID was from a familiar area code in Pennsylvania. She looked toward the student, waved a hand seeking forgiveness, and then took the call.

"Hello."

"Hi, Cassie, it's Anna. Have you got a minute?"

"Anna!" she answered. "Hello. What a surprise!" She looked back at the student who was giving her an impatient stare. The students were not allowed to have their cell phones on at school. Cassie figured she'd get the double-standard lecture as soon as she hung up the phone. Kids were a lot bolder these days.

"Listen, Anna, I have a student here in the office." The student gave her a sneer. "Can I call you back?"

"Okay," said Anna. "We can talk later, but it's important. I need to talk to you . . . *soon*."

Cassie knew Anna well. Since Anna was a child, she was always easy-going, never wanting to cause a fuss, never seeking attention, and never wanting to be in the way. The urgency in Anna's voice likely meant trouble. "Wait a minute," she said to Anna as she placed her hand over the receiver and lowered the phone.

"Can we resume this discussion later?" she asked the student. "I need to take this call." The young girl leaned her head backward in disgust. "Sure, whatever," she complained as she rose from her chair and headed for the door. While Cassie tried to negotiate a quick follow-up appointment, the student was already feeling put out and would have nothing of it. Rolling her eyes, the young lady walked out of the room, slamming the door as she left. Cassie knew she had some damage control to do when she finished the call, but this was an unusual event. *Anna knows I'm at work*, she thought. *Why would she be calling in the middle of the day? There must be something wrong with Dad.* As her thoughts evolved into worry, she stood up and locked the door to her office, then returned to her desk and picked up her phone.

"I'm sorry, Anna," she said. "I was in a meeting with a student. But I am free now. What's wrong?"

"Dad's test results came back today," said Anna, "and I'm afraid it's bad news."

"What is it, Anna?" Cassie asked with concern.

The Phone Calls

"Dad is dying," said Anna. "He probably has only a few months left."

It was the news Cassie anticipated. She knew Dad had not been feeling well, and he was planning to have some tests. She had talked to him several weeks before.

"Is he in the hospital?" she asked.

"He was in the hospital for a few days before he even called me," replied Anna, "but he is back home now. They expect him to be able to stay there for awhile before his condition deteriorates to where he needs special care."

Cassie had watched her mother-in-law die in a nursing home alone. It was painful for her to watch. The thought of her father going through that same ordeal was more than she could take.

"Anna, we can't put him in a nursing home," said Cassie. "I can't stand the thought of that. We simply can't let that happen."

"We're not at that point yet," said Anna.

"But we will be soon," said Cassie. "And what can I do? I'm two thousand miles away."

Anna understood Cassie's concern and assured her she would do everything she could to take care of him. Anna still lived near her father, and she didn't have a full-time job. "Cassie, don't worry," said Anna. "I'll take care of him." Anna was sincere, but she was also aware that the task could easily overwhelm her.

Cassie felt her grip on the phone ease a little, because she knew when Anna said she would take care of someone, she meant it. It was her gift. "I guess I need to get back there to see him as soon as I can," said Cassie. "We have spring break in a couple of weeks; maybe I can come then." Spring break had always been a family time, but Cassie was going to be alone this year since her daughter, Lisa, was going to Florida with friends, and her son, Jason, had joined the Navy and was now stationed overseas. "Do you think that would work out okay?" she asked.

"I think that would be good for Dad," replied Anna. "He really misses seeing you."

"Did he say that?" she asked.

"Cassie, Dad would never impose on any of us like that," answered Anna. "But you know he misses all of us whenever we're not there."

"I know he does," said Cassie.

"Come as soon as you can," said Anna.

Cassie was torn between her love for her father and responsibilities at

The Package

home. She was not one to shirk responsibility, which usually made decisions fairly straightforward. However, her day-to-day responsibilities were now in conflict with a sense of responsibility to her dying father. She struggled to find a compromise. "Okay, I'll probably come during spring break," she said. "I'll let you know what my plans are as soon as they firm up."

"Okay," said Anna.

"I'll call Dad at home tonight, okay?"

"I'm sure that will make his day," said Anna. Cassie didn't reply. "I'll talk to you soon, okay?"

"Yes," answered Cassie. "Thanks for calling me."

"Okay, Cassie. I love you."

"I love you too," Cassie replied warmly. "Bye."

"Bye," said Anna.

Cassie returned her cell phone to her purse and sat back into her chair and replayed her conversation with Anna. She knew she needed to plan a trip in the weeks ahead. It would be an opportunity for her to spend some quality time with her father. Cassie loved her father dearly, and she chided herself that it took a life threatening illness to get her to think about how to address her uneasiness with him—and herself.

For most of her adult life, Cassie had enjoyed a close relationship with her father. But when she and her husband, Mark, relocated to Sacramento ten years ago, the two thousand mile distance took its toll. She thought to herself, "Distance is cruel to families." As she pondered this further, she was saddened by a realization that, in her case, distance had met its obligation.

Yet, beyond the physical distance, the last few years had evidenced a widening gap of a different and more seditious nature in their relationship—Cassie had been intentionally avoiding closeness with her father. It was a self-protection mechanism that had kicked in to protect her from her own shame. Distance, in an unexpected turnabout, had actually transformed itself into a comforting ally. With her life filled with nearly unmanageable chaos, distance—both real and emotional—had allowed her to hide her weaknesses from everyone, especially her father. Cassie was embarrassed, ashamed, and felt that she had disappointed him. She had failed at one of the most fundamental things in life that her father had valued the most—marriage. Cassie was divorced.

After twenty-three years of marriage, Cassie's husband came home from work one day, packed his bags, and told her he was leaving her. She was devastated. But when he told her *why* he was leaving, she rose from her

The Phone Calls

despair and became angry. He was having an affair with a woman he met at the gym where he worked out. Cassie screamed and cried and threw things he owned out of the house onto the front lawn. But none of her antics impacted anything beyond her own emotions. Mark intended to divorce her. In the beginning, his guilt made it difficult to face. But the angrier she got, the easier it became.

When Mark was finally gone for good, she cried herself to sleep every night for weeks. Even though she had a sense of loneliness in her marriage for years, the actuality of being alone was much more difficult. Yet, far worse than the solitude for Cassie was her sense of failure. It was more than a month before she could even tell her father that Mark was gone.

Cassie and Mark had been regular churchgoers, but attending church became almost more than she could bear. At an earlier time, she had been the head of the women's ministry. Having been a leader for other women made dealing with her failure much more difficult. She recalled once telling a close friend, "How can I even show my face at church again?" Her self-reflection was even more indicting. *Why did Mark need another woman? Why wasn't I enough?* she wondered.

As Cassie forged her way through this disaster in her life, Mark decided he wanted to come back. He felt guilty and wanted to make things right. At first, Cassie wasn't sure what to do. She struggled with this decision. For her children, perhaps reconciliation would be best. But did she need a husband for whom she was no more than a salve for his conscience?

Cassie sought advice. She respected her father's wisdom, so she discussed the situation with him. He was attentive and empathetic, but gave her no direct answer to her dilemma. He spoke only about forgiveness and second chances. In retrospect, she understood why he gave her no answer. He always allowed his children to find answers for themselves. Reconciliation was too difficult for her to face, though, and she decided to move on with her life without Mark. Her decision was made with determination but not without regret. She knew she would likely question it for the rest of her life.

While her father had never told her what she should do, Cassie had convinced herself that he believed she had made the wrong choice. She felt ashamed and had decided the best way to avoid it was to avoid her father. Shame tossed her to one side to say she should have forgiven Mark, and to the other side saying she should forgive her father. In fact, the shame was so real to her that it had become more than a feeling. It was as though

The Package

shame were a person with whom she lived. Many nights she cried herself to sleep in its grip.

———•◆••◆•———

Anna Patrick hung up the phone and sat alone in her home office. She rested her chin on her folded arms on the desk in front of her and thought through the conversations she had just finished. The call to Stephanie had been agonizing, as she could sense the turmoil within her sister even after she hung up the phone. *Cassie did what Cassie always does*, she thought, *gets the information, makes a plan, and executes.*

Anna thought about how different her sisters were. Cassie was matter-of-fact, determined, and invulnerable—or so she seemed. Stephanie was off-the-wall, unpredictable, and out of control like a beautiful flower floating on a rushing stream. Both of them seemed trapped within themselves and yet, to her chagrin, they didn't even seem to be aware of the cage.

Anna couldn't overlook these issues, however, for she knew the pains carried by her family were real. But she had an unwavering confidence that the possibility for healing was likewise as real. She remembered her father had once said, "The answers are simple; they just aren't easy." She smiled when she realized her ears actually heard her own voice say those words aloud. They were wise words, indeed. But she knew the truth instilled in them was purposed to be invisible until revealed at the time chosen by the Author of truth.

Anna also knew the next few months were going to be unpredictable in every realm—physical, emotional, and spiritual. She closed her eyes and began to pray. *Lord, I know healing is as real as the chair I'm sitting in. I know it is there, even though I can't see it. God, please heal my father of this illness. I know a time will come, Lord, when you need to bring him home to you. I accept that. But there are things still remaining to be done in our family, things needing to be resolved. Please bring him back to health as a sign to Cassie and Stephanie that you are real, and that you love them more than they know.* Anna also prayed for the emotional well-being of her sisters, and that God would reveal his truth and open their eyes to his glory.

As for my husband and my children, Anna continued, *please keep us together as one, shine the light on our darkness, bring peace to those who are troubled; and let us never forget that the strength of our family rests in your strength, and our success in life can only be measured by our success in you. Amen.*

The Phone Calls

A loud voice broke the silence. "Mom, are you taking me to soccer practice, or is Ethan taking me?" It was Anna's son Nathan. She stood up and went to the kitchen where Anna's oldest son, Ethan, was studying.

"Ethan, can you please take Nathan to practice today?" she asked.

"I have a lot of studying to do, Mom," he replied without much thought. But a few moments later, Ethan remembered the news about Grandpa earlier in the day, looked at his mother, and reacted to her immediate need. "Sorry, Mom," he said comfortingly. "I can take him. I can study later tonight."

Anna smiled at her son graciously and kissed him on the forehead. "You are a good son," she said. As the boys rushed out the door, Anna thought about the trials she had endured with her own family. Her husband, Craig, was an airline pilot. Her relationship with him was solid. He was a man of deep faith who believed in the Word of God and lived it to the best of his ability.

Craig had spent most of his career on flights where he would fly out and return on the same day. But now he piloted international flights where he would be away overnight; his crazy schedule had put a strain on the family. In fact, the pressure on Ethan drove him into hanging out with a bad crowd, and that led to some trouble. It involved illegal drugs. Anna didn't want to know the details; she only wanted to get him help. She tried not to condemn him. Craig put him in a drug rehabilitation program that helped him get back on track. He was a good kid, but with the stress he was under, she and Craig had to keep an eye on him—not for their sake, but his.

Anna returned to her office and again prayed for her three men: Craig, Nathan, and Ethan. She prayed for them to be strong in the Lord and in the power of his might. She believed praying made a difference. Again, she thought back to the phone calls she had just made. Relationships were broken; and guilt, loneliness, and fear reigned. Her father and her sisters needed far more than a little help.

They needed intervention.

4

EMERGENCY ROOM

The evening had been difficult, and it was well after midnight when Anna finally sat down at her kitchen table to rest. Her father had been admitted to the hospital after an episode earlier that night. Fortunately, amid its occurrence, he still had the presence of mind to call 911. Even though he was weak when help arrived, he had made the trip to the hospital without further incident.

Anna's evening began with a phone call from the hospital. Anna, Craig, and her two sons hurried to the car and rushed there as quickly as they could. Along the way, she made short phone calls to both of her sisters to apprise them of the situation as best she knew it and promised to follow up with more information as it developed.

When they arrived, Craig stopped the car near the emergency room entrance. Anna and her two sons jumped out and rushed through the door. While she briefly waited for the triage nurse, who was finishing up with someone ahead of her, Ethan and Nathan took seats in the waiting area. Once the line cleared, she stepped forward and said, "Hi, I'm looking for Jim Mullins. He was brought in by an ambulance earlier tonight."

The triage nurse made a few quick entries on her keyboard and scanned down her computer screen with her finger. "Yes," she said. "He came in several hours ago. Are you a family member?"

"Yes, I'm his daughter."

"Please wait here for a moment, and I'll get someone to help you," she said, rising from her chair and exiting through a door behind her. As she waited, Anna caught the eye of her sons and tried to smile reassuringly, but she suspected they saw worry hiding behind her feigned expression. A few moments later the triage nurse reappeared and said, "Please take a seat for a few minutes. Someone will be right out to get you."

As she turned toward the seating area, the entrance doors slid open and

Craig entered. Anna took his hand and led him to where the boys were sitting. A few minutes after they sat down, a nurse entered the room through a set of frosted glass automatic doors and looked toward the triage nurse, who pointed at Anna across the room. The nurse walked over to Anna and asked, "You asked to see Mr. Mullins?"

"Yes," answered Anna, rising to her feet.

"I can take you back now," she said. The nurse turned and headed back toward the doors with Anna lagging behind. Anna hurried and caught up with her and whispered, "Can my family come with me?"

"It would be better if we limit the visitors for now," said the nurse. "We're pretty busy tonight. Okay?"

Anna nodded, turned and waved to her family to let them know she was going in alone, and continued to follow the nurse back through the same automatic doors from which she had appeared. As they entered the patient care area, the nurse, whose name tag identified her as Julie, escorted Anna down a hallway having curtained rooms identified by numbered placards hanging from the ceiling.

"He's right down here in room seven," said Julie. "He's comfortable now, but he has had a pretty rough evening. He's still a little disoriented, so don't be surprised by that."

"I understand," said Anna. "Do we know what happened?"

"Not for sure. We know that he was feeling lightheaded and had some discomfort in his chest. You'll need to talk to Dr. Butler if you want to get more details. She's the attending physician tonight."

"Can I talk to her now?" asked Anna, just as they stopped outside room seven.

"I will let her know you are here. It may be a while before she can get to you. Like I said, it's been a busy night."

"Will he go home tonight?" asked Anna.

"The doctors have completed their initial assessment, and they've decided to admit him for observation and further tests. We're waiting for Admissions to identify a room and complete the necessary paperwork."

"Thanks, Julie," said Anna.

"You can go in and see him now," said Julie as she turned to resume her duties. As she walked away, she realized and reacted to Anna's kindness—having made the effort to call her by name. With a warm smile, she turned toward Anna while walking backwards and said, "You're welcome. And they told us about 10 minutes ago that they thought he would move to the floor in about an hour. If I can do anything else for you, just let me know."

The Package

Anna acknowledged her offer with a nod and watched Julie walk away. Turning toward the curtain surrounding her father's bed, she stood motionless for a moment and then slowly eased it back. His eyes were closed when she entered, but the sound of the curtain hooks rattling in the metal track roused him. Having seen him as recently as the previous weekend, she was surprised at his appearance. He seemed to have deteriorated substantially in a few short days, and his countenance evidenced his stressed condition.

"Hi, Dad," said Anna.

"Anna," he said softly. "Thanks for coming."

"You okay, Dad?" she asked.

"Just feeling funny," he answered. "Something not right."

"Well, we'll get you fixed up and feeling better soon," she said.

"Here by yourself?" he asked. Dad was clearly using the minimum number of words possible.

"No, Craig and the kids are in the waiting room. They suggested that only one of us come back here for now—until you get to your room."

"Maybe in a few minutes," he said.

"I think they said about an hour."

"An hour?" he muttered. "How did you know I was—?"

"You had the hospital call me," she said.

"I did?"

Anna recalled what Julie had said about him being confused. With that in mind, she decided to limit the conversation, opting instead to let him sleep. He was indeed disoriented, and she pondered whether it was related to his condition or caused by one of the medications he had been given.

"You look tired, Dad," said Anna.

"I am, honey. Just fell asleep when you—"

"Why don't you get some sleep, and we'll see you tomorrow then?" she said. "Would that be okay?"

Dad acknowledged her suggestion by simply closing his eyes. Anna kissed his cheek, stepped out, pulled his curtain closed again, and started walking back toward her family. As she approached the exit back to the waiting area, Julie called out to her. "Did you still want to speak to the doctor?"

"Yes, please, if I could," she answered.

"Wait here for a minute," said Julie as she quickly disappeared around a corner. Anna waited a few minutes, and Julie returned with another young woman who turned out, to her surprise, to be the doctor.

42

Emergency Room

"Hi, I'm Dr. Butler. Julie said you wanted to speak to me."

"I'm Anna Patrick. I'm the daughter of Jim Mullins, in room seven."

"Let's sit down here for a moment if you don't mind." She directed Anna toward a set of cushioned chairs that were there for this very purpose.

"I assume you are familiar with your father's chronic heart condition?" the doctor asked.

"Yes," said Anna, "I believe they told him it was something called cardiomyopathy."

The doctor was happy to see Anna understood what they were dealing with because the news wasn't good, and it would be easier to explain to someone who could grasp the seriousness of the situation. The doctor began, "Ms. Patrick—"

"Please call me Anna," she interrupted.

"Okay, Anna, your father's heart is weakening, and his overall condition is deteriorating. This is not unusual for someone with this disease. I suspect he came very close to fainting this evening, perhaps due to some overexertion that resulted in an inability of his heart to pump sufficient oxygen to his brain. He complained about being lightheaded and indicated confusion."

While the doctor had seemed young to Anna initially, that particular concern was diminishing. As Dr. Butler spoke, Anna became more and more comfortable with her competence. She possessed a confidence in her manner that was reassuring.

"Now," continued the doctor, "I have given him a sedative to help him sleep and recuperate as best he can. We have called his cardiologist, and he would like us to run some tests to determine any further actions we should take. For now, he is resting comfortably, and we will admit him for observation and to complete the requested testing. Is that clear? Do you have any questions?"

"How much time does he have?" asked Anna.

"I am sure you realize this disease will not go away," she said. "It is a chronic illness."

"How long?" she asked again.

"There's no sure way to tell. These things are extremely variable. But you clearly understand that his condition is quite serious."

"Please, just tell me," said Anna, seeking a straight answer.

"It could be hours or weeks—perhaps a month. His cardiologist may be able to provide you a better answer. But there is really nothing we can do

The Package

now but wait and see." The doctor hesitated for a moment to see if Anna had any further questions, and when it appeared that she did not, the doctor stood to her feet and asked, "Is there anything else I can do for you?"

"No, thank you very much," said Anna. "I appreciate your help."

With that, Dr. Butler smiled and scurried off. Anna was thankful for her kindness but felt vulnerable as she watched the doctor vacantly advance to the next patient on her roster. Anna was aware that the emergency room staff saw tragedy happen every day. For them, this day was like any other. But for Anna and her family, ordinary days seldom occurred in hospitals. Now fearing that the day of her father's death was imminent, she contemplated a simple truth. *No one alive experiences that day more than once*, she thought. *We all have only one father.* Indeed, this was no ordinary day for her.

Anna rejoined her family in the waiting room and explained what was happening. Ethan and Nathan wanted to see Grandpa before they left the hospital and, under the circumstances, Anna thought it seemed prudent. So they decided to remain in the waiting area until they moved him to his room. Anna stepped away from her family to a quiet hallway, turned on her cell phone, and called Stephanie. She answered the phone on the first ring, as she was sitting by her phone anxiously awaiting the call. The caller ID let her know who was calling.

"Anna, how's Dad?" she asked, sidestepping the usual salutations.

"Well, Steph, the doctor said Dad's heart is weakening, and he probably became lightheaded from a lack of oxygen. Perhaps he nearly passed out. He's sleeping now, but they don't know what to expect from here."

"He'll get through this, right?" asked Stephanie.

"There is no sure way to know," said Anna. "Look, if I were you, I'd come as soon as possible. It may or may not be necessary. I honestly don't know. But if it were me, I wouldn't want to second-guess myself later."

"I've already booked my flight. I leave at 6:00 a.m. from JFK, which means I had better get some sleep. I have to get up at three in order to make the flight, and it's after nine now. Anything else I should know?"

"Not that I can think of," said Anna. "So I'll see you in the morning then?"

"I'll come to the hospital straight from the airport," answered Stephanie. "What room is he in?"

"We're waiting for him to be assigned to a room," said Anna. "I'll text you when I find out the room number."

Emergency Room

"Okay. Thanks, Anna."

"All right," she replied. "I'll see you tomorrow. Good night."

"Good night," said Stephanie.

As Anna hung up the phone, she became fascinated by the fact that Stephanie had already made travel plans. It seemed like an uncharacteristic move.

Since the three-hour time difference with Pittsburgh made it a little after 7:00 p.m. in California, Cassie was finishing dinner when she received Anna's call. Anna repeated to Cassie most of the same information she had told Stephanie. It was clear to Anna that Cassie understood the critical nature of her father's condition. However, Cassie was not hinting at a need to react quickly to Anna's news. Cassie told Anna that the school administration would frown upon suddenly leaving in the middle of the school year for a simple illness or a hospital visit. Driven by commitment as a core value, Cassie believed that exceeding the expectations of your management was expected. But Anna prodded her to consider alternatives. "Cassie, I have to be honest. I am pretty worried about him. He doesn't look good to me. I told Stephanie that if I were in her shoes, I would come. I can't tell you, with any kind of a clear conscience, anything different. But you have to make that decision. I understand it's difficult for you." Anna hoped she had provided the needed persuasion.

"Let me think about it," said Cassie, "and I'll call you back."

"Tomorrow, I hope," said Anna. "I mean, if you call me tonight and I don't answer, just leave a message. I'll turn my cell phone off before I go to bed, and I'll pick up your message in the morning. If you need to reach me urgently for some reason, call my home phone. Will that work?"

"Yes," said Cassie. "I'll let you know what I decide. Good night and get some rest. Thanks for keeping me informed."

"Good night, Cassie."

"Good night. Call me if something changes."

Anna folded up her cell phone and slid it back into her pocket. She returned to the waiting room and found Craig and the boys passing the time by numbly watching the hospital channel on the television. As Anna sat down next to Craig and took his hand, he smiled at her and squeezed her hand to reassure her. It was the first positive feeling she'd had in several hours, and she was grateful for it.

It was nearing midnight when they finally moved her father into a room. Afterwards, the four of them paid him a brief visit and sat very quietly, trying to avoid rousing him.

45

The Package

Ethan broke the silence and whispered, "What's going to happen, Mom?"

"I don't know," said Anna. "I really don't. Nobody does."

Anna's father flinched and mumbled some unintelligible words that seemed to be part of a dream he was having. At his first utterance, they all stared anxiously at him from their various vantage points across the room, anticipating that he would awaken. To their disappointment, he silently dropped back into a deep sleep. For about ten minutes more, the four of them stood gazing at him, quietly sharing incongruent feelings of sorrow and gladness. They were saddened by his condition yet glad to be near him.

When they finally drove home, Anna rested her head against the seat of the car and closed her eyes. In her stillness, she felt and heard the periodic rumble of the tires rolling across the seams in the highway beneath them. That empty monotonous message seemed appropriate for the difficult day it had been. As she opened her eyes, she looked across the car at Craig, who was alert and in control. His lips were moving as though he were speaking, yet there was no audible voice. Without asking, she knew why—he was praying.

Again, she closed her eyes and thought of her father's unstable heart. His heart was dying; her heart yearned for God's intervention. Believing that he possessed the power to intervene, she prayed to ask why he hadn't. As she finished her petition to God and opened her eyes, she again looked across the car and saw her husband still praying. She glanced toward the back seat where her two weary sons were beginning to nod off to sleep. She smiled and then repented to God for her complaints. A brief look around the car had made her realize how grateful she truly was—grateful for the family that God had given her.

5

THE PROMISE

The next morning brought blue skies, and Jim awoke to the sun-drenched blossoms of a redbud tree just outside his hospital room window. *How fortunate*, he thought, *to be so near a second floor window providing such a spectacular closeup view.* But while this scene from the woodlands provided a comfortable familiarity, the repetitive beeping of the heart monitor beside his bed was a foreign sound. The nurse on duty had enabled the audible option on the unit, and it had been chirping for several hours. This noisy contraption was a persistent annoyance, yet it was this same clamoring that provided evidence of the last echoes of life within him. Jim smirked as he considered the irony—did he actually want it to stop?

A few months ago, when the doctor told him he had a bad heart and was dying, he had taken the news well. The rare disease that was killing him had a mysterious sounding name: restrictive cardiomyopathy. This disorder, he had learned, was a disease of the heart muscle that caused the walls of the ventricles to become stiff, thereby reducing the heart's efficiency. At the time of his diagnosis, the doctor advised him that many of his symptoms could be treated, but the only real cure was a heart transplant. His heart would weaken over time until it could no longer do its job.

Jim had elected to forgo the transplant option. He realized his decision was a self-imposed death sentence, yet he felt that there were many younger people who needed a new heart worse than he did. Death was not something he welcomed, neither did he fear it. Many of his friends had argued contrary positions with him, but he was settled in his own mind. Nothing now remained but to walk through the short time left in his life. He simply needed to embrace his situation, which was a lesson he had learned long ago.

Again becoming aware of the beeping heart monitor, Jim looked for the nurse's call button. He was distracted from his search when Anna entered the room. Anna was the most sensitive of Jim's daughters, and the strain of his current circumstance was evident in her face. While his energy was diminishing, he still could garner enough to generate a smile for her and greet her with a childhood nickname, "Anna-banana."

Anna tilted her head and smiled, aware that her father had just made a short journey to a happier time. The brief rush of joy she felt was gratifying, but her anxiety quickly snapped her back to the present, causing her eyes to well with tears. This reaction conflicted with Anna's predetermined plan, which she had concocted just before she entered the room. She had hesitated there to gather her emotions and assert her will over them; sadness would not be her master. In fact, crying was the last thing she wanted her father to see. Yet, despite her earnest intent, he had disarmed her in less than a minute by a smile and a single word.

Anna tried to hide her reaction by leaning over his hospital bed, giving him a gentle kiss on the cheek, and placing her cheek against his. Putting her arms on his shoulders as if to give him a hug, she held on to him and on to her emotions long enough to whisper in his ear softly, "I love you, Daddy."

Jim was weak but still aware of his surroundings. He had made a deliberate attempt to brighten Anna's mood when she walked through the door, but the unsteadiness in her voice made him fear he may have dampened it. "It's okay, Anna," he said reassuringly. "I know you're sad—and scared. But this is my time."

Anna drew back, gazed into her father's eyes, and said, "Daddy, I will be okay. You need to worry about you!"

"Anna," he answered in a raspy voice, "I'm not worried at all."

Of Jim's three daughters, Anna was best equipped to accept and understand this statement. Her present relationship with him was built upon a foundation of shared tragedy since they had both endured the loss of their wife and mother respectively. Their concurrent suffering had created a unique bond within the family.

Because of this, before Anna married, she stipulated to her soon-to-be husband that they must live near her father. While the circumstances of her sisters' lives had taken them to cities far away, she was determined to stay near her father, feeling that he had suffered enough loneliness in his life. Though she understood that her priority would need to be her new husband and family, she felt that her father needed her support as well. He had never told her that explicitly, but Anna recognized that he would never

The Promise

make such a request. In her heart though, she truly believed that he needed a family connection close at hand.

Even beyond the shared time at the cabin and their close proximity, Anna and her father shared a faith in Jesus Christ that, to each of them, was the substance of life itself. They both heard the voice of God within their own spirits, and they trusted his voice speaking to them through the other. Therefore, Anna shared her father's assurance regarding his future.

"I know you're not worried for you, Dad. I just don't want you worrying about me. Okay?" said Anna as she moved to the chair across the room to place her sweater on it.

"Okay," he answered, hesitating for a moment, "Anna-banana."

Jim laughed at himself as Anna turned back toward him with her hands on her hips and a giggle. But as she watched him, his laughter deteriorated into a coughing spell. He motioned for some water, and she responded by filling a plastic cup from a pitcher on his table. Adding a straw and quickly handing it to him, he took a few sips and the coughing subsided as quickly as it came. His hand holding the cup began to shake, and Anna retrieved it, returning it to the table. He closed his eyes for a few moments to relax and ensure his coughing would subside. As he lay there quietly, he heard his breathing settling back to normal. But then another, more irritating sound again caught his attention—the monotonous beeping of his heart monitor. "Anna, could you please get someone to come in here and turn that beeping off?"

"Dad," she answered, "why don't you just relax and let them do their jobs? They're the experts." It took less than one second of an impatient look from her father for Anna to understand the message and comply. She considered pressing the call button but then decided to make a trip to the nurse's station, thinking that a few minutes to calm her emotions might be beneficial.

As she walked to get assistance, Anna decided that she needed to refrain from making any further suggestions. She realized that her father had made up his mind about his situation, and he had always been difficult to dissuade when he possessed such a mindset. She also decided that if her father wanted to keep the mood light, she would try to find that same attitude within herself.

Something within her nature sought to care for him, compelling her to make things right—to somehow make him well. But the painful reality of his condition was becoming undeniable. Letting go was what she needed to

49

The Package

do. She knew she could not prevail in this situation, nor did her father want her to. He was at peace. While she understood what he needed from her, she struggled to let it be truth inside her.

Anna returned to the room with a nurse who made the necessary adjustment to the monitor. She thanked the nurse as she left the room and then addressed her father. "Dad, Stephanie will be here soon," she said. "She caught the early flight from JFK. As soon as she heard you were admitted last night, she caught the first flight she could get on."

"I'm glad she's coming," he said. "Have you talked to her much lately?"

"We've had maybe three or four conversations over the last few months," she said.

Jim hesitated for a moment and then said, "Did you know she called me last month?"

Indeed, Stephanie did tell Anna of the call, and she had conveyed that the conversation had gone well. Since Stephanie had confided in her, Anna attempted to question her further about the conversation, but Stephanie hit her usual shutdown point and quickly digressed to meaningless chatter. This frustrated Anna. Feeling that the time was waning for Stephanie and her father to put the past behind them, she was disappointed in herself for not being assertive enough to press this point with her.

After Anna's call with Stephanie ended, Anna related her frustration to her husband. Craig usually provided sage advice, and in this case, he suggested that she let it be. "God will work what he wills," he said, "in the season in which he desires it. Simply pray and put it in his hands." Anna didn't always heed Craig's advice because it challenged her own desires. But in this case, Anna knew he was right.

Anna's focus returned to her father's hospital room, where her father was waiting for an answer to his question about the phone call with Stephanie. "Stephanie told me she called you," she answered, "and that you two had a nice conversation."

"That, we did," Jim said. He considered the intended lack of depth in that description. His voice evidenced his disappointment as he repeated it to himself, "That, we did."

Recalling that she had earlier bought a magazine in the gift shop for her father, Anna retrieved it from her purse and handed it him. He thanked her for it and laid it aside for later perusal. They continued talking for about an hour, recalling assorted minutia from their memories, but making no further mention of the present difficulties in their family relationships.

The Promise

They reminisced about old friends, children, grandchildren, and happier times.

Conversation was slow and tedious for Dad, and his weariness soon became evident. Anna suggested they take a break, but he insisted on continuing, enjoying every moment of this treasured time with his daughter. Anna was taking pleasure in the moment as well, knowing all the while that she was fighting a nagging discomfort that sought to wipe the smile from her face.

The conversation was suddenly broken when, without warning, Stephanie entered the room with a flair that Anna had come to describe with the single word that characterized it. "Stephanie!" cried Anna.

"Hello, I'm here," said Stephanie. "How is everyone? Great, I hope!" Stephanie gave Anna a courteous hug. "It's good to be here finally. Nothing like that 4:00 a.m. arrival at the airport to make a 6:00 a.m. flight! And the best part is when airport security selects you for further inspection. It's as if you won something. Lucky me!"

Stephanie's complaining brought an irritation to the surface for Anna, a feeling of frustration caused by Stephanie's consistent portrayal of herself as a victim. This depiction was a dichotomy, however. If Stephanie actually believed that everyone and everything victimized her, she somehow managed to conceal it beneath an almost abundant exuberance. Perhaps Stephanie believed the flashy appearance might deter anyone from seeing anything of her real character. Anna wasn't sure.

In truth, Stephanie was aware of the deception, and she had become prolific at masking her feelings. In fact, she had become so proficient that her true character was often a stranger to herself. Yet, even if that truth could somehow be made evident to her, it was irrelevant. Stephanie had abandoned truth long ago as an unattainable fantasy—everything had become relative.

"How are you, Daddy?" she asked, kissing him on the cheek.

"Well," he said, "this isn't my best day."

"Yeah, me neither." Anna was stunned by Stephanie's response and gave her a stern look of disapproval. Stephanie back-pedaled quickly, saying, "I mean, with the news about you coming here last night and all—I was really worried. I'm just glad I finally got here to see you." Looking toward Anna, her gaze sought her approval. Anna rolled her eyes at first but eventually nodded her head in consent.

The Package

Dad reached up and took Stephanie's hand. "I'm very glad you're here, Stephanie," he said. "We have a lot we still need to talk about."

It had been only a few minutes since she arrived, but Stephanie was already feeling out of sorts, detecting the nuance in her father's statement. She was aware that he was seeking a means to repair the damage that had been caused by years of neglect. But the residue left from past events was something that Stephanie hid deep within herself, tucked away undetected. Now her father threatened to pull the refuse from out of the shadows, and her discomfort was tangible.

"Right," said Stephanie. "We've got lots to catch up on. Did you guys have lunch yet? I'm starving."

He knew her question was an attempt to skirt the issue. While Jim was well-acquainted with the chasm existing in his relationship with Stephanie, he also knew that he would be unable to remove the pain of their rift on this day. He had tried to deal with their issues in their prior phone call; but like a child who had seen a ghost, Stephanie ran from the topic. Jim eased off and suggested that the topic could be discussed later, but time was now growing short. For now, he only hoped to apply some medicine that might enable healing in the future. It was not important that he see it, only that it happened. His hope was not for today but for tomorrow.

"Dad," repeated Stephanie. "Are you hungry?"

He gently shook his head no.

"Okay then, let me check with the nurse and see when they feed you around here," said Stephanie, leaving with the same flourish she came.

"I'm sorry, Dad," said Anna, "I don't know what's with her today."

"She got up and went to the airport at four in the morning," he said, smiling. "She struggled through security. She's been through a lot."

"But this isn't about her, Dad," she retorted. "I'm really sorry. I'm sorry she can't see that."

"Anna," said Dad, "the first thing you said to me when you came here today was 'I love you.' It was the first thing she said too. She just doesn't know how to use the same words you do."

Anna looked into her father's eyes. Even now—even in this mournful place in his life, he was still teaching. She felt ashamed to be physically strong and yet so weak, while her father in his weakness exhibited a strength to which she could only aspire.

"You're right, Dad," she said. "I don't know what's with *me* today. I'm sorry."

The Promise

"Everything in God's creation has its own unique beauty," he said. "Our job? We're expected to find it."

Anna was moved and determined that she would capture this proverb alongside a plethora of other profound sayings he had deposited within her memory. She kissed him on the cheek and whispered in his ear again, "I love you, Daddy."

"The king is enthralled by your beauty; honor him, for he is your Lord." Anna looked at her father curiously. "It's from Psalms," he said. Anna smiled to thank her father for the compliment.

Reappearing with the same vigor as her exit, Stephanie revealed that she had unearthed another crisis. "They do not intend to feed you until 1:30. I told them that that 1:30 was totally unacceptable because you need to eat to maintain your strength, and that is simply much too long to wait. So, I'll just have to go get you something to eat. What do you want? Just tell me what you'd like, and I'll go get it for you."

"Stephanie, I am fine," he said, smiling. "I don't need to eat right now. I'm not very hungry."

"Well," she said, picking up her purse and preparing to leave. "I'm only making sure they are not taking advantage of you. I mean, 1:30 is utterly ridiculous." Turning to her father before she left, she asked, "Are you sure you don't want something?"

He stared at Stephanie intently and then raised an outstretched hand toward her. "Stephanie," he said, "come here. Please."

Stephanie stood motionless for a moment but finally ambled toward her father and took his hand. Pulling her closer, he stared into her eyes and said, "Stephanie, I appreciate that you are doing everything you can to show me how much you love me." He squeezed her hand and shook it gently. "I love you too."

Stephanie was taken aback. As she considered his assessment of her actions, she realized that he was right. In some masked fashion, she knew she cared about her father. While she was unaware that these feelings were driving her actions, her father had perceived it. The fact that he seemed to be able to see inside her, sensing emotions of which she was unaware, rattled her security. She felt as though she were standing in the room naked.

"Listen, uh . . . I'll be back in a few," she said, releasing his hand and beginning to back away. "I need to go. I mean, I need to go get something to eat. You're really sure you don't want something?"

"I'm sure," he replied.

The Package

Stephanie looked at Anna and asked, "You need something?"

"No, I'm good," said Anna.

"Okay, be back in about forty-five minutes," said Stephanie as she moved toward the door.

"Wait!" Jim had called out with all the strength he could muster. "I think Anna wants to go with you."

"I do?" said a surprised Anna.

"Yes, you do," he said. "Now go."

Anna stared at her father for a second with a puzzled look on her face. Stephanie, still reeling from her vulnerability, sought to make a quick exit. "So, are you coming or not?" she asked.

As Anna gazed into her father's eyes, he raised one eyebrow. Anna had several succinct memories that provided clear interpretation of that message. "Okay, I'm coming," she replied.

Stephanie's angst finally pushed her to walk out the door.

"You need anything while I'm out, Dad?" asked Anna.

"I need you to seek beauty where it appears it can't be found," he said, smiling.

"I understand," said Anna.

"I need to get some sleep," he said. "Take your time, okay?"

"Okay," said Anna. She smiled at him, waved, and left the room.

Cassie pulled into the hospital parking garage and was relieved to have finally arrived. Like Stephanie, she caught a predawn flight, but the time difference between Sacramento and Pittsburgh allowed her to arrive no earlier than mid-afternoon. At a layover in Atlanta, she had phoned Anna, and Anna had apprised her of their father's status. She knew his condition was deteriorating and surmised that this visit with him would likely be her last.

Cassie considered the missed opportunities in her life. Had she been too involved in her own life to find time for her father? She considered the probability that everyone experienced similar regrets at the end of their parents' lives. Perhaps this was normal—perhaps not. She wasn't sure.

Upon entering the hospital lobby, Cassie stopped by the information desk to obtain her father's room number. Anna had provided it to her in their earlier phone conversation, but she was unable to write it down at the time; given the emotions of the day, she had forgotten it. She waited her

The Promise

turn in line, and the receptionist looked at her, smiled politely, and asked, "Can I help you?"

Before Cassie answered, she heard a voice across the lobby shout, "Cassie!" Cassie looked up to see Anna striding toward her with open arms. As she embraced Anna, she noticed Stephanie walking up behind her.

"We're just coming back from lunch," said Anna. "You just get here?"

"Yes, I was just asking for Dad's room number. How is he?" asked Cassie.

Anna directed her with a head nod, and Anna and Stephanie began to walk to the elevator with Cassie following. "We left him a few hours ago to get something to eat. He said he needed some rest, so he asked us to take our time. We're just going back up."

As they walked toward the elevator, Cassie realized she hadn't talked to Stephanie, an oversight that she felt she should correct. "Hi, Stephanie," she said. "Sorry, I'm a little distracted. How are you?"

"I'm fine," said Stephanie, feeling relieved to know that she was not invisible. "Thanks for noticing."

Cassie stopped dead in her tracks, searching for a potent retort. Stephanie and Anna, who had continued momentarily without her, turned and looked at her curiously. Cassie scowled at Stephanie briefly, and with a wave of her hand, she walked past them while speaking under her breath. "Forget it," she said. "It's not worth it."

"What's that?" demanded Stephanie, not hearing what she said, but clearly capturing the meaning.

Cassie halted again and snapped back toward her. "Nothing, Stephanie. I didn't say anything to you. Now do you suppose that you could just let me get through this without creating an incident? Would that be okay?" Cassie turned and resumed her path to the elevator without waiting for an answer.

Anna looked at Stephanie, who was infuriated. She then grabbed her by the arm and dragged her slightly to get her moving again. They all arrived at the elevator and stepped inside without saying anything more. While it was a short ride to the second floor, the lack of subtlety in the silence made it seem much longer. Finally, the bell rang, the doors opened, and they walked out onto their dad's floor. Anna directed Cassie by pointing ahead of them and saying, "Dad's down this hall and then to the right—room 210." As Cassie began to walk down the hall, Anna leaned toward Stephanie and made a suggestion. "Why don't we wait here and give Cassie a few minutes alone with Dad?" She pointed toward a waiting area near the elevators.

The Package

In other circumstances, Stephanie might have found numerous reasons to resent this suggestion. However, in this case, she welcomed it. The verbal joust with Cassie had irritated her, and in just a few short minutes, she already found herself needing some space to regain her composure. "Yeah, sure," said Stephanie. "Works for me."

Cassie hesitated, looked back at them, and reflected on how much she appreciated Anna's insight. There were times where she simply knew the right thing to do. "Thanks, I would appreciate some time alone with Dad. Give me a few minutes and then come on back," she said. She proceeded down the hall and disappeared around the corner.

As they each took seats in the waiting area, Anna observed Stephanie's demeanor. Stephanie forcefully picked up a magazine, dropped it on her lap, and then started flipping through it mindlessly; she obviously wasn't reading the publication. It was something to pass the time—and to cope.

Cassie tapped on her father's door and slowly entered his room. He was drowsy, but the sound roused him enough to see her enter. Smiling, she ambled up to his bed, brushed the hair on the top of his head with her hand, and said, "Hi, Dad, how are you?"

"Cassie," he replied warmly.

"Yep, it's me," she said. "Here at last. Sorry it took so long to get here."

"It's not just around the corner, is it?" he said, smiling.

She looked down and away from her father's eyes as a feeling of guilt for living so far away overtook her. "No," she said, "it's not around the corner, Dad. I'm sorry."

"How are the kids?"

"They're good," she replied. "And I'm doing okay too. I am looking forward to spring break. I need the time off."

"I'm looking forward too," he said.

Cassie understood what Dad meant. Personally, though, she struggled with his resignation to this disease. "Dad, don't say things like that. I want you to get well and get out of here. Maybe you'll get better."

"Cassie," he said, "you are an intelligent girl. You know that won't happen."

"Dad, you more than anyone I know believe in miracles. Why not for you?" she asked. "Why no miracle for you?"

He reached out and patted her hand. "I've asked God for my miracles," he said, "and I trust that he'll perform them."

The Promise

"What miracles?" she asked.

"Greater miracles than the one that could raise me from this bed!" he declared.

"Dad, I don't understand."

"You will," he said.

"I will?—How?—When?"

"In his time."

"I'm sorry," said Cassie. "I don't know what that means."

"You will, sweetheart. You see, that's one of the miracles," he said while closing his eyes and smiling; it was as if he were imagining something wonderful.

"Dad, please," she said. "Why can't you just explain it to me?"

Still smiling, her father opened his eyes and looked at her. He reached up with his hand and gently brushed her cheek with his fingers. "Do you remember when we visited Grandma's farm when you were little?" he recalled. "Remember seeing that calf being born?"

"Yes, of course I remember," she said. "I think I was about six."

"You and I had talked about it beforehand," he said. "You knew what to expect, you walked out into the field with Grandpa and me, and you watched as that mama delivered her calf."

"It was amazing!" said Cassie, recalling the moment of birth. "I loved that calf. It was the cutest thing. Poor Grandpa had to keep it forever because I wouldn't let him send it to the slaughterhouse. It was mine."

"You knew what to expect," he reminded her, "and yet you were amazed and awed by the miracle of birth."

"That's true, Dad," she replied. "But what does that have to do with any of this?"

Anna and Stephanie eased the door open and looked into the room. "Okay to come in now?" asked Anna.

"Sure," said Cassie.

Dad whispered to Cassie, "Some things are too wonderful to explain," he said. "You simply have to experience them for yourself."

Anna and Stephanie drew closer and stood next to Cassie beside their father's bed, one on each side of her. It was the first time the four of them had been together in the same room at the same time for many years. Jim scanned the room and made eye contact with each of his daughters, one by one. "You're all here—together."

Cassie glanced at Stephanie, realizing that they were all there, but they were certainly not together. She looked back at her father who was dying, and suddenly all the difficulties of the past seemed insignificant. What could she do to ease his pain? Cassie reached her hand out to Stephanie, who was surprised at this conciliatory act. Stephanie hesitated, looked at her father, and then responded by taking Cassie's hand. Cassie did likewise with Anna.

"Yes, Dad," said Cassie, "we are here together—all of us."

Stephanie took Cassie's lead, looked at her father, and said, "Dad, is there anything we can all do for you?"

Dad smiled, having prepared himself for this very question. "Yes, there is," he replied. "I need to tell you some things while you are all here together."

"Sure, Dad," said Cassie. "What is it?"

"There are a few legal matters to discuss," he said. "I have instructed my attorney to liquidate all my assets and provide each of you with a third of my estate."

Cassie, regretting that her father had to spend this time going over his legal preparations said, "Dad, we don't need to discuss this now. It doesn't matter."

"Yes, it does matter. These are things that you need to know. My estate should be worth about $320,000. Each of you should receive a little over $105,000 after my death. That sum includes everything but one item."

"What's that?" asked Cassie.

"The cabin," he replied. "I have placed it in a trust."

"What do you mean?" said Stephanie. "What kind of a trust?"

"I took out a mortgage to extract the equity from the cabin. I placed the cabin into the trust along with enough money to cover its cost for about eighteen months after my death. At that time, my executor will be directed to sell the cabin unless one of you chooses to take ownership—in essence, to buy it."

Cassie looked curiously at each of her sisters, wondering if either of them possessed any insight into this whole cabin trust scenario, but she quickly concluded from their facial expressions that they were just as confused as she was. She looked back at her father, recognizing that he had planned this with forethought and purpose. *Why?* she wondered.

"All the details are in the legal filings," he continued. "Is that clear?"

"Why, Dad?" asked Anna, voicing the question on everyone's mind. "Why keep the cabin?"

"Stephanie," he replied, "you asked if there was anything you could all do for me?"

"Sure, Dad," said Stephanie, affirming her offer.

"I want a promise from each of you," he said.

"A promise? To do what?" asked Cassie.

"Your mom and I bought the cabin for our family," he explained, "and we shared a lot of time and many good memories there together. It is a special place to me." Jim hesitated, realizing that the request he was about to make would require one of the miracles for which he prayed. He looked again at each of his daughters, one by one. "I want each of you to promise me," he said, "that you will set aside at least one more time—one last summer weekend to spend together as a family at the cabin—just the three of you."

Dad saw that Cassie's face revealed a lack of enthusiasm for the idea. While his health was fading fast, this moment was critical enough to demand his full attention and focus. "What's wrong, Cassie?" he asked.

"Dad, I think what you're trying to do is great," she said, carefully choosing her words. "Noble, even. I commend you for it. But I don't think it's a good idea. I don't know that I want to do that."

Stephanie was relieved that Cassie had voiced her similar feelings, allowing her to remain silent on the matter. The whole idea was revolting—she hated the cabin. Besides, the relationship strain with her father alone was reason enough to deny his request. But then, in a twist of fate, something inside Stephanie aroused her childhood jealousies. Cassie had said no—and that provided a unique opportunity to one-up her big sister, the family icon. The idea of making Cassie look uncooperative was appealing, and watching her sister squirm might overcome the lackluster accommodations for a simple weekend. So, rather impulsively, Stephanie said, "Okay, Dad. I'll do it. If it's that important to you, I'll go. I promise."

The malicious plot began to unfold to Stephanie's delight. As predicted, Cassie was floored by Stephanie's answer, and she gaped at Stephanie in bewilderment. Stephanie responded by providing Cassie a smug expression, which was fuel for the fire.

Anna was simply befuddled. Had she guessed their individual responses, she would have confidently predicted the opposite of what actually occurred. Anna was perplexed by her sisters' answers. She looked back to Cassie, who still appeared stunned by the turn of events, and she waited for her to respond further. Instead, Cassie stood speechless.

The Package

Anna refrained from providing her positive response to her dad's wishes, knowing that agreement with Stephanie would leave Cassie alone in her rejection of his request and increase the already intense pressure on her. As she waited, she watched Cassie attempt to catch up with her own feelings. Finally, Anna tried to coax a response from her. "Cassie? What do you want to do?"

The pressure caused Cassie to step away from the bed for a moment to think. The last thing she wanted was to disappoint her father, but she had somehow blundered. Predicting that Stephanie wouldn't agree and foreseeing the explosiveness of such a situation, she had taken control. She had played her role as the eldest, spoke up confidently on behalf of all three of them, and drew the only logical conclusion: it simply wasn't a good idea. But in an inconceivable turnabout, Stephanie had agreed to go. Cassie was now faced with three difficult choices: one, she could disappoint her father; two, she could make a promise she knew she would not keep; or three, she would step up to fix what was broken. None of these options was tenable; yet, as she considered each of them, she realized only one was acceptable. She could not disappoint her father, and she would not lie. Only one option remained—facing her issues with Stephanie. She eased back to his bedside with resignation. "I'm sorry, Dad. I—"

"Cassie!" exclaimed Anna in disappointment.

"May I finish, please!" snapped Cassie. Anna relented.

"I'm sorry, Dad," said Cassie. "I shouldn't have said it wasn't a good idea. I will do what you've asked. I'll go. I promise."

"Me too, Dad," Anna said excitedly. "I promise."

Jim successively looked at his three daughters and then looked up to heaven and smiled. This first miracle was provided. He considered how it had transpired. So often, he pondered, we think we act with our own free wills when in reality, we are simply responding to God's leading. He takes us where we need to go even when we resist going there on our own, yet we wrongly convince ourselves that we go by our own choice. Jim found his picture of God expanding. However, it always expanded and never grew smaller. Jim thanked each of his daughters for their love and for their promises. Each one of them kissed him before he went back to sleep.

Very late that evening, Cassie received a call in her hotel room from Anna telling her that her father had passed away. She had expected it. It was as though he had willed himself to remain until he said what he needed to say, said good-bye, and went home. While she and Anna both knew his time grew short, the reality of his passing was still painful, and they cried together over the phone.

When Anna and Cassie finished their conversation, Anna left for Stephanie's hotel. Anna felt that she should deliver this news in person because she felt it might be particularly difficult for Stephanie. She walked up to her door, stood for a brief moment to gain her composure, and reluctantly knocked on it. Answering the door in her nightgown, Stephanie saw Anna standing there and began to shake and back away, sensing what this visit meant. "Oh, God, no!" she said, breaking into tears and collapsing to the floor. Anna sat down on the floor beside her, held her, and cried. "He's gone, Steph," said Anna as Stephanie cried louder. "Dad's gone." Anna pushed the door closed with her foot, and they sat and held each other for awhile. A clock radio needing the time set was perched on the nightstand, and its flashing red numerals were casting shadows in the room. The dark scene it painted reminded Anna of another achingly similar one—the cabin on the night of the accident.

After Stephanie's tears subsided a bit and she began to get a grip on her emotions, Anna convinced Stephanie to go back to her house for the night. Stephanie had chosen a hotel because she resisted being dependent on anyone. But she didn't consider at the time how significantly her father's death would impact her if it happened while she was alone.

For most of the night, Anna sat with Stephanie, who intermittently cried and sobbed but said very little. Anna resisted intervention; it was not necessary to explain to Stephanie her own feelings. Stephanie knew that a door had closed forever that she needed to walk through, and Anna was painfully aware of it. The situation seemed hopeless to Stephanie, but Anna knew that God could overcome this obstacle. She couldn't imagine how he might do it, but she knew he could. So her intervention on that night was a silent one—she prayed.

Though Anna stayed close by her side, Stephanie felt completely alone. Even though she courted loneliness every day of her life, she had not felt it this intensely since her mother died. She knew she had things to say to her father that she was unable to say. Unexpressed feelings buried within her seemed cursed never to see a resurrection. What was it that kept her trapped inside herself? Why could she not open up to others? Why could she feel no peace?

The Package

In fact, all that Stephanie could feel was pain, sadness, loneliness, and despair. Her life could be summed up in one simple word that encompassed it all: hopelessness.

The next three days were a torrent of activity preparing for the funeral service. While Stephanie continued to stay with Anna, Cassie remained alone at her hotel. They all met together several times to discuss the arrangements. During that time, Stephanie barely interacted with anyone, often sitting alone or walking about numbly. For once in her life, she was surprised to find that she appreciated Cassie. Cassie was in command and worked through the funeral arrangements with the funeral home, dealt with the pastor who was officiating, and selected the music and who would play it. She processed through the whole situation with deliberation and strength. For that one moment, Stephanie was envious of Cassie.

Over three hundred people attended the funeral service, which was a celebration of his life. That was Anna's contribution. While Cassie made the necessary decisions, Anna lobbied for her desires to make the ceremony upbeat—as positive as possible for a funeral.

After the funeral service, a limousine carried the three girls to the small graveside service. They were there alone with the pastor, which was how Cassie wanted it. Jim was to be buried in a plot next to Denise. Neither Cassie nor Stephanie had been to this place since their mother died, and a flood of memories rushed in as they stood together gazing at their mother's tombstone. This was particularly painful for Stephanie.

A few minutes later, the limousine took the girls back to their own cars, and they agreed to meet at a small Italian restaurant. This was the only time since their father died where they were together without decisions to make or places to be. It was the only time they had visited and relaxed together in years. The conversation was minimal. In fact, it was a very quiet dinner.

As they were finishing, Cassie spoke to Stephanie. "So, we're the proud owners of a cabin in Pennsylvania. How about that?"

Stephanie's lackadaisical attitude was evident in her demeanor.

"Well, in spite of an apparent lack of enthusiasm," continued Cassie, "it seems we all have a promise to fulfill. Anybody have a suggestion for a date?"

Anna was anxious to get them together soon and said, "How about Memorial Day weekend?"

The Promise

"That's right at the end of the school year," replied Cassie, "and with the flights from the west coast, I need a longer weekend than that. If I'm coming . . . I mean, when I come, I'd rather it be for a little more than just a two-day weekend. I can do almost anything in the summer."

"What do you want to do, Stephanie?" asked Anna.

"I want to forget the whole thing!" she replied.

"Stephanie!" said Anna, who was clearly distraught.

"I didn't say I wouldn't do it," said Stephanie. "You asked what I wanted to do."

"Okay, what dates work for you?" she asked.

"Anytime in the summer is fine," said Stephanie. "My schedule is pretty open right now. Whenever."

"Well, we always went to the cabin as kids on the Fourth of July weekend," said Anna. "Anybody got a calendar?"

Stephanie pulled one from her purse and opened it up. "The Fourth is on a Friday," she said. "That's a three-day weekend."

"Okay," said Anna. "How about we arrive Thursday evening, and we'll stay at the cabin for three days, leaving on Monday."

"When Monday?" asked Cassie.

"Well," said Anna, "you wanted to make sure the trip was worth your travel time, so how about Monday evening?"

"Look, we promised Dad a weekend," said Stephanie. "This is turning into five days."

"It's actually only four," said Anna. "You think that's gonna kill you?"

"It might," replied Stephanie.

Cassie had removed her calendar from her purse as well and now had it open. "Okay," she said. "I'll book flights to get there on Thursday, July 3, and leave on the evening of Monday, July 7. Are we agreed?"

"Stephanie?" said Anna.

"Oh, all right," said Stephanie, "if you two goodies need to spend four days, I'll do it." Stephanie gazed intently at Cassie and glanced back toward Anna. "If World War III breaks out at the cabin, do we get a pass?"

"No passes," said Anna. "We all promised. So, do we have agreement?" Cassie and Stephanie both nodded affirmatively. Anna chose to ignore the rolling of the eyes that accompanied Stephanie's nod. Anna motioned to the waiter. "Could we get our check please?" Both Anna's sisters reached for their wallets. "Nope," said Anna, "this one's on me. No negotiation."

"Why?" asked Cassie.

The Package

Anna growled her answer with her best gangster accent. "Because-a then you-a owe me, and I'll-a track you-a down like-a dogs if you don't-a show up. You-a got it?"

"I-a got it," said Cassie, playing along.

"You-a got it?" said Anna, glaring at Stephanie.

"I'm shakin' all over," groaned Stephanie as she wagged her head in disbelief.

Anna and Cassie laughed out loud together at Stephanie as the waiter arrived with the bill, which Anna paid with cash. "Ready to go?" asked Anna. Both Cassie and Stephanie nodded. They rose from their seats and moved toward the door, negotiating their way through a busy evening dinner crowd that had gathered and was waiting for an open table.

Once outside, the three sisters looked at each other, traded hugs, and reluctantly parted ways. As Anna got about halfway to her car, she turned back toward them. "I love you guys!" she shouted, waving energetically. "See you on the Fourth!"

6

PREPARATION

An early July sun rose over the hillside above the cabin beginning the day of the promise—the day that the three sisters would arrive. A few hours later, a car pulled into the gravel driveway and eased to a stop. The car door opened, and the first arrival of the day set foot onto the property. Anna stood, removed her sunglasses, and drew a deep breath into her nostrils. The morning breeze smelled of pine needles as it blew her dark brown hair across her face. The aroma of pine was a familiar smell in this place, and it caused her to stop for a moment and relax her folded arms onto the top of her car door. *I love this place*, she thought. *Maybe as much as Dad did.*

Anna stepped back, closed her door, walked to the edge of the forest, and stretched her arms over her head. She cherished the freedom she felt beneath the canopy of the stately trees. In her imagination, the myriad creeks and rills separating the slopes near the cabin were like arteries providing life to the quiet reaches of the woodland. For a moment, she paused and quieted her thoughts to meditate on the peacefulness surrounding her. As she stood motionless, the engulfing silence was suddenly amplified by a lone singing songbird, which was soon joined by a gentle wind discovering the leaves.

Oh, the delight in visiting this place, thought Anna, *a place with beauty that calms the soul. Here, traffic jams, demanding schedules, and the pressures of everyday life hold no power.* Her plan was to exploit the beauty of this day in solitude before her sisters arrived, and she intended to make the most of that opportunity.

Preparing to unload the supplies from her car, she stepped up on the porch, held the screen door open with her foot, and unlocked and opened the door. As she returned to the car for her first armload, she heard the sound of the wood screen door slapping against its frame and echoing throughout the hollows. *If a home had a voice that could declare its presence,*

The Package

she thought, *that would be it.* It was a dichotomous sound, harsh in its presentation but warm in its intent. She smirked as she popped her car trunk open and began the process of lugging everything into the cabin.

Her feelings about spending the extended holiday weekend with her sisters were as disparate as the smack from the screen door. Her anticipation was countered with trepidation, and this contradiction made her time of solitude all the more precious. There would be time to sense her own spirit and to speak with God about the coming family summit.

Anna had convinced her sisters that arriving on Thursday evening before the Friday holiday would give them more time together. In retrospect, she considered that waiting until Friday might have been wiser. There were more activities on the Fourth of July to distract everyone from the depth of their emotions. She hoped there would be no fireworks until the next evening.

When Anna finished the tasks of putting away the weekend's supplies, settling herself into her bedroom, and changing clothes, she embarked on her planned trek through the woods. About three miles from the cabin was an old friend to whom she owed a visit, a friend that she and her sisters had named Pinnacle Ridge.

When Anna and her sisters were children, they gave names to nearly every place they hiked and played. It was an easy way to tell somebody where you were going or where you'd been when you were out in the woods. The place they named Pinnacle Ridge was a large, rocky protrusion from the green hillside that overlooked an expansive river valley. It was a favorite childhood stomping ground where Anna and her sisters would sit for hours and share their innermost thoughts and feelings. It was the right place to ponder Anna's hopes for the weekend to come. Since the time she was a child, if she or her sisters had a wish, Pinnacle Ridge was the place to go. Anna was anxious to get going. She had been planning this hike for several days. She grabbed a bottle of water from the cabinet she had just stocked and set off on her excursion.

Pinnacle Ridge was so named because it was the high point of the ridge that ran along the edge of the valley, and it had a ledge overlooking a meadow nearly eighty feet below it. Anna recalled a warning from long ago. "The Pinnacle is a dangerous place," her father would say. "Make sure you stay back from the edge." The girls heeded that advice and were always careful not to run or play near the edge, but they did like to venture out to sit on the edge with their feet hanging above the void.

Preparation

The hike to Pinnacle Ridge began on a path alongside the brook running near the cabin. When Anna was young, the family—particularly the girls—ran up and down that path so many times as to keep it clear of vegetation. Even in recent years, Anna knew her dad had often gone out and taken walks along it. It was a flat, gentle, and easy walk. As Anna began her hike upstream, she found the Creek Path a little overgrown in places, yet there was still enough of a defined path to keep the walking easy.

The Creek Path continued along the edge of the stream for about a half mile. At that point, it emptied onto a logging road that was once accessible from the main road near the cabin. As Anna approached this juncture, the path she was walking on became less defined. Once she arrived, she was surprised to see that the logging road was no longer there.

When they were kids, the place where she stood had been a dirt and gravel road with no vegetation to speak of, except for a smattering of grass between the twin paths traversed by the tires of the logging trucks. Now, she was startled to see that the only remaining evidence of that road was a long ribbon of much smaller trees growing along its previous course. She kicked her heel into the ground and scratched away the thin covering of dirt, grass, and moss on the surface. Just beneath this organic veneer was the familiar gravel roadway. The forest might have been evicted for a season, but it had moved back home.

It was at this intersection point where Creek Path ended. In its day, the old logging road continued to follow the creek bed upstream and because of this, the girls called it Creek Road. Anna's foray up Creek Road was still reasonably negotiated, as most of the trees along the path were still small. But as happens in any mature forest, numerous large trees had fallen across the path. With no loggers around anymore to remove these obstacles, Anna had to scramble to get over or around them. She still found this feasible and in fact enjoyable.

The trail continued in this manner for nearly a mile. At this point, the old logging road had ended at the beginning of a mature forest of ash trees. Stephanie first named this place Ash Grove, based on a song she had learned in elementary school by the same name. The large ash trees were tall and majestic here, and they had bountiful branches. In the fall, these trees dropped a very large number of leaves, making this grove an ideal autumn playground.

Anna continued her hike through Ash Grove. The hiking was easy here since the canopy of the trees had choked out most of the forest undergrowth. She knew that come October, walking in the leaves might be like wading in snow. But today was easy. As she scuffed her feet along her path, she scared up several cottontail rabbits, a few squirrels, and even a groundhog. At one point, she stopped when she heard the loud rat-a-tat sound of a pileated woodpecker. It was a large bird she had only seen a few times in her life, as its intense reverberation in the trees meant you would hear one from a distance far more often than you'd see one nearby.

The path to Pinnacle Ridge continued through Ash Grove, and about midway through, it began a steady climb uphill. The creek that the trail had followed here forged a sudden deep gouge in the hillside and veered to the right, away from Anna's destination. She continued her steep climb for about ten minutes until she arrived at the beginning of the next leg of her journey.

Pine Hill was aptly named for a very large grove of white pines growing near the top of the hill Anna was climbing. As children, Pine Hill was the ideal place for a game of hide-and-seek, in that you could sneak around the trees during the game and remain hidden for hours. Being the youngest, Anna disliked the game. Her two older sisters were more skilled at changing hiding places than she was, and that resulted in a lot more time spent seeking than hiding.

The pine forest had matured since Anna had been here last. Walking around in the trees, she estimated that there might be twenty or thirty acres of what were now thirty or forty-foot tall pine trees. Navigating through this forest was more difficult than she remembered since the breadth of the trees had expanded, making many of the paths between them impassable.

Nearly an hour into the journey, Anna walked out of the pines and entered into a large area with very few trees. Since it was nearly at the top of the hill, it was given the name Upper Meadow. It was about a ten minute walk across the Upper Meadow to Pinnacle Ridge, down through a small rill, across a tiny stream, and back up a gentle slope.

In the spring and summer, the Upper Meadow boasted a number of groupings of wildflowers. There were wild daisies, coneflowers, and in the wet areas around the small stream were clusters of day lilies. But the Upper Meadow was dominated by various types of tall grasses, which flowed like a sea in the breeze. The Upper Meadow was a beautiful place.

Ten minutes later Anna finally arrived at her childhood refuge. She walked out onto Pinnacle Ridge, sat down, and took a long drink from her water bottle. The hike seemed a little shorter than she expected, but she hadn't made this journey in many years. *Everything seemed larger when I was a child*, she thought. She smiled, realizing that nearly everyone shares this perception.

As she stood and scanned the horizon from this vista, she was surprised by how different everything looked. She was fascinated at how much twenty or thirty years can change the entire look of the forest. It was still a beautiful place, but it *was* different. She crept toward the edge and gazed down at the Lower Meadow at the base of the cliff. A grove of trees had grown up at its base, and she could barely see the meadow through the tops of those trees.

Anna sat down on the rock for awhile to enjoy the view and the fresh air. She watched as a parade of large white cumulus clouds marched past her in procession on their deep blue street. An occasional high-flying jet would draw a slender white ribbon into the sky. It was a lovely July day, and the ridge was a welcoming companion.

Anna sat on the rock for nearly an hour before her eyes noticed something that caught her curiosity. It was sitting in the small scrap of the Lower Meadow that she could barely see through the trees. She stared at it for a few seconds, pondering what it could be. Finally, she realized it was a pile of wood planks strewn across the ground and overgrown with weeds.

She rested her back onto the rocky ground and directed her attention again to the blue sky. As she pondered the things she had seen here, a sudden realization hit her. It caused her to sit up and reassess what she had seen in the Lower Meadow. Comparing her memories with what she now observed, she came to realize that the strewn planks in the grass were all that remained of the Old Barn.

The Old Barn in the Lower Meadow was an abandoned outbuilding, which was in poor condition even when they were children. The Lower Meadow, and hence the Old Barn, could be visited by continuing down the ridge about one hundred yards to the right and scrambling down the rocky slope. Anna and her sisters had accomplished this innumerable times as children, and upon doing so, they would go to the Old Barn to play together and talk.

Looking at what was left of it, Anna's thoughts again turned to her sisters. She hoped their mutual relationships were not like the Old Barn. It was worse than neglected, worse than abandoned. It was beyond hope—now no more than a collection of broken and rotting pieces. There was virtually nothing of value left. It was unsalvageable.

The Package

As though she were standing watching herself, she realized the negativity of that kind of thinking and banished the thought. She determined to replace it with a positive one. She recalled that when they were children, Cassie believed if you took a pine cone from Pine Hill, closed your eyes, and made a wish as you threw it over the cliff, your wish would come true. On this day, Anna didn't need a pine cone. She didn't need a wish. She needed help—divine help.

Anna stood up, looked to the heavens, and prayed with a very loud voice that she knew no other person would hear. At each pause in her voice, it was as though nature itself echoed her very heart.

"Lord Jesus . . . I trust in your ways . . . and while I may not always understand them . . . I will not lose hope." Quietly, she repeated the final words to herself, "I will not lose hope."

Anna often spoke to God, but she usually did not "hear" an answer. But as Anna thought to begin her trek back to the cabin, she stopped to scan the horizon one last time. She suspected she might never see this vista again. As she stood taking in that last gaze, the gentle breeze that had been stirring in the trees all morning hushed to a strange stillness. In that moment, she sensed a voice in her spirit saying, "I AM with you."

As if with purpose, a strong gust of wind rushed across the forest below her and up the ridge, causing her to shift her weight to keep her balance. A dead limb cracked and then crashed to the ground somewhere in the forest below. Anna smiled at God and thanked him for the reassurance. Dancing down off the rock, she began the hike back, singing songs to God and laughing.

"God was not in the fire, not in the wind, but was heard in a still small voice," she said aloud. A renewed confidence burgeoned inside her spirit, and the knowledge that she was not hiking alone put a spring in her step.

Cassie sat in a waiting area at O'Hare International Airport waiting for her connecting flight. It was already mid-afternoon, and it was going to be late in the evening by the time she finally arrived at the cabin. She had spent the last few months mentally and emotionally preparing for this trip. Yet with all the thought and rationality she could muster, she still did not know what to expect.

For Cassie, the fact that she and Anna were on good terms was a positive aspect. While they had not been close in recent years, the time before and during Dad's funeral had given her a new respect for Anna. She had matured into a woman who was simple but wise. There were numerous occasions on the last trip where she had seen Anna bring sanity to insane situations. Cassie was glad Anna would be there. She felt Anna embodied the one chance they had for a civil weekend.

On the other hand, Cassie saw Stephanie as unpredictable. Cassie knew they had made some progress the last time they were together, but it was a few small steps on a very, very long journey. She knew she had some fence-mending to do. She wondered if those fences would end up being boundaries to protect relationships or walls to preclude them.

That aside, Cassie determined that she would have an open mind about the whole weekend. She had the self-awareness to know that determination was one of her strengths. However, that same awareness also told her that when intense feelings wound themselves into the mix, she could get frustrated—sometimes *very* frustrated.

Stephanie has strengths too, she thought, trying to nurture a positive attitude. *Passion, for instance—she's very passionate about things.* Then worry crept back in as she considered that assessment further: passion often creates intense feelings. While trying to be positive, she had come full circle back to her own weaknesses. "It could be a long weekend," she said out loud.

"I'm sorry. What did you say?" asked the lady sitting next to her in the airport.

"Nothing, sorry," said Cassie, realizing how tangible her thoughts had become. "I guess I was thinking out loud."

Spending a weekend at the cabin wasn't Stephanie's idea of a vacation, or even a fun weekend away. Numerous times she had toyed with the idea of disregarding the promise she had made to her father. She certainly couldn't disappoint him any further than she already had throughout her life. And she considered it probable that her sisters might someday be happier if she didn't participate. Even for someone who loved to live life without rules and threw caution to the wind, there was still a feeling inside her that still believed that promises should be kept. So she clung to that belief and motivated herself to board the plane for Pittsburgh.

As she sat on the plane staring out the window across the countryside while listening to her MP3 player, Stephanie had to face the simple fact

The Package

that she was emotionally unprepared for this weekend. She wasn't sure she even had the ability to prepare for it or that she should prepare for it. By the time she exited the plane into the Pittsburgh airport, she had worked herself into a tizzy and became overwhelmed by it all.

Walking down the concourse to the baggage claim area, Stephanie resolved that she was too tired to deal with her emotions tonight. *It won't hurt anything if I wait until morning,* she reasoned. *I'll simply call Anna and stay here to get a good night's sleep before I take this on.* She proceeded to the rental car counter, cancelled her reservation, and checked into the airport hotel.

Stephanie called Anna from her hotel room and made up the best excuse she could fashion without being honest about her apprehension. She could hear the disappointment in Anna's voice. Stephanie had anticipated this, and she was disappointed in herself for not having the guts to go through with staying with her sisters that night. But she could not overcome the urge to postpone the conflict she anticipated. *Even tomorrow is far too soon,* she thought.

———

Anna hung up the phone feeling disappointed, but also remembering her thoughts earlier in the day about the wisdom of getting together early. Maybe this was as it should be. Maybe everyone needed to sleep on it for one more night.

7

FIRST NIGHT

It was getting late when Cassie arrived at the cabin. The normal four-hour flight from the west coast had seemed endless with the addition of a planned three-hour layover in Chicago. As she finally pulled into the driveway, she was surprised to see only one car outside, expecting that she would be the last to arrive. She removed her bags from her car, walked up the three steps to the porch of the cabin, and breathed a sigh of relief. *Finally here*, she thought.

Cassie entered the door and was surprised to find an empty room. She expected Anna to be standing at the door waiting.

"Anna? Are you here?" she called out.

Anna rushed into the room from down the hall. She paused for a moment while Cassie set down her bags and greeted her with a warm embrace. "Cassie!" she said. "How are you? I am so glad you are here. I've been here most of the day, and I've got to tell you, it was getting a bit lonely. It gets pretty dark here."

"Well, your big sister is here now." Cassie caught a whiff of a pungent aroma in the room. "What's that I smell?"

"I was brewing some tea before bed," said Anna. "It's a new exotic blend I'm trying. Want some?"

Drinking something with such an unpleasant aroma was not an engaging idea, but Cassie had resolved that she would get along this weekend. It was counterproductive to start off on the wrong foot. "Okay," said Cassie. "I'll give it a try. Let me put my bags away." Cassie began gathering her bags. "You in the back bedroom?" she asked.

"Yes. I figured you could settle in Dad's room," said Anna as she retreated to the kitchen stove to pour the tea.

Cassie hadn't even considered the sleeping arrangements. Sleeping in her parents' room had a sense of awkwardness about it, but she could not

The Package

conceive of a logical reason to challenge the idea. Her hesitation made Anna aware of her discomfort.

"Is that okay with you?" asked Anna.

"It's fine," said Cassie. "If you think that . . ." She was still evaluating other possibilities, but acquiesced. "It's fine."

"Leave the bags for now," said Anna. "We can get them later."

Cassie took Anna's suggestion and set the bags on the floor near the entrance to the hallway leading to the bedrooms. This hallway left the room at the point where the living room melded into a kitchen. The kitchen had an island for cooking with an elevated counter attached to its backside for eating. At the counter were three stools, and Cassie availed herself of one and sat across the counter from Anna as she finished preparing their tea.

"So how was your trip?" asked Anna.

"Pretty good," said Cassie. "We had an equipment delay on the Sacramento to Chicago leg, but I had a long layover before my Pittsburgh flight anyway, so it turned out okay. I told the man at the rental counter I was driving an hour up into the mountains, and he gave me a free upgrade to a four-wheel drive."

"That's good."

"Well, it sure made driving the gravel roads out here a little easier. He was really nice."

"Maybe he thought you were cute," laughed Anna as she finished pouring tea for the two of them and then nodded to suggest they move to the living room sofa.

"Be serious," said Cassie, joining her on the sofa. "I said he was nice. I didn't say he was blind."

"You're too hard on yourself," said Anna. "It's not like you're . . . you know . . . unattractive."

Cassie glared at Anna, indicating that she had noted the backhanded compliment.

"Sorry," said Anna.

Cassie tried to set that conversation aside by picking up her mug and taking a sip of tea. However, her taste buds revolted, and she quickly pulled the cup away from her mouth. Although the possibility had escaped Cassie's consideration, the taste was actually worse than the smell.

"How's the tea?" asked Anna. "Do you like it?"

"It's different," said Cassie. "But I'm not a big tea drinker anyway—

mostly coffee." No longer interested in its contents, Cassie examined her mug. The logo of the steel company that had employed her father was emblazoned on the side in bright colors. Thinking of him, she looked around and realized how empty the cabin felt. Anna sensed her change in mood.

"It's hard, isn't it?" she asked.

"What?"

"Being here—surrounded by Dad's things."

Cassie sighed with regret. "I wish I hadn't told him I didn't want to come," she said. "He was dying, and that was all he wanted from me—to come here. It was so important to him that we all came here this weekend."

"You told him you'd come," said Anna, as she leaned a bit closer, "and you're here."

"I still haven't dealt with the fact that Dad is gone," said Cassie, looking toward the hallway. "I keep expecting him to walk into the room. I always thought of him as the man of steel. Somehow I guess I thought he'd live forever."

"Working at a steel mill doesn't make you ironclad," said Anna. "You've been away for a long time, Cassie. I mean, on the outside, maybe he looked like the man of steel, but on the inside—the inside was gold."

Cassie set her mug on the coffee table, rose to her feet, and walked around the room looking at family pictures on the shelves. She walked by the kitchen counter and slid her hand along it as she passed.

"I do have some great memories of this place," she said.

"Yeah, me too," said Anna. "Remember when Dad and Mom bought this place—the surprise trip?"

"That was so funny," said Cassie, laughing. "Stephanie thought we were going to Disney World. And we ended up here, in the middle of nowhere. She was so disappointed."

Anna rose to her feet and confronted Cassie. "Well, that's understandable," she said. "You were what, ten years old at the time? Steph was only seven; I was five. There's a big difference between a seven and a ten-year-old, you know."

Anna's defensive reaction took Cassie aback. Anna rarely said anything that could be construed as critical. "Hey, it was just funny at the time," said Cassie, trying to ease her concern. "I wasn't criticizing her."

"It seems like you're always picking on Stephanie," said Anna.

Cassie recalled a rule that Mom had taught them when they were kids. When the family got in the car, no one was allowed to say anything nega-

The Package

tive for five minutes: no whining, no complaining, and no criticism. It was simply a way to get things off to a good start. "Hey, hey, hey!" reacted Cassie as she moved back to a chair sitting next to the sofa. "I just got here. Don't we have a five-minute rule? I thought we had a five-minute rule."

Her appeal to the family rule made Anna realize that she was criticizing Cassie's critical nature. She had been called on her duplicitous remark.

"Okay, sorry," said Anna, who figured that the only way she could save face was to find a way to reinterpret the rule. "I thought it was two," she said with feigned seriousness.

"You nut!" said Cassie, hurling a throw pillow at Anna. "Always have to make a joke, don't you?"

"Hey, I wouldn't want to have to be so serious all the time like you," said Anna. Cassie's sneer accused her again. "Oops," said Anna, looking at her watch. "Still one minute to go."

Anna turned her watch toward Cassie and pointed to it, Cassie's stern look melted into a smile, and then they both laughed out loud. Anna retrieved the sofa pillow from the floor, and they sat together for a moment as the laughter subsided.

"So, how are Craig and the kids?" asked Cassie.

"Well," replied Anna, "Craig is off on a three-day international jaunt. I thought it was difficult being married to a pilot who only did 'out-and-backs' at every hour of the day. But he's flying international now, and it's worse. Here's to moving up." Anna raised her mug in a mock toast and took a sip. Cassie picked up her mug and responded in similar fashion but was careful to avoid taking another drink.

"And the boys?" asked Cassie.

"Nathan is away at a two-week soccer camp," answered Anna. "And Ethan's on a retreat with the youth group from church. I thought it was crazy when they scheduled it on the Fourth of July weekend. I mean, it was always a family weekend for us as kids." Anna thought for a moment as she took another sip of tea. "As it turned out," she conceded, "it was for the best. I would have struggled to get here this weekend if that hadn't happened. God seemed to have a plan of his own."

The idea that God somehow had plans at this level of detail was too much for Cassie's theology. She believed that she decided her own affairs out of her own free will. She had come here because Dad had asked her, not out of some act of divine intervention. She perceived that Anna simply liked to spiritualize everything.

First Night

"Maybe it was just good fortune, Anna," replied Cassie.

"Maybe God had a plan," she retorted.

Cassie decided that she shouldn't derail things the first evening with a useless theological debate. "Okay, I guess it's . . . it's possible," she sneered.

Anna also realized that this debate had no fruitful conclusion. She was concerned, however, that Cassie's doubt was becoming a chronic pattern. Yes, Cassie's nature was to question everything, and she lived her life based on her reasoned answers. But in the last year, Anna had seen Cassie doubting the one thing that she had never questioned—herself. Clearly, the divorce was a seminal event that had shaken Cassie to her very foundation.

"So, what about you? How are . . . you know . . . things?" Anna had tried to choose her words so carefully that she had become tongue-tied.

"Why do you have to ask that way?" snapped Cassie.

"I don't know," said Anna, realizing she had hit a nerve. "It's just awkward."

"Awkward?" Cassie was irritated. "Because I don't have the perfect family and perfect life like you—that's awkward for *you*?"

Anna had heard the "perfect life" accusation before, and it aggravated her. "I've never said we were perfect," she answered. "I've never even thought so." Cassie didn't respond. "Look," said Anna, "I'm sure it's been hard since Mark left. And I'm sure you're dealing with fear every day with your son in the service and stationed overseas. Look, I want to talk to you about it. But I don't know how."

Cassie glared at Anna for a moment, but the truth stopped her in her tracks. She looked away.

Anna thought it an opportunity to reach out to her. "It just seems like you shut everyone out. Why do you do that?" she asked.

Cassie struggled to reveal her feelings. "Anna, I spent twenty-three years washing clothes, cooking meals, raising kids, and working a job at the high school. Most of those years, I dealt with cold indifference from Mark. We'd go to church, and everyone would think we were the happy couple."

"I'm sorry, Cassie," said Anna. "None of us knew."

"I hid it from everyone. But now . . . now that he's gone . . . everyone knows . . . I feel totally exposed. I've failed my kids, my family . . . everyone."

"Why do you think that?" said Anna. "I don't blame you; nobody blames you."

Cassie looked at her with pain in her eyes. *If only that were true*, she

The Package

thought. Her daughter, Lisa, was a rebellious teenager. Seeing early indications of trouble, Cassie had reacted by heavily restricting Lisa's activities. But the tighter Cassie held on, the deeper Lisa's rebellion went. Adding insult to injury, Cassie's husband Mark undermined her. Mark avoided conflict at all cost. "Kids will be kids," he would say. "Let them make their mistakes and learn from them." And that disengaged, permissive approach endeared him to Lisa. Cassie often wondered if the strain of dealing with Lisa might have been what drove Mark into infidelity. He detested Cassie's rigid view of life, and he had turned Lisa against her. It was painful to admit.

"Lisa blames me," she told Anna. "She's always seen things Mark's way. When he left, she blamed me. She said I was too religious for her dad. Can you believe that? Too religious! 'Dad doesn't need a priest, he needs a wife,'" she said mocking Lisa's accusations. She paused for a moment, trying to understand her own feelings. "You know, Anna, it's amazing. I thought we shared a faith in Christ. I thought he believed as I did when we got married. Turns out, what he really believes in wears a size two. I don't understand why people can't see that, especially Lisa."

"Do you really think that?" asked Anna. Cassie looked indignant. "What I meant was, do you really think you are too religious?"

"I don't know," she replied. "I mean, I've never even been the Christian I thought I ought to be. Mark thought I was too strict about things. But, the truth is, even Dad once told me I was too religious."

"Dad told you that you were too religious because being a Christian is not about going to church," said Anna.

Cassie felt invaded and betrayed. "How do you know that's what he told me?" she asked. "Did you and Dad talk about this?"

"Cassie, that's what Dad told *everyone*."

"You?"

"Yes."

"I guess *you* listened," said Cassie sarcastically.

"I tried."

"So it's just that simple," she said as she rose from her chair, moved to the kitchen, and dumped her tea into the sink. "I didn't listen, and you did; and that's why you're living the perfect life."

Anna had overlooked this characterization the first time, but Cassie's sarcasm now motivated a terse response. "Cassie, my life is so far from perfect," she snapped as she jumped to her feet. "I was always the little sister,

First Night

always wanting to be accepted—to be as important as everyone else. I was only fifteen when Mom died, fifteen! And where were you? Off at Boston College! I was here, right here in this cabin trying to take care of Dad. One of my kids was in drug rehab a few years ago; did you know that?" Cassie looked at her but provided no response. "Well, *did* you?"

"No," said Cassie, feeling embarrassed.

"And you think my life is perfect!" Anna shook her head in disgust.

"Anna, I only meant that—"

"It has taken me years to figure out who I am; someone other than Jim's daughter, or Craig's wife—or *your* little sister. I've learned that I am a child of God, and he sees me for who I am, as Anna; and he loves me. And while my life is *not* perfect, God knows who I am."

Anna's defensiveness was uncharacteristic—her response took Cassie aback. Perhaps, Cassie considered, the anxiety posed by the weekend was affecting Anna too. She back-pedaled. "I didn't mean to attack you, Anna. I'm glad you've found your answers. Right now, I am just feeling so inadequate." Struggling for words, Cassie walked back in the living room and took a seat on the sofa. Anna sat down next to her. "I just need to . . . I don't know," said Cassie. Anna encouraged her with a warm smile, and Cassie continued. "I just need to find a way to enjoy a four-day weekend with my sisters. When is Stephanie coming anyway? I thought she'd be here."

"Tomorrow morning," said Anna. "She flew into Pittsburgh tonight. But she said she wasn't coming out to the 'boonies' in the middle of the night. She said she'd be here in the morning."

"I still can't believe she's actually coming," said Cassie.

"Why?"

"When's the last time she ever did anything for anyone else?"

Anna knew that Cassie's condemnation was essentially true. For years, Stephanie had deliberately isolated herself from the family. But Anna had determined that she would remain positive.

"Look," said Anna, "Steph may have her issues with Dad—and us for that matter—but she loved him. When Dad ended up in the hospital, she dropped everything and was there by his side. In fact, she was the one who asked if there was anything we could do for him."

"Dad sure came up with another one of his surprise answers," said Cassie.

"Yes, he did."

The Package

"I just figured he'd smile and say no. Dad never needed anything."

"Cass, that's not true," said Anna.

"You know, the man of steel."

On the surface, Anna understood Cassie's assessment. Their father *was* the man of steel. He was tough, strong, and independent. He was a fearsome negotiator and a solitary voice standing against the crowd. He set expectations for himself and generally achieved them. But the accident had changed him forever. Yes, he still possessed every characteristic that Cassie had come to know, yet something else inside him had come alive. Anna had seen the transformation happen before her eyes—here in this cabin. She knew her sisters had missed it.

"Cassie, right after the accident, after the memorial services and the visitations were over, when you went back to college, Dad came here for a month."

"I knew that," said Cassie. "Nobody bothered to tell me at the time; but when no one answered the phone for a week, I finally called Uncle Todd, and he told me where you were." The ill feelings had always inhibited discussion about that time in their lives.

"I'm sorry, Cassie," said Anna. "I should have called you. But I had a lot going on here—I was overwhelmed."

"I thought going back to school was the right thing to do," said Cassie. "Maybe I shouldn't have. I guess I didn't expect that all of you would simply disappear."

"Well, Dad felt he needed to come here," explained Anna. "Stephanie refused to come. She was so angry about losing Mom. The Davises said she could stay with them while he was gone, so Dad let her have her space."

Cassie wondered why Anna was dredging this up this story.

"I know you know all that," Anna continued, "but I've never told you about that month—about what happened."

"Are you about to tell me why we're all here?" asked Cassie.

"Maybe," replied Anna. "I'm not sure I know."

"Providence? Or God's plan?" said Cassie sarcastically.

"I don't know, Cassie," said Anna.

"Maybe it's only because Dad made us all promise to come this weekend."

"Or maybe not. Look," continued Anna, realizing that further discussion was futile, "let's save this for another time. It's been a long day. I'm exhausted, and it looks like we have the whole weekend together. I think I'm going to turn in." Anna smiled at Cassie to release the tension.

First Night

Cassie understood. "Good night, Anna."

"Night, Cassie."

Anna headed toward the hall but stopped and pointed to a phone sitting on a small stand. "And look!" she exclaimed. "Modern conveniences come to the mountain—a phone. And it even has buttons on it!"

"Oh, I brought my cell," said Cassie.

"You really have been away for awhile," said Anna. "Here? The only bars your phone will see here is if you take it down to the Chug-a-Jug on Route 8."

"I thought you were going to bed!" joked Cassie.

"Right." Again, Anna started walking to her bedroom. But before she exited the room, she turned and placed her hand on the corner of the hall and laid her head against it, looking back at Cassie. "Cassie?" Cassie looked toward her. "I'm glad you came."

"Yeah, me too," replied Cassie. "We've got a lot to catch up on. Good night, Anna."

As Anna retired for the night, Cassie sat quietly for a moment and looked around the room. She rose up and ambled along the mantle of the fireplace, which had many family pictures that had accumulated over the years. She paused at each picture and looked each one over until she reached a portrait of her father. She picked it up, gazed at his image, and recalled that moment in the hospital when she made her promise. A few moments later, she gently placed the portrait back on the shelf saying, "Good night, Dad."

Cassie picked up her bags from the floor. Before she proceeded down the hall, she hesitated and turned about for a moment. Her eyes found a room full of dying memories that were once again being given new life inside her. Eventually, her focus again fell on her father's portrait. She stared at it for a few seconds with a smile on her face and turned out the lights.

8

FOURTH OF JULY

Anna woke early and read for a little while before going to the kitchen to prepare breakfast. She was just finishing when Cassie came into the room and looked deeply into the simmering pot on the stove. She then panned her gaze up to Anna. "Oatmeal?" asked Cassie. "Is there a message here? I was hoping for Frosty O's. You know, for old time's sake."

"Frosty O's? Are you kidding? Those things were like 500% sugar. My kids ate them one time, and they had *me* climbing the walls. I mean, no one would eat those things unless they—you are kidding, right?"

"Yes, I was kidding," said Cassie. "But you didn't have to go all the way to oatmeal. It's like the perfect food for everything that ails you."

Anna filled a bowl and handed it to Cassie. She stirred it slowly as she stared into it. Even its appearance was distasteful. "I don't know," said Cassie, "maybe I wasn't kidding."

Anna became defensive. "If you didn't want oatmeal, you could have helped a little in the planning, you know. I didn't know you were so picky."

"Relax, Anna, oatmeal is fine." Anna was unconvinced. So Cassie put a full spoonful into her mouth and feigned delight. "Hmm!"

"You are such a pain," said Anna as they both laughed together.

Just then, they heard the sound of a car door outside. Moments later, the door to the cabin popped open, and Stephanie flowed into the room laden with bags as if she were on a three-week vacation. She dropped her bags, looked at her sisters over her sunglasses, and spoke in an irritated tone. "Hang on. I've got to pay the cabbie."

"You came in a *cab*?" decried Cassie.

Stephanie delivered a stern look and walked out the door.

Anna watched Stephanie exit and snapped back toward Cassie. "That didn't take long."

"What?"

Fourth of July

"You and Stephanie."

"Anna, she came in a *cab!*"

Anna had expected difficulties. But conflict raged before they barely finished one sentence. "Could you please just lighten up on her for one weekend? The five-minute rule applies to Steph too."

Cassie was indignant.

"Right?" demanded Anna.

Cassie sighed and relented. "All right, I'll work on it."

Stephanie reentered the room, returned her wallet to her purse, and expressed her frustration. "I cannot believe that. Ninety-three dollars for that trip. Oh well, what should the fare to nowhere be, anyway?"

Anna stepped toward Stephanie, hugged her, and said, "Hi, Steph. I am so glad you're here."

Cassie offered dispassionately. "We were just discussing the merits of oatmeal."

"Great!" said Stephanie. "It's good to know the important issues of our time are being discussed right here in the heart of Hicksville."

Stephanie's eyes met Cassie's for an awkward moment. Cassie spoke first. "Nice to see you, Stephanie."

"Hello, Cassie. How are things on the left coast?"

"Well, Sacramento is quiet compared to the insanity of New York. I don't know how you can stand to live there."

Anna winced.

"Well," said Stephanie, "living there is not nearly as insane as visiting this place. I can't believe I let Dad convince me to do this. But I'm here now, so where should I put my bags?"

"You're in the middle room," said Anna, glad for the change in subject. "I'm in the back."

"And where are you staying?" asked Stephanie.

"In Mom and Dad's room," replied Cassie.

Stephanie was annoyed with what she perceived as Cassie's arrogance. Staying in Dad's room said plenty about Cassie's view of the world—and the family. "Perfect," she sneered.

"What was that supposed to mean!" yelled Cassie to Stephanie as she exited. Failing to get an answer, Cassie turned to Anna. "What was *that* supposed to mean?"

"I don't know," she answered. "Please, Cassie, remember why we are here."

The Package

"My staying in Dad's room was your idea," said Cassie.

"I know. I'm sorry."

"What in the world was Dad thinking?" mumbled Cassie under her breath.

Stephanie returned to find Anna and Cassie eating their oatmeal but saying nothing. "So, you girls are having oatmeal?"

"Yep," said Anna, hoping to avoid revisiting the oatmeal discussion again.

"Okeedokee," said Stephanie with a pasted on smile. Her feigned enthusiasm met with disapproval as Anna rolled her eyes. "Do we have any fruit?" she asked.

"I have some bananas," she said, smiling and shaking one of them in the air. Finally, Anna had something somebody wanted.

Stephanie considered the bananas but then said, "I'll eat the oatmeal."

"Actually, it's not *that* bad," said Cassie, trying to say something positive. To her chagrin, this met with two disapproving stares. "*Seriously*," she insisted.

"What a ringing endorsement," said Anna.

"Especially coming from the family critic," added Stephanie.

Cassie found that characterization annoying, and she was winding up for a fiery response when she saw Anna's pleading eyes. Cassie had opened her mouth to respond, so she adapted by filling her mouth with a large spoonful of oatmeal. "Hmm," she said flatly.

"So Stephanie, your flight was okay?" asked Anna.

"It was cheap," said Stephanie. "You'd think they could spring for snack bags containing at least three pretzels."

"I flew all the way across the country," said Cassie, "and I got a package of crackers with six, count them, six crackers in the package."

"They obviously knew you were special," said Stephanie, picking at the numbers.

This was going to be much more difficult than even Anna had imagined. "So," she interjected, "what do you girls want to do today? We have a whole weekend together. I'm excited about it. Aren't you, Cassie?"

"Sure," she replied.

"Stephanie?" asked Anna.

"I'm working on it," she replied. She then looked at Cassie with distaste. "Just don't make me think about it."

"Look, this wasn't my idea," erupted Cassie, who had finally had

Fourth of July

enough. "I've got a lot to deal with back home. I promised Dad I would do this, and I'm trying to make the most of it. If you want to complain about it, don't complain to me."

"Okay," snapped Stephanie. "Lighten up. I don't see why you have to—"

Cassie interrupted and then both girls argued simultaneously.

"Everyone take a deep breath here!" shouted Anna, trying to take control.

"If we can only find a way to get through this weekend without killing each other," muttered Cassie.

"Come on, Stephanie," said Anna. "We'll have fun together. It's the Fourth of July. Let's go to a parade."

"I just arrived in the outskirts of nowhere and now you want to drive me to *downtown*?" said Stephanie.

Anna gave her a disapproving look, and Stephanie reacted and spoke with a contrived excitement. "But it will be so much fun. How about you, Cassidy?"

"Where did you want to go, Anna?" said Cassie, redirecting her response away from Stephanie.

"I was thinking Millvale," said Anna. "They have a parade and fireworks every year. It's a cute little place."

"Millvale is like thirty miles away, isn't it?" asked Stephanie.

"Everything is not a block away like it is in New York," said Anna. "You're not in Oz anymore, Steph. Welcome to Kansas."

"This is Pennsylvania," she replied.

Anna stared at her intently and shook her head in disbelief. "Good grief, it's a metaphor," she said. "Am I the only one around here with any sense of humor?"

It was clear that Anna was going to press until everyone relented, so Cassie finally yielded. "We had better go get dressed, Anna." Anna agreed and left the room as Cassie picked up the oatmeal bowls and began to rinse them out in the sink.

Stephanie, despite her faults, had some degree of compassion for Cassie. She knew the divorce strained Cassie, not because she had any real knowledge of the situation or circumstances, but because she knew Cassie couldn't accept anyone else faults, let alone her own. Stephanie watched Cassie for a minute before she spoke. "You okay?" she asked.

"I'm *fine*," replied Cassie.

"I know you've had a lot to deal with," said Stephanie.

The Package

"You *think*?" snapped Cassie sarcastically.

"Look," said Stephanie, "I may be a total jerk, but it doesn't mean I don't care."

Cassie was taken aback by Stephanie's honesty. It disarmed her. She simply could not construct a reply.

"You'd better get dressed," said Stephanie.

"Yeah. I'll do that," said Cassie. It wasn't a warm response, and Cassie wasn't proud of it. But the concepts of trust and Stephanie were incongruent.

"We'll probably be half the crowd there," continued Stephanie. "Wouldn't want them holding up the whole parade on account of us needing to use the street to get there."

Stephanie saw that Cassie managed a bit of a smile as she exited for the bedroom. *That almost looked like a crack in the royal armor*, she thought. Still holding her oatmeal bowl, she decided to give it a try. She slid a spoonful into her mouth and was surprised by the taste.

"Actually," she said aloud, "this stuff is pretty good."

9

MEMORIES

It was late that evening when the girls returned to the cabin. Stephanie was laughing as she came through the front door and turned on the lights. Cassie and Anna followed close behind. "No, I did *not* think the back way was more fun," Cassie said to Stephanie. "Especially in the back seat. My stomach is in knots. What was I thinking letting you drive?"

Anna was finally having fun. Cassie and Stephanie appeared to have put a moratorium on family warfare for at least a few hours, and Stephanie's grand prix return to the cabin was an unexpected bonus. "I love hilly roads," said Anna. "That reminded me of when Dad took us that way as kids."

Cassie went to clean up a few remaining items in the kitchen as Anna sat down on the sofa next to Stephanie. "Remember that time Dad flew over that hill in the car, and you popped up in the air and hit your head on the ceiling?" asked Anna.

"Remember?" replied Stephanie. "It still hurts to think about it."

"Mom gave him a lot of grief about that," said Anna. "She told him it was very dangerous. I know Dad felt bad about it."

"Yeah, sure he did. Clear until the next day when he and I were driving back to town. He looked over at me, grinned from ear to ear and said, 'Keep your head down this time, honey.'"

Cassie finished in the kitchen and reengaged in the conversation. "I'm going to get changed," she said, "maybe even go to bed. It's been a long day. Between the parade, the walk at Baker Park, dinner, and the fireworks, I'm pretty tired."

"Oh, come on, Cass," said Anna. "I was hoping we could make some hot chocolate and stay up late, you know. Maybe even a revenge match of Monopoly."

The Package

"You're kidding, right?" said Cassie. "Monopoly takes like four hours to play."

"Okay, scratch the Monopoly," replied Anna. "You in, Steph?"

"Hot chocolate is about as good as the night life gets around here," said Stephanie. "And, surely, Cassie, you can't pass on such a wholesome, idyllic, family experience." Cassie wasn't relenting. "Come on, Cassidy, I know you're *old*, but it is only ten-thirty. Besides, if you go to bed, we're just going to sit here and talk about you. Won't we, Anna?"

"Yep," Anna said with glee.

"About *what*?" asked Cassie, displaying a playful impatience by standing with her hands on her hips. In reality, she was indeed curious.

"Well, we could talk about Daniel Zabosky," said Anna, giggling like a teenager. "You remember Daniel Zabosky, don't you Steph?"

"How could you forget *Daniel*?" said Stephanie, speaking his name as if it were poetry.

"You mean like, when Cassie was down at the lake on the pier with him?" asked Anna.

Cassie now knew what event they were talking about, but she wasn't sure how they knew about it. "What are you two talking about?" she asked.

"What *are* we talking about, Anna?" laughed Stephanie.

"I think were discussing a kiss, Stephanie. I believe I recall that little goody-two-shoes sister of ours kissing Daniel. And I do mean *kissing* him."

Cassie was embarrassed, though she understood it was silly to feel that way. She had kissed someone when she was a teenager, so she finally decided to play along, "Tell me you girls were not there watching. You saw that?"

"No, we didn't see it," said Stephanie. "But I sure saw it. Anna covered up her eyes. You know, young minds, so impressionable."

"We spent almost every weekend up here that summer," said Cassie defensively. "I only kissed him that one time."

"Sure, we understand," said Anna. "Imagine our luck, seeing a once in a lifetime event. I mean, her luck, you know, because—"

"You didn't see it," quipped Cassie.

"Right," said Anna.

"You guys spied on me; that is so not cool," said Cassie as they all began laughing together.

As the laughter began to subside, Anna and Stephanie returned to the sofa and continued with another round of the good-natured ribbing. "And then there was that time when Cassie went over to the neighbors and—"

Memories

"Time out!" shouted Cassie. "Enough Cassie-bashing. I am going to change clothes. But when I return, I will be ready to recall a few bruising memories of my own!"

Anna watched Cassie until she left the room. When she was out of earshot, she continued. "So do you remember when Cassie—"

"Ah, ah, ah!" said Cassie as she popped out of the hallway, wagging an accusing finger. "Now I told you, not while I'm out of the room. I'm liable to put something in your beds." She gave them both a knowing smile and left the room.

As the sneakiest one of the three, Cassie had occasionally taken steps to make sure her two little sisters understood that she was the boss. She was clever, and could usually manage to hide a snake or mouse in their beds without being caught. She always provided some plausible explanation which, when coupled with well-contrived innocence, provided a believable alibi. At least her parents bought it, even though her sisters suspected otherwise. With their suspicions now confirmed, they looked at each other with a shared understanding.

"Okay, that's good enough for me," said Stephanie. "I'm waiting."

"Yeah," said Anna.

After a few moments of vivid recollection of the sheer terror that can be caused by a small rodent, Anna had a sudden realization—they had actually convinced Cassie to put off going to bed. With that in mind, Anna decided it was time to start the party. "I think I'll make the hot chocolate," she said, "using Mom's secret recipe."

"Whipped cream?" mocked Stephanie. "Some secret. Better keep that one under lock and key. Wouldn't want to see the family fortune lost to some unethical vending machine looking for an extra nickel."

"It's tradition," said Anna. "We have no choice. It's deeply ingrained in the genetic codes locked up in our brain cells."

"The genetic codes locked up in our brain cells?" replied Stephanie. "I think the key operational word here is 'locked up.' And if you keep talking like that, locked up is what you'll be."

"Oh, hardee-har," said Anna.

"I am going to go get changed as well. I'll be back in a New York minute."

"Don't take the makeup off yet!" said Anna.

"Why?" asked Stephanie.

"I'm young. I scare easily." Anna busted out laughing. Stephanie had taken that one hook, line, and sinker.

The Package

"Locked up, I tell you. It's happening," said Stephanie, shaking a finger toward her as she left the room.

Anna continued to laugh as she began mixing the cocoa into the milk heating in the pan. She had bought some cookies from the bakery to indulge in at some point in the weekend, and this seemed like the right opportunity. "Do you girls want some cookies with your hot chocolate?" shouted Anna so that she could be heard down the hallway.

"Cookies?" shouted Cassie. "Are you sure you don't want to turn out the lights and start a campfire on the living room floor?"

Anna's eyes widened. "That's a great idea!"

"Unbelievable!" said Stephanie, continuing the fun. "I just found a straightjacket back here!"

"You two have absolutely no imagination," shouted Anna. At that moment, Cassie strolled into the room wearing a bizarre combination of nightclothes including leopard patterns combined with paisley, satin, and flannel. Anna tried to hold back her laughter but couldn't. "Okay, I'll take it back. You have lots of imagination—lots."

"Since when did you become the fashion police?" replied Cassie without hesitation. "Here, I'll stir the chocolate. Why don't you go dress down?" she suggested as she took the spoon from Anna. She hesitated, and then continued, "If that's possible."

"Excuse me?" said Anna.

"Your honor," mocked Cassie, waving her hand up and down Anna's frame. "I believe the evidence speaks for itself."

"Oh, this is good. I'm trying to create memories here, and you two are being Laurel and Hardy. Okay, I'll go." She started to leave the room but returned with great urgency. "You ever cooked hot chocolate before? I mean, without burning it?"

Cassie put the back of her hand to her head and feigned distress. "I know it's incredibly complicated. You'd better hurry."

Anna said, "Make sure you add the whipped cream and stir it in just before it boils, and then take it off the . . . heat . . . right . . . away." Her words slowed as she noticed Cassie glaring at her. "Or not," she said with a sneer before making a quick exit.

Cassie felt inept because Anna was giving her detailed instructions for making hot chocolate. She was only doing it in jest, but it caused insecurity to rise up inside her. "At least I still know how to make hot chocolate without fouling it up," she muttered to herself.

Memories

"What did you say?" asked Stephanie, who had entered the room mid-sentence.

"Nothing," said Cassie. "Just talking to myself." Stephanie took a seat on a stool at the counter. "Do you want cookies?" asked Cassie. "I didn't hear your answer."

"The real question is," pondered Stephanie, "do I want to completely kill my diet this weekend? I'm pretty sure the cotton candy I ate today didn't count."

"Right, it's mostly air anyway," said Cassie.

"Was that like a Freudian slip?" asked Stephanie.

"What are you talking about?"

"That's exactly what you said that day with Dad. When we went over the hill in the car, and I hit my head." She mocked Cassie's voice. *"Don't worry that she hit her head. It's mostly air anyway.'* Who needs enemies? I have an older sister."

"Good grief," said Cassie. "That was like thirty years ago. Get over it."

Cassie's reply was a little terse, and Stephanie considered whether there was a deeper meaning behind it. But even she was beginning to enjoy the evening and decided this would be a silly place to derail it.

"Now for the third time," Cassie asked impatiently, "do you want some cookies?"

"I guess," Stephanie answered. "I'll restart the diet tomorrow." Cassie set a plate of giant soft-baked chocolate chip cookies on the counter, and Stephanie reconsidered the diet when she took her first bite. "Or maybe not."

From across the counter, Stephanie saw that the hot chocolate was just beginning to boil. "You need to add the whipped cream now," insisted Stephanie. "Right now! Right now! Right now!" Cassie quickly stirred the whipped cream into the chocolate and then took the pan off the heat. Stephanie didn't ease up on her. "Man, that was close. I thought you had this under control. You almost missed it."

"Almost," said Cassie. "Story of my life."

"What?" asked Stephanie. "What are you talking about?"

Anna reentered before Cassie could answer the question. "How's it coming?" she asked, looking intently into the hot chocolate. "Great! You girls rock!"

"Yes, an incredible achievement," declared Cassie as she lifted her wooden spoon into the air in mock triumph.

The Package

"She almost blew it," said Stephanie, who stopped speaking suddenly when she found a spoon pointed at her nose.

"Well it looks like perfection to me," said Anna. "Let's pour." Anna retrieved the mugs from the cupboard and Cassie poured the chocolate. "Marshmallows!" said an excited Anna. "Anyone want marshmallows?"

"If you have some, sure," said Cassie.

"Are they the little ones or the big ones?" asked Stephanie.

"Little ones," answered Anna.

"Great," said Stephanie. "The big ones just bounce off my nose."

Anna looked at Cassie, and they began to snicker and snort. It was like having a fastball cross the plate in slow motion so you could easily hit it out of the park. "There's got to be some sort of a rule here, right?" said Anna. "It's way too obvious. Don't you think?"

"Cute," said Stephanie dryly. Then she laughed and said poetically, "I mean my nose."

They all laughed as they each took a mug of hot chocolate and retreated to the living room. As they settled in their seats, Anna looked at Stephanie and asked, "Now where'd we leave off?"

"I think you were just about to tell another Cassie-tale," said Stephanie.

Cassie brought her game as she had promised. "Whoa. Why is everybody picking on me tonight? I mean, Anna's the youngest. Isn't it tradition to pick on the youngest?"

"Tradition?" mused Stephanie. She turned to Anna with a fabricated regret. "Anna, I'm sorry, but if it's tradition, we have to do it. Right?"

"Now hold on just a second—"

"So Stephanie," said Cassie, "remember when we were all up here for the weekend running through the woods, and you fell into that old well? Anna turned around, didn't see you, and then started screaming about your having disappeared and that you must have been snatched by aliens."

Cassie and Stephanie expectantly looked at Anna for an explanation. "I was scared," she replied. "I heard this noise, then Stephanie screamed, and I turned around and she simply wasn't there anymore."

"You were practically hysterical," said Cassie, who was laughing so hard that her side was beginning to hurt.

Stephanie's suddenly turned toward Cassie. "I notice here, Cassie, that it seems that you weren't very concerned about me."

"What are you talking about?" asked Cassie defensively. "I ran back to find you, but I couldn't get Anna to stop screaming. That scared me more than the fact that I didn't know where you were. It was like science fiction only scarier."

"I had just seen a movie where exactly that happened," said Anna. "I didn't know. I was only a kid."

"Ah, the classic 'I am the poor misunderstood youngest child' syndrome." Cassie was truly on her game.

Stephanie recalled the incident from her point of view. "And there I am lying in the bottom of a dry well with a huge knot on my head trying to figure out what happened. Strange, isn't it? I always seem to find a way to get hit on the head."

"Well," said Anna, "I was sure glad you only fell in a well."

"That's thoughtful," said Stephanie.

"Well, it beats being abducted by aliens," said Anna. "Cassie ran fast to go get Dad. I was relieved when we got you out."

"You!" exclaimed Stephanie. "It was a miracle I didn't break my neck."

The girls sat for a moment considering the whole episode and their bantering about it. They maintained a momentary seriousness until Cassie began to snicker, and they all fell into a joyous laughter.

"We had a lot of fun growing up together, didn't we?" said Anna.

The smile faded from Stephanie's face, she took a sip of her hot chocolate, and then sighed. "It was simpler then."

Cassie understood the profound nature of her statement. The complexities of life had overwhelmed them. There *was* something they had lost, a closeness they had once possessed that had needlessly escaped them. "There were some really good times," she said. "We were so close—we told each other everything."

"Daniel Zabosky?" argued Stephanie playfully.

"Well, *almost* everything," admitted Cassie.

Moments after those words left Cassie's mouth, there was an ominous crack of thunder that had the sense of judgment of Cassie's words. A reverberating rumble echoed throughout the cabin.

"It sounds like it might storm," said Cassie as she set down her mug and headed toward the hall. "I'd better check the windows in the bedroom. I had them open."

After Cassie left the room, the mood quickly subdued. Stephanie rose from the sofa and moved to the window to look into the dark night sky. "Is there supposed to be bad weather tonight?" she asked.

"I don't think so," replied Anna. "But you can always get a pop-up storm this time of year."

"I still hate it when it storms," said Stephanie. "Too many bad memories."

Anna knew that she meant memories of the accident. In the Mullins family, that solitary word could be spoken in isolation from all others, and its meaning was unambiguous. It had happened in a thunderstorm, and storms were still reminders.

"The storms don't bother me so much any more," said Anna, "but I still hate driving in bad weather—especially at night. It's so hard to see."

"I guess I closed them earlier," said Cassie, returning from the bedroom. "But I don't remember doing it." A subdued Anna was gazing into her mug while Stephanie stared out the window. "Is something wrong?" she asked.

"We were talking about Mom," said Anna, "and, you know, the accident."

"What brought that up?" asked Cassie. "The storm?"

Stephanie seethed. "Every storm reminds me of it. I think about Mom's car smashed into that tree lying in the road, and through the pouring rain, I can see her struggling to get out of the car. It's unbelievable she survived that only to get hit by another car. That guy that hit her—what an idiot! He probably had a few too many for the road—probably flirting with his girlfriend. He sure wasn't paying attention."

"We've been through this before," said Anna. "That's not what the police report said."

"Who cares what they wrote?" she erupted. "It was just another accident for them."

Anna was watching a surprisingly pleasurable evening begin to fall apart. Stephanie was going off-line. Anna hoped to reach her before she became a familiar emotional wreck. She tried to ease Stephanie toward the truth. "He wasn't able to see Mom's car around that curve in the rain, and Mom couldn't see the tree in the road, either. You can't blame him for the accident—or her death. How could he have known?"

"I can blame him if I want!" shouted Stephanie. "Don't tell me how I need to feel!"

Anna gave a glance toward Cassie seeking her intervention.

"It was difficult at the time," said Cassie. "I was pretty angry too. I mean, we weren't kids anymore, but it was so sudden and so final. Dad was devastated."

Anna tried to build on the opening. "He found his way through it, though, here—God helped him through it."

Memories

"Sure," said Stephanie. "God helped *him* through it. Where was God that night? Where was God when *Mom* needed him? She was completely alone. He wasn't with her. I'm not sure he's there at all."

"Of course he's there," said Cassie. "You know that. He's there. He may not always do what we want—he certainly hasn't always done what I wanted—but he is there."

"Is that your prepared speech?" snapped Stephanie. "You've lectured me every time I've seen you for the last ten years about my living with one guy after another, how I'm living in sin. And now look at you: you go to church, and your husband gets up one day and runs off with another woman! Is that your God, Cassie, one who leaves you alone? Why would I want that?"

"Stephanie!" chided Anna, knowing Stephanie had crossed the line from feeling pain to inflicting it.

Cassie was stunned, but stammered out the best response she could. "I . . . I don't know . . . I don't know what to tell you. I don't have answers to all your questions, Stephanie."

Seeing Cassie reeling energized her. "Well, why not? I'd like some answers. When Mom died, I was alone. Dad left me in Pittsburgh to come here. You went back to college. If there is a God, he wasn't there; I was alone. He wasn't there then . . . and he isn't here now!" Cassie had disengaged and moved across the room to sit in a chair away from the fury.

"Stephanie, please," appealed Anna.

"You have no answers, either," shouted Stephanie, now directing her ire toward Anna. "You sit in your ivory tower looking down on the rest of us and try to tell us how to think and feel. You're as bad as Cassie is. The truth is, there *are* no answers. I'm going to bed. It's getting stuffy in here."

"Stephanie! Please wait!" shouted Anna as Stephanie stormed out of the room. Anna walked dejectedly to a seat near Cassie. Both girls sat in silent disbelief, each wondering how the evening could have deteriorated so quickly.

"She is so angry," Cassie said intolerantly. "I can't deal with that."

"Maybe she has her reasons," said Anna.

"Her *reasons*?" said Cassie. "It's been *how* many years?"

"Too many for her," said Anna. "Or not enough."

Cassie didn't comprehend the nuance of the statement, but she didn't pursue it. What Stephanie said about her divorce was difficult to hear, and the words echoed in her mind. "Is that your God, Cassie, one who leaves you alone? Why would I want that?" Her words were cruel, but the truth was still the truth, and she had to admit it.

The Package

"She's got one thing right," said Cassie, "I used to think I had all the answers. I don't understand what happened at home. Being a Christian sure doesn't make things simple."

"It actually does make things simple, Cassie. It just doesn't make them easy."

"Why are you talking in riddles?" asked Cassie. "What in the world are you talking about?"

"It's not complicated, Cassie. Being a Christian requires we accept God's forgiveness and do what he says. It's a simple idea."

"Okay," said Cassie, unsure of where this was going.

"Living a Christian life, though, that's a different story. Jesus told us, 'If you love me, the world will hate you.' Life wasn't easy for Dad, and it isn't easy for me."

"Well, it *sure* isn't easy for me," said Cassie. "In fact, I'm barely making it."

"Do you want to talk about it?"

"That's sweet—I do—but I'm tired, and I get melancholy when I'm tired. And Stephanie's got me a little worked up too. Right now, what I need is a good night's sleep."

"Okay," said Anna, "we'll talk later. You go on; I'll clean up."

Cassie started toward the hall but turned back to Anna. "What are we going to do about Stephanie? How do we talk to her?"

"We wait for her to talk to us. And we—you and I," said Anna as she pointed toward heaven, "we talk to him."

"Whatever," said Cassie. "Are you sure you don't want me to help?"

"No, I'm fine. You go on to bed."

"Thanks, Anna. Good night."

Cassie walked down the hall to turn in for the night, and Anna began cleaning up the kitchen. Taking her own advice about prayer, she stopped and looked toward heaven. *I'm sure you know what you're doing,* she prayed. *But would you like to let me in on it? You and Dad—you and Dad cooked this whole thing up, didn't you? It is taking all my strength to hold everyone else together.* In her spirit, the statement echoed with significance. Was that really her responsibility? She again looked heavenward and asked, *Is that a fault— or a gift?*

10

THE NIGHTMARE

Stephanie was standing in the woods in a heavy, pouring rain amid the flashes and rumblings of a raging thunderstorm. Her soaked, uncombed hair and streaming mascara merged to create chaotic dark veins across her face. The noise of the deluge falling around her was so intense that it sounded like loud static on a mistuned radio.

Stephanie sought to get out of the rain but wasn't sure where she was or how she happened to be there. Moving forward, trying to find her way, she was suddenly knocked to the ground by a shattering loud noise and blinding light as lightning struck a tree beside her. Looking up in the flickering darkness, she could see that the lightning had split the tree to the ground, and the ensuing ferocious wind appeared to be weakening it further. A subsequent large gust cracked the tree at its base, and it began to cascade toward her.

Stephanie quickly bounded out of the way of the tree as it accelerated toward the ground, finally jarring the earth with an ominous crash. In the aftermath, Stephanie found herself on the ground gasping for air. Finally relaxing and attempting to regain her senses, she became aware of a dim, diffuse light throughout the trees around her that was growing steadily brighter. She turned her head toward its source, and through the rain, she saw two headlights approaching.

She looked along the length of the tree toward its former top and realized it had fallen across the highway. In the distance, across the road, she saw a sign slowly appear from the darkness as the lights brightened. It said Pennsylvania Route 8. Within moments, the car came rushing around a curve, the brakes locked up, and the car began skidding toward the tree lying in the road. The front fender on the driver's side slammed into a tree branch with a crash that burst the headlamp and spun the passenger side of the car against the trunk of the tree. The horn began a steady continuous blast as the car came to a stop.

The rain pounded against Stephanie's eyelids to the point where she could barely see without wiping the rain from her face. As she pushed the rain aside with her sleeves, she recognized the car. She eased toward it, and the farther she advanced, the more certain she was that this was her family's car. As the reality of the situation mounted, her walk changed to a trot and finally to a run that ended when she slammed into the driver's side door.

Wiping the window with both hands, she could see her mother slumped motionlessly over the steering wheel. She jerked the door handle, but the collision had wedged the front fender into the door—it was jammed. She frantically tried the rear door—it was locked. She ran around the back of car to try the other doors, but they were inaccessible, blocked by the tree.

She ran back to the driver's window and beat on it repeatedly. "Mom!" she yelled. "Mom! Wake up!" She continued beating on the window to no avail, as her mother was unable to answer. "Mom, please wake up," she begged as she finally slumped alongside the door to the ground in anguish, continuing to beat the palm of her hand against the door in futility.

And then, in a disturbing translation, Stephanie found herself sitting in the passenger's seat. Her ears were filled with the sounds of the rain splattering on the metal roof, the car horn blaring, and the thumping sound of the still-oscillating wipers. Mom moaned and slowly raised her head from the steering wheel, causing the horn to cease its blaring. "Mom," she said. "It's Stephanie. Don't worry, Mom. I'll get you out of here."

"Stephanie," said her Mother weakly. "Please help me, Stephanie. Please. Help me."

Stephanie tried to get out of the car. She struggled with the doors and windows, but for some reason beyond her comprehension, she could not open them. Terrified, she screamed for help as she beat on the windows of the car. But no one but Mom was there to hear her.

"Stephanie," pleaded Mom.

"Yes, Mom, I'm here," she said crying, struggling to remain positive.

"The pain—please help me," Mom said again. Stephanie dropped her head against Mom's shoulder and began to cry frantically. Making one final effort, she kicked the passenger window repeatedly with her foot trying to break the glass until her energy waned. "I can't get out, Mom," she cried. "I'm sorry. I can't get out!"

The Nightmare

Suddenly, the inside of the car began to brighten and Stephanie sat up in expectation. Through the driver's side window, she saw two bright lights quickly approaching. They rapidly grew brighter until Stephanie heard a squealing sound so loud it made her cover her ears. She looked at her mother. Even with her life waning, there was concern in her eyes. "Mom?" she yelled.

And then suddenly, as if in slow motion, there was a sound like the percussion of a skyrocket that eventually dissolved into a thousand separate sounds and flashing lights of all sorts of shapes and colors. The colors faded to an utter black darkness, and the loud sounds gave way to a composite tinkling sound, like hundreds of small pieces of glass falling to the ground in random sequences. Following that, there was a rushing sound that began softly and became intolerably loud within seconds. It seemed as if the sounds of the entire event were occurring in reverse until the noise vanished.

A startled Stephanie sat up in her bed. The window in her bedroom flashed with a brief white light, and a distant rumble of thunder reverberated in the room alongside the rain still pelting her bedroom window. Sitting in the dark, she wiped her hair from her face, felt the sweat on her cheeks, and then rubbed her index fingers against her thumbs assessing the moisture on her hands. Perhaps it wasn't sweat—maybe it was tears.

"It's only a nightmare," said Stephanie, trying to calm herself as she tried to settle back into her pillow. "It was only a dream," she said, "a dream." Lying motionless for a few moments, she focused on relaxing the pace of her breathing. As her stress eased, she began to weep. Her mother had pleaded with her for help, yet Stephanie could find no way to save her.

The nightmare was familiar. It had repeated itself over the years—nighttime storms seemed to trigger it. It was unrelenting in its pattern; she could never save her mother. However, on this night, Stephanie pondered an aspect of the dream she had never considered before. She realized that she had somehow saved herself—or had she?

The storm raged intermittently until just after midnight, and the morning brought clearing skies. Stephanie's restless night left her unsettled, and the uneasiness she felt when she arrived at the cabin had been amplified by the storm. Her faithfulness to her promise waned as her will succumbed to the obvious truth—she could not endure this place any longer. After dressing and gathering her things, she crept into the living room,

The Package

thinking she might avoid a conflict with her stealth. As she walked along the shelf that held the family portraits, she was arrested by the image of her father. She stared at him with disdain and tried to excuse her failure.

"Dad, why did you ask us to come here?" she whispered. "This place—this place—is so full of you and Mom—of life and death. How can I make sense out of all that? I want to. I simply don't know how." Unseen by Stephanie, Cassie had entered the room with a stretch and a yawn.

"Don't know how to do what?" asked Cassie. "Who are you talking to?"

"No one," answered Stephanie, feeling a bit embarrassed. "I mean, myself, I guess. There's no one else here."

Cassie had worried about Stephanie's state of mind all night. "Are you okay?"

"Yeah, I'm fine," said Stephanie, aware that her response was far from the truth. "Listen, can I take your rental?"

"Where?"

"I can't stay here. It's just too much. It's confusing, and I need to breathe. I simply need to get away from here."

"You're leaving?"

"Yes. I mean, everything inside me is shouting I should go. I know I probably should stay, I mean, I promised Dad I would, but—"

"Stephanie, I want you to stay!" The statement stunned Stephanie, but its forcefulness even surprised Cassie.

"What?" replied Stephanie.

"Do I have to repeat it?" said Cassie. She looked at a confused Stephanie and put forth another sincere attempt. "I want you to stay." Stephanie's eyes reflected her inner conflict. Cassie entreated her, "Okay?"

"Why?" asked Stephanie.

Overnight, Cassie had wrestled with an inner voice that demanded resolution. Stephanie needed help—Cassie could no longer deny it. Cassie's needs were different but just as real. She needed her sister.

"You're not the only one who is confused, you know," confessed a contrite Cassie. "I need you."

"*You* need *me*! *I* don't even need me!" she shouted helplessly. "I can't figure out my own problems, let alone yours. You don't need anyone."

The truth of that indictment was unavoidable, and the words cut deep. "Why are you doing this?" asked Cassie.

Stephanie shrugged her shoulders and shook her head side to side. She had no explanation.

The Nightmare

Cassie relented and removed the keys from her purse. "Here. Here are the keys to my rental. Take it where you need to go. If you need to go back to New York, leave it at the airport, and I'll have Anna bring me to pick it up. Do what you need to do."

"Cassie, you don't have to feel sorry for me—"

"I'm not feeling sorry for you," said Cassie, cutting her off. "I'm feeling sorry for me. Sorry that I have allowed myself to become so cold."

The iron-willed Cassie is sorry she is cold? mused Stephanie. She was stunned by this admission and wondered what prompted it. "Look, it's great this is working for you," she said, "but I need to go. Thanks for the car. I'll get it back to you somehow."

"You have the phone number here?"

"Yes."

"What should I tell Anna? Do you want me to wake her?"

"No, please don't." Stephanie regretted disappointing Anna, but she could not face it. "Just tell Anna . . . tell Anna I'm sorry." Cassie thought she caught a glimpse of reconsideration, but it yielded as Stephanie walked out the door saying, "I've got to go."

Cassie watched from the window as Stephanie put her bags in the backseat and got into the car. She started it and pushed the accelerator so hard that the tires spun in the gravel. Anna was sitting in bed reading her morning devotional, and the noise hastened her trek to the kitchen where she found Cassie sitting at the counter with her face in her hands.

"Who was that?" asked Anna.

"Stephanie."

"Where's she going?"

"She doesn't know."

"*What?*"

"I think she's going home."

"Without even saying good-bye?"

"If she had her own car," said Cassie, "I'm not sure either of us would have seen her at all this morning. She had to wait on me to get up so she could leave." Anna walked over and peered out the window at the spot where the car once sat, and she looked more discouraged than Cassie could remember. Cassie tried to comfort her. "She said to tell you she was sorry."

"Oh, Steph. Why'd you have to go and do this?"

"I'm sorry, Anna. It's probably my fault. I know that more than anybody else, you wanted this weekend to be special. It looks like we've ruined it for you."

The Package

Anna's emotions flashed. "Cassie! Stop taking the blame for everything. It's not your fault. We are not here for me." Cassie dropped her head. Chiding her had not achieved the intended result. "Look," Anna continued gently, "I admit I was excited and a little bit surprised that you both came. But Dad asked us to come here, and I believe he had a reason. It wasn't for him; it was for us."

Cassie looked dejected and moved away from Anna toward the living room. Quietly, she said, "He probably only wanted us to get together and work things out between us so we can be like a normal family—you know, people who actually *talk* to each other."

Anna heard the resignation in her voice. She followed her to the living room and sat near her. "I don't think that's it, Cassie."

"Then what?"

"Cassie, you called Dad the man of steel. That's how you saw him, right?"

"Yeah, I guess so."

"When Mom died, he reacted like Stephanie. He simply had to get away. So we came up here."

Cassie had never considered Stephanie's similarities to her father. She had always seen them as polar opposites. The idea that they could be similar was a fascinating observation.

"I said the other night I had never told you about that month after Mom died," said Anna. "Would you like to know what happened?"

"Sure, if you want to tell me," replied Cassie.

"Dad was so weak, so unsure of himself—of what to do—and he was angry. He spent most of the first week sitting on the front porch staring into empty space. I thought he was going to totally collapse. He would sleep half the day and stare the other half. I was scared. I was hurting too. But I couldn't find time to think about me because I was so scared for Dad."

"But after that week, something happened. Dad picked up a pen, and he started writing. He had a journal he carried that he would write in occasionally, but on that day—that day his writing became a passion. And then the writing became reading, and you know what he read?"

"His Bible?" guessed Cassie.

"That's right, his Bible. On the second Sunday here, we went to church, and the pastor asked him how he was doing. And can you guess what he said?" Cassie shrugged. "He said, 'God and I are talking about it. I'll let you know.' It was so simple and honest, but kind of scary too."

The Nightmare

"That week, Dad started getting up early in the morning and taking long walks. And then he'd come back to the cabin, and we'd make tall glasses of iced tea and talk about things. He started asking me how I felt, and he held me and comforted me as we cried together about Mom. We also shared memories and laughed about things we had done together. Every day, though, Dad would read his Bible and write in that journal."

"After another week went by, I finally got up the courage to ask Dad what he meant at church when he said he and God were talking about it. His eyes cleared and his face glowed as he looked at me and said, 'At times like this, you have a choice. You can be angry with God and blame him for all your pain, or you can embrace God and let him comfort you while you endure it.' He said, 'I told God I wasn't sure I needed him. But I finally came to the truth: be it by God's hand or the hand of the enemy, pain comes in our lives. And it becomes our choice to either wallow in the darkness alone or be comforted in the light with him.' He told me, 'I have chosen to live in the light.'"

"There's a lot of truth in that," said Cassie, who was visibly moved.

"It sure was a lot for me to consider. But I went and wrote down what he said so I wouldn't forget it. It helps me find my way through the tough times. As the days wore on, Dad grew stronger and stronger, read his Bible, wrote in his journal, and talked with me for hours about what he was learning. He'd get out his harmonica and play hymns at night while we watched the sunset and then the stars twinkling in the sky. It was a profoundly sad but somehow peaceful time."

Cassie began to sense the depth of that time for her father and the importance of Anna's sacrifice. Cassie had returned to college, and throughout the years had often struggled with guilt over that decision. Anna had covered for her. "I'm really glad you were here for him."

Anna smiled in appreciation as she continued. "In the years after that, Dad would tell people that this cabin is where he found his faith. What he meant was, this was where his Christianity became real, where it became a relationship and not just a religion."

"I knew Mom's death really impacted him," said Cassie. "I knew he had changed. I didn't understand it completely, I guess."

"Cassie, Dad tried to share what he had learned with all of us. When we were together, though, it was always about whose kids were doing what, who was going where on vacation, and who was getting a promotion. Nobody was much interested in what Dad had to say. Me too. I was only

The Package

with him more when he got sick, and I spent the time listening and remembering. I'm a forty-year-old fledgling."

"That *is* a lot to think about," acknowledged Cassie.

Anna drew the story to a succinct conclusion. "I think that's why Dad wanted us to come. He hoped we would find the same thing he did here. I only wish Stephanie hadn't gone. She . . . I just wish she'd stayed."

"I wish she'd stayed too. I tried to tell her that . . . I haven't been . . . I don't know—"

"It's okay, Cassie, the words will come." Anna could see that Cassie's attitudes were changing, and she wanted to encourage her. "You and I still have three days together, right?"

"If you still want to stay with only me," said Cassie.

"Cassie, 'only you' is more than enough. Did you bring your bathing suit?" Cassie nodded yes. "I thought we might walk over to the creek for a swim, a picnic, and maybe a long talk about 'things'."

Cassie understood. "That would be good," she said.

As they left to get changed, Cassie's thoughts shifted to the creek where she and her sisters spent many summer days together. "I wonder if the old tire swing is still there."

"Cassie, it's been over twenty years."

"Maybe kids have replaced it now and then." Anna's doubtful look made Cassie laugh. "Hey, it's possible."

"Well, it better have some good strong rope because—I hate to tell you this, sister—you ain't the skinny kid you once was."

"Oh, that helps," she said as she neared her bedroom.

Anna followed her down the hall saying, "I'm kidding. I'm kidding!"

11

MYSTERY NOTE

Cassie and Anna returned from their picnic and swim in the late afternoon. Cassie stepped up onto the porch and saw a peach-colored form attached to the door. She removed it and examined it. Being extremely farsighted, she extended her arm and with a glance barely made out the words "Sorry We Missed You" in the upper left corner and the name of Jim Mullins in the upper right corner. In the scribbled remarks, she could make out the word *package*, but that was all. She concluded it was from the post office and dropped it into the picnic basket she was carrying. Anna followed her into the door as Cassie went to the kitchen.

"Well, Anna, that was fun," said Cassie as she set the picnic basket on the counter, removed the notice from inside, and placed it beside the basket. "I like that rope thingy even better than the old tire swing. Of course, I'm a little too old to be falling off such things. But it was fun."

"Yes, it was," said Anna. "What was that on the door?"

"It's a notice from the post office saying there is a package there. It has Dad's name on it. I guess someone had to sign for it, and we weren't here." Cassie picked up the notice to examine it further, but without her glasses, she quickly became distracted and returned it to the counter. "I'm kind of surprised that Dad would be getting a package here at this point. Maybe it's something he had on backorder."

Anna set down her towels and blankets and relaxed on the sofa. "Thanks for a great day, Cassie. I had a lot of fun."

"I did too," said Cassie. "And thanks for the opportunity to talk. There's almost no one I can talk to about the divorce and how I'm really feeling. I don't know why I didn't see that you were there for me all the time. I wanted talk to Dad about it, but I felt like such a terrible person. There's such a stigma around being divorced in the church."

"Dad would have understood," said Anna. "He reached out to you. You pushed him away. I offered to come to see you, and you told me not to come. I respected what you wanted."

"I know I did," said Cassie. "I've pushed everyone away. It's crazy. I mean, it doesn't help, but I keep finding myself doing it."

"Everyone has to find their own path."

"Do you know what one of the hardest things is?"

"What?" asked Anna.

"Sitting in that high school guidance office every day trying to help kids find what they should do with their life—what college they should attend, what career they might pursue, and what courses they should take. As I get ready in the morning, I look at myself in the mirror and ask, 'What do I know about making the right choices, what things to invest my career, my time, or my life in?' Everything I've invested in is gone. What can I offer these kids? I was so glad for the summer break."

"Everything isn't gone, Cassie. The same way God softened Dad, he can soften you, and you can be stronger, wiser, and more capable than you have ever been. You cannot see that far ahead, but if you will walk with him, he will take you there."

"I don't know if I know how to do that," said Cassie.

"You walk with him, and he will take you there."

"You make that sound so easy."

"It's simple but not easy."

"Ah yes, that again."

"Ready to get dressed for dinner?" asked Anna.

"Dinner? Are you kidding? I just ate enough picnic junk to make me sick. Maybe later." As Cassie answered, they heard a car pull into the driveway. Anna walked to the window and peered through the blinds. "Is someone here?" asked Cassie.

Anna exclaimed excitedly, "It's *Stephanie!*"

"Oh, my goodness. She came back," Cassie marveled, wondering what could have caused Stephanie to return. For the first time on this trip, she began to wonder if perhaps Anna were right. Maybe there really was some deep purpose. "What's happening?" Cassie asked, more to herself than Anna.

"What do you mean?" asked Anna.

Before Cassie could answer, Stephanie peeked through the front door and moseyed into the room toting her bags. "Hey, ladies. Mind if I hang out with you two for a few more days?"

Cassie stared in disbelief. She thought this scenario impossible.

Mystery Note

"Stephanie, what are you doing back here? I mean, I'm glad to see you, but you said that—"

"I know what I said. I was going home; I really was. But I decided to do some shopping in Pittsburgh before I left, then I thought I'd get an ice cream, then I thought I'd get my hair done—and then I remembered where I was—and then I remembered how I laughed with you guys last night and how long it had been since I had laughed at all. I figured, what could it hurt to spend a few more days with you two?" She turned to Anna privately, "I mean, it might hurt Cassie if I punch a big one right between the eyes, but *I'm* probably safe." She sneered at Cassie. "She's such a girl."

Anna threw her arms around Stephanie and wouldn't let go. "Oh, Steph, I'm so glad you came back."

"I can't believe you came back!" exclaimed Cassie. "You are *completely* unpredictable!"

"Well, that's at least one thing you can count on me for."

"But you *hate* this place!" replied Cassie. "You told me you *had* to leave!"

"I do hate it," said Stephanie, "and you told me you needed me."

Anna panned her eyes toward Cassie. "*You* said that?"

"Well, yes, I guess I did say it." Cassie was still uneasy with this confession, but it was the truth.

"A weak moment, I guess," said Stephanie.

"You mean you came back here because I said I needed you?" asked Cassie. "Did you take a wrong turn somewhere?"

Stephanie was disappointed, yet she believed what Cassie had said that morning, even if she was uneasy with it now. She laughed as she began to take her bags back to her room saying, "I knew I could count on you, Cassie."

As Stephanie left the room, Anna pondered both Stephanie's return and Cassie's confession—she couldn't decide which was more astounding. "Wow!" she said to Cassie. "Could you rewind that please? I'm not sure I just heard what I thought I heard."

"I've seen stranger things," said Cassie, "I can't remember when, but I'm sure I have."

"You're one to talk! Let's go get dressed." Anna picked up the towels and they headed for their bedrooms.

Stephanie returned to an empty room. "Hey this isn't funny, where'd you girls go?"

The Package

"We're back here changing," called Anna from the bedroom. "Are you hungry?"

Stephanie raised her voice to be easily heard down the hall. "A little. You girls getting ready to eat dinner?"

"Cassie said she's still stuffed from our picnic," shouted Anna, "so we thought we'd wait a few hours. Is that okay?"

"Sure, I'll just have a snack to hold me over."

Anna shouted, "There are some potato chips in the picnic basket that's sitting on the counter. Help yourself."

Stephanie opened the picnic basket and pulled out an open bag of potato chips. She set it on the counter and took out a handful. As she munched on a few, she saw the notice from the post office lying on the counter. As she looked it over, her eyes suddenly widened in amazement. She shouted with urgency, "Anna, what's this on the counter?"

"What are you talking about?" asked Anna.

"This notice from the post office! Where'd you get this?"

"It was on the door when we came back from our swim," answered Anna. "Why?"

"Did you look at it?" Stephanie asked frantically. "I mean, did you read it?"

"I did, sure," answered Cassie, who had finished changing and entered the room. "Why?"

Stephanie was befuddled by their lackadaisical attitude. "There was a package delivered to *us?*—*here?*—*today?*"

Cassie laughed at this ridiculous idea. "Okay, we've got one of those 'mostly air' moments going here." Cassie, now wearing her glasses, took the notice from Stephanie as Anna entered the room. "See it clearly says right here that the package is—" Cassie stopped, stunned. She turned to Anna in amazement.

"What is it?" asked Anna.

"This package wasn't delivered *to* Dad," said Cassie. "It's *from* Dad." Anna looked over Cassie's shoulder at the notice.

Stephanie overcame her astonishment, took the notice from Cassie, and studied it one more time. "Okay, so let me get this straight. This says there is a package at the post office for Cassie Carlisle, Stephanie Mullins, and Anna Patrick. And it says it was sent by Jim Mullins—"

"—Dad," said Cassie.

"How is that possible?" asked Stephanie. "It's been months since the funeral."

108

Mystery Note

"The man of steel," said Cassie.

"Of gold," corrected Anna.

"What?" asked Stephanie. "What are you two talking about?"

Before either of them could answer Stephanie's question, a firm rapping on the front door caused them all to shriek. Coupled with the apparent delivery from "somewhere beyond," the knock on the door was eerie.

"This is getting way too strange for me," said Stephanie. She said to Cassie, "You're the oldest. *You* get it."

"Why me?" asked Cassie. "It's great how I'm the oldest only when it's convenient."

The rapping repeated, and Anna responded courageously. "Oh, for Pete's sake, I'll get it." She answered the front door as Cassie and Stephanie looked on in suspense.

The door opened to reveal a familiar face. "Oh, Pastor Riddick," said Anna. "Won't you come in? My sisters are here, and they will be so glad to see you."

"Really?" he answered. He was puzzled, since he had never met either of them formally.

"Oh, you have no idea actually," she mused as she escorted him into the room. "Pastor Riddick, these are my sisters. This is Cassie; that's short for Cassidy."

"Hello, Cassie," he said, shaking her hand.

"And this is Stephanie."

"Nice to meet you Stephanie."

"Ladies," said Anna, "this is Pastor Riddick. He was Dad's pastor when he stayed here. I met him years ago when Dad and I were here together. You remember him from the funeral, right?"

Cassie didn't remember him, but thought admitting it might be viewed as impolite, so she tried to mask it. "Ah, yes, well actually . . ." She stumbled over her words and looked to Stephanie for help.

"Actually," continued Stephanie, "we were talking about that just before you arrived and, uh . . ." She pitched it back to Cassie.

"Yeah," said Cassie, reengaging. "We were discussing some of the people there and, well . . ." Truth triumphed and she confessed. "No, I don't remember."

"Yeah," agreed Stephanie. "I mean no, sorry."

"It's okay," he said. "I intentionally kept a pretty low profile. Jim and I were close, but I never knew many of his family or friends in Pittsburgh. It was nice to see Anna there, though—at least one familiar face."

109

The Package

Anna took the notice from Stephanie and showed it to the pastor. "Sorry," she said, "we're a little bit out-of-sorts. You see, we found this notice from the post office saying a package was delivered to us today. And, strangely, it says the package is from Dad. Apparently, we had to sign for it, so they took it back to the post office."

"So you don't know what it is?" he asked.

"We're at a bit of a loss to explain it, frankly," she continued. "We had just discovered the note when you knocked. Actually, it kind of spooked us a little bit. You know, city girls, out alone in the country, strange packages—"

"Oh, I am so sorry," he said. "I didn't mean to scare you. Look, I won't keep you. I knew you were here and thought I'd stop by to say hello. Thought maybe you'd like to join us for church tomorrow morning—9:30 sharp." He addressed Anna directly, "I am sure everyone would love to see you again." He looked at Cassie and Stephanie. "We would love to have you ladies come too. Imagine . . . all of Jim's girls together."

Anna knew Stephanie hadn't been to church in years and feared putting her in a difficult position. "Look, we appreciate it, but Stephanie isn't much into going to—"

"Maybe we should go," said Stephanie.

"What!" replied Anna.

"I figured you'd want to—too unpredictable?"

"Cassie?" asked Anna.

Cassie had seen unusual events happen this weekend, and seeing Stephanie at church would be a miracle in itself. "I wouldn't miss it," she replied.

"Well . . . okay then," said Anna to the pastor. "It looks like we'll be coming tomorrow morning. I hope come-as-you-are is okay, because I don't think any of us brought church clothes."

"Sure. It won't be a problem," he replied. "I promise."

"Great," said Anna. "Thanks."

"Oh, you are so welcome," he said. "I can't wait. It'll be a special Sunday for us. Okay then, good night."

"Pastor, wait," said Cassie. "How did you know we were here?"

"I'm sorry," he asked. "What do you mean?"

"You said you knew we were here and thought you'd stop by. How did you know we were here? How did you know we'd be here?"

The pastor squirmed and stammered. "Well, actually, I didn't know . . . I mean I did know because, uh . . . Well, to be honest . . . your dad told me

Mystery Note

you'd be here." Cassie, Stephanie, and Anna were all surprised by his response. He quickly smiled, waved, and walked out the door. "See you tomorrow!"

12

SUNDAY MORNING

Anna pulled the car into the parking lot of Valley Church about five minutes before the start of the service. Stephanie had slept late and taken too much time getting ready. Within a few seconds of their arrival, Anna and Cassie popped open their doors, gathered their purses, and hastily walked toward the church door, which was propped open and sat at the top of five concrete steps.

Stephanie lagged behind, still sitting in the backseat and looking at the sign on the front lawn through her window. "Tyranny and Liberty" apparently would be the topic of Pastor Riddick's message. She thought this a fairly innocuous topic—a holiday-oriented sermon that shouldn't trigger too much discomfort. Having avoided church since she was a teenager, she didn't need to feel condemned on this visit. As she had second-guessed her promise to her father, she questioned what made her commit to do this— something so inconsistent with her character.

A rapping on the window in front of her face startled her. It was Anna. "Are you coming?" she yelled. Stephanie opened the door. "Sure," she said flatly. "I'm coming."

As they approached the building, Stephanie looked the church over and found it to be much as she had expected. It was a small white church consisting of one large sanctuary surrounded by a number of smaller Sunday school classrooms and offices. It was similar in appearance to many other churches in the area, and Stephanie wondered what had motivated her father to choose this one.

As they entered the door, they met a woman who was the head of the greeters that day. "Good morning, ladies," she said. "I'm Doris Carson. You're Jim Mullins' daughters—right?"

"Yes, we are," answered Cassie.

Sunday Morning

Doris shook her hand and handed her a bulletin. "Pastor told me to keep an eye out for you."

"I'm Cassie."

"I'm Doris—oh, I'm sorry. I already said that, didn't I? Well, we are so glad you decided to join us this morning."

"Thanks," said Cassie. "This is my sister—"

"Anna, right?" she said. "It's been a few years, Anna, but it's great to see you again."

"Nice to see you again too, Doris," replied Anna. "How is Bob?" she asked.

Doris smiled pleasantly as she pointed into the main sanctuary. "He is doing fine. He's sitting up there on the third pew on the right waiting for me to join him." She leaned toward Anna and gave her a slight hug and whispered to her, "You are such a sweet girl to ask."

Suddenly the large pipe organ gracing the front walls of the sanctuary began playing the prelude to the opening hymn. Doris quickly moved on to Stephanie, took her hand, shook it gently, and said, "Doris."

"Stephanie," she shouted in reply.

"Come on, follow me," said Doris with an excited urgency. She led the queued threesome—Cassie, Anna, and Stephanie—to an empty pew halfway to the front, and they all filed in. Having brought up the rear, Stephanie was now on the aisle next to Anna. She pondered the risk and benefits of sitting there—away from the aisle, she could minimize interaction with others; near it was the security of a quick exit.

Suddenly the organ hit a staid chord, everyone stood at attention, and the congregation began singing the opening hymn. The girls all stood and joined the chorus as Anna handed Stephanie a hymnal opened to hymn number 306, "Faith of Our Fathers." As Stephanie followed along in the hymnal, her ears harkened to the enthusiastic singing of those around her. She was especially fascinated by one lady sitting two rows behind her, who Stephanie thought redefined the standard for tone-deaf.

Faith of our fathers, living still,
In spite of dungeon, fire, and sword;
O how our hearts beat high with joy
Whene'er we hear that glorious word!
Faith of our fathers, holy faith!
We will be true to thee till death.

The Package

Stephanie continued her detached critique through most of the second verse and marveled that people could sing such gloomy material with unbridled enthusiasm. Anna bumped her with an elbow and nodded her head toward Stephanie's hymnal, encouraging her to sing. Stephanie mouthed the words silently, providing a faux smile whenever Anna looked at her.

After the opening song, the service progressed with announcements, communion, a second hymn, and then an offering. Stephanie got out her purse to contribute to the offering. *Maybe a dollar or two*, she thought.

Anna perceived Stephanie's sense of obligation and fear of unwarranted attention, so she leaned toward her and whispered in her ear, "You don't have to give anything if you don't want to." Stephanie sensed that this was a test—to see if she wanted to. Confidently, she complied with the perceived requirement, pulled two dollars from her purse, and dropped them in the plate. *I am leaving no room for anyone to criticize me*, she thought. She then passed the plate to Anna, who responded by rolling her eyes and passing the plate on to Cassie without a contribution. Stephanie realized that she had only outwitted herself. Anna was the youngest, but she wasn't clueless.

As the service progressed, Stephanie assessed Pastor Riddick. He had been polite and friendly the night before. His long tenure in the church was evident, however, and he exhibited a stately presence. He spoke with formal tones instilling respect and honor. Comparing his present demeanor with the previous night's relaxed manner proved to be a fascinating exercise.

Checking the order of service in the bulletin that Doris had handed her, Stephanie readied herself for the sermon as Pastor Riddick stepped forward. He opened his Bible, placed it on top of the rostrum, and placed his sermon notes alongside it. Smiling warmly at the congregation, he raised his hands and said, "Let us stand and pray." The congregation responded in near perfect unison. "God," he prayed, "may you delight in our worship and may your word go forth and accomplish its purposes. Amen." The entire congregation again answered in unison, "Amen" and dropped back into the pews with the same unanimity.

Pastor Riddick began reading passionately from his notes. "When in the course of human events," he declared, "it becomes necessary for one people to dissolve the political bands which have connected them with another and to assume among the powers of the earth, the separate and equal station to which the Laws of Nature and of Nature's God entitle them, a decent respect to the opinions of mankind requires that they should declare the causes which impel them to the separation."

Sunday Morning

Stephanie thought it impressive that he could speak with such fluidity. It nearly overcame the fact that she had no idea what he actually said.

"These, my friends, are the opening words to the Declaration of Independence. The signing of that renowned document is what we celebrate on this Fourth of July weekend. With our parades, cookouts, festivals, and fireworks, we commemorate that moment in time when we declared ourselves no longer to be the bond servants of tyrants but descendants of the Most High God, from whom we derive an inheritance of freedom.

"What, you might ask, is the relevance of this earthly occasion to our spiritual plight in the world? Much, I would answer you. For the things of this earth are only shadows of those things that are eternal. They are imperfect images, described by the apostle Paul as a poor reflection in a mirror. So what might we see in this poor reflection that is the Fourth of July? What might we see in that distorted mirror that is our Declaration of Independence? What spiritual lessons can we derive from our celebrations of this occasion?

"The first lesson is this: whether in the unseen spiritual world or in the physical world that daily besieges our senses, there are truths that transcend. As in the physical world of our forefathers, there exists in the spiritual world a real and present evil that seeks to destroy our lives. In both worlds, this is tyranny—that evil that demands the sacrifice of liberty in exchange for an apparition called peace and safety. Sadly, those who agree to such an exchange find themselves possessing neither liberty nor security.

"The second and more abiding truth is that liberty is the passion of the heart of man. The innate desire to be free to act on one's own will is indisputable. Our earlier reading of the Declaration outlined the belief that people have a right to the separate and equal station to which the Laws of Nature and of Nature's God entitle them. But what is this right? And what or who has granted it to us? And once we have it, what is our duty to it?

"Daniel Webster, our fourteenth US Secretary of State once said, 'God grants liberty only to those who love it, and are always ready to guard and defend it.' Clearly, Secretary Webster thought that the possession of liberty was bound with an obligation. God granted liberty only to those who were willing to suffer to possess its benefits.

"One needs look no further than the boundaries of our own state to see the most palpable historical event that elucidates this truth. On December 18, 1777, only eighteen months after the Declaration of Independence was signed, George Washington and his Continental Army arrived at Valley

Forge, Pennsylvania, for the beginning of a winter encampment that has come to best signify the price paid by the brave soldiers that fought for our independence.

"So poor were the conditions at Valley Forge that Washington at one point declared, 'unless some great and capital change suddenly takes place . . . this Army must inevitably . . . starve, dissolve, or disperse, in order to obtain subsistence in the best manner they can.' Typhus, typhoid, dysentery, and pneumonia were among the killers that took as many as two thousand men that winter.

"It is critical to note that these anguished soldiers already enjoyed the liberty that was affirmed by the Declaration, and yet they suffered in its defense. In fact, the liberty that they had been granted by those in authority was not because of any action on their part. Yet this fact did not deter their suffering but rather enhanced it.

"When these men enlisted for service in the Continental Army, they knew they might suffer death at the hands of the British soldiers. How much harsher the reality was of dying slowly in defeat—not at the hand of the enemy but by the wrath of nature. I often wonder how many of these soldiers questioned their own judgment as they lay starving, freezing, and dying.

"On this Sunday morning, I implore you to examine your own life and to learn the lessons taught to us by these men. Like these soldiers, spiritually, we have been set free from the tyranny of sin by actions not of our own choosing. Jesus Christ, with his outstretched arms on the cross of death, purchased for us eternally a liberty beyond that which can be secured by any earthly compact.

"Like the people who lived in this land on July 4, 1776, we are all faced with a choice. We must choose whether to align ourselves with tyranny to derive its apparent benefits of safety or with liberty, which, though provided freely, comes with obligation.

"So what must we do? As Daniel Webster declared, we are obliged to defend liberty against tyranny in this earthly realm. But, more importantly, and of eternal significance, we must be willing to defend the liberty we have in Jesus Christ against all enemies. This is a battle that demands our present attention. But in order to fight and win this battle, we must know and understand our enemy.

"Ephesians 6:11-12 declares, 'Put on the full armor of God so that you can take your stand against the devil's evil schemes. For our struggle is not

Sunday Morning

against flesh and blood, but against the rulers, against the authorities, against the powers of this dark world and against the spiritual forces of evil in the heavenly realms.'

"As Christians, we must know that our enemies are not flesh and blood, and we must act according to that knowledge. If your brother offends you, forgive him. He is not your enemy. If one harms you in some manner, forgive him. Your battle is not with him. Our enemies are not of this world. Always be reminded that your offender is enlisted in the army of a tyrant and knows not how to do anything except that which his evil commander demands.

"The apostle Peter tells us, 'Finally, all of you, live in harmony with one another; be sympathetic, love as brothers, be compassionate and humble. Do not repay evil for evil, or insult with insult . . . but with blessing.' We may often find ourselves at a disadvantage in life by living this way. But it is what true liberty demands. Sometimes the cost is high.

"So, then, what benefits do we derive from choosing to be in the service of liberty?—or, in the spiritual realm, in the service of God Almighty? Do we deprive ourselves of the blessings of liberty by being his servant? No, we do not. In fact, serving him is the essence of liberty itself. They are inseparable—one and the same.

"In like manner to those soldiers of long ago, by serving him we derive for ourselves the ultimate blessings of liberty. For them, it was the blessed but imperfect country we inhabit today. For us, it is far more. It is the surety of boundless perfect liberty, which is the assurance of life eternal in the presence of God himself.

"And as for our lives today, we can look again to the apostle Peter for what to expect. Beginning in 1 Peter 4:12, he teaches, 'Dear Friends, do not be surprised at the painful trial you are suffering, as though something strange were happening to you. But rejoice that you participate in the sufferings of Christ.'

"As you live a life in service of Christ, you will find many times—maybe most times—when you have a sense of peace and safety. You may also find times when you are actively engaged in battle against the forces of evil. But you may also find your own personal Valley Forge, a place where there is no war going on around you, no enemy to drive away, and no attack to overcome. Nevertheless, you may find yourself suffering greatly for no apparent reason. It may cause you, like those soldiers, to wonder if you made the right choice.

The Package

"As Christians, we need to know that we have a sure and confident commander who can comfort us in the battle beyond that of any earthly officer. Know that the liberty you possess is not dictated by the circumstances surrounding you. Know that those in the service of a tyrant are not your true enemy. And finally, know that your suffering, even without an apparent lack of purpose, is in the ultimate service of liberty. And the liberty of which I speak is the true liberty that we have in Christ. He is our eternal rest. Amen."

As the pipe organ began playing the prelude to the final hymn, Stephanie contemplated Pastor Riddick's words. He had expressed confidence in a belief that suffering is normal, almost to the degree that suffering should be an expected and desired consequence of life. This idea—that suffering can be of benefit—revolted her.

Stephanie had always questioned how a loving God could allow suffering to occur in the world. In his sermon, Pastor Riddick had suggested that God not only allowed suffering, but that he took some sort of morose delight in it. Stephanie considered the accident in this context. Did God intend for it to happen? Did he plan it? This thought strangled her perceptions of God.

"Good morning," said a voice, snapping Stephanie back from her emotional discord. "I'm Bob Carson. I was a friend of your Dad's." Stephanie realized the closing hymn had finished, and she mindlessly held an open hymnal in front of her. Bob stood in the aisle next to her.

"Oh, hi," she replied. "I'm Stephanie." She eased past him into the aisle to allow Anna and Cassie to greet him. "And these are my sisters, Anna and Cassie." As Bob successively greeted Anna and Cassie, numerous other people began closing in to welcome them. Many knew Anna from previous visits, and she introduced Cassie and Stephanie to them. While everyone she met was kind, the focused attention became too much for Stephanie.

"Can I have the keys?" asked Stephanie. "I need to get something from the car."

Anna removed the keys from her purse and handed them to Stephanie, who made a beeline for the door. She gave brief, courteous nods to those who greeted her as she passed, but she was clearly on a mission to leave. As Anna spoke to another acquaintance, she introduced Cassie, who was watching Stephanie's exit from the church. Cassie responded politely, then leaned toward Anna and whispered to her, "We'd better go."

Anna scanned the room for Pastor Riddick, hoping to say good-bye,

118

Sunday Morning

but she didn't spot him. She and Cassie excused themselves and made their way to the car, finding Stephanie sitting in the backseat waiting. They piled into the car and began the drive home.

The initial part of the ten minute ride back to the cabin was somber, especially in the backseat. Anna briefly told Cassie how pleased she was to see Bob Carson. He was Dad's friend, and he was battling cancer when she had last seen him five years earlier.

Anna pulled the car into a gas station on the way home. "Anyone need anything?" she asked. Both Cassie and Stephanie shook their heads no. While Anna pumped the gas, Stephanie looked at Cassie sitting in the front seat. She thought she saw tears in Cassie's eyes, which Stephanie considered a rare occurrence.

"You okay?" she asked.

"The truth?" asked Cassie. Stephanie shook her head yes. "That message—it felt like getting my wisdom teeth pulled," said Cassie. "I'll probably be better because of it, but it wasn't comfortable."

Stephanie nodded in agreement and watched Cassie drift back into reflection. *Tyranny and Liberty*, she thought. Even for Cassie, the sermon hadn't been as innocuous as Stephanie had expected. It prodded at open wounds. Stephanie had suffered a great deal—pain had been wrongly inflicted on her—and life had labeled her a victim. But faced with the dissonant concepts of a loving God and purposed suffering, she pondered a question that simply defied resolution. *In her life, who was the tyrant?*

13

REVELATION

The cabin door burst open and Cassie lunged into the room. While Cassie knew that she should probably have availed herself of the restroom facilities at the church or even the gas station, she had elected to wait. "I'll be back in a minute," she called to her sisters as she scurried across the room toward the hall.

Anna and Stephanie followed through the door at a far more leisurely pace. Stephanie set down her purse, dropped onto the sofa, and filed her nails, continuing what she had been doing since the time they left the church parking lot. Anna moved to the kitchen to plan lunch. After she wiped the breakfast crumbs from the counter, she paused to talk to Stephanie, whose filing was becoming feverish. Anna wondered how she could have any fingernails left.

"So Steph, what did you think of the service?"

Stephanie spoke flatly amid her filing, "The pastor's a nice man, and the people were nice too."

Anna recognized that Stephanie had artfully dodged the question. "That's true. They're very sweet," said Anna. "But what did you think of the service?"

Stephanie ceased filing, glared at Anna for several seconds, and then shrugged her shoulders. "It was nice," she said before resuming her filing. Anna took a break from her kitchen duty, walked into the living room, and sat down next to Stephanie. "Come on Stephanie, talk to me! What did you think?"

Stephanie continued without reaction for a few seconds and then glanced at Anna, then back at her fingernails, never breaking her rhythm. She hoped Anna would get the point. Finally, she dropped her hands into her lap and glared at Anna. "Maybe I'm not sure, okay? It's been a long time since I've been in church. It actually felt a little weird."

Anna had hoped that their visit to church had been a positive experience for Stephanie, thinking it might open the door to discuss meaningful topics. Anna struggled for a response, and Stephanie could see her uneasiness. Irritated with the whole line of questioning, Stephanie chided her. "Is that okay? Isn't that what you wanted to hear?"

In retrospect, Anna could see that Stephanie had attempted to avoid a confrontation about church, and she had pushed her unnecessarily. "You're right," said Anna. "It was very nice."

Cassie returned from the restroom feeling quite relieved but oblivious to the tension in the room. "So what shall we make for lunch? What do we have left, Anna?"

Anna sighed, jumped up from the sofa, and regrouped. "Well, there are some hot dogs, and we still have those baked beans from our picnic yesterday."

"Do you think those things are still good?" asked Cassie.

"They're baked beans," assured Anna. "They're invincible."

As Anna pulled the baked beans from the refrigerator, there was a knock at the door. Stephanie stopped her filing, stood to her feet, and moved toward the window.

"Who is it?" asked Cassie.

Stephanie peeked between the slats of the window shade and saw Pastor Riddick, who was exhibiting an annoying enthusiasm. She'd spent the morning at church. Wasn't that enough? She turned to Cassie and sighed. "It's the pastor." Her imagination flirted with the unrealistic notion that someone might suggest they not answer the door. Instead, Cassie flung her hands in the air as if to say, "I'm busy here," and Anna gave her no response. So Stephanie flipped her nail file into the air, caught it in her hand, and walked towards the door saying, "I'll let him in."

"Should we make him lunch?" Cassie asked Anna, unsure of the protocol for such an occasion.

"No, let's just sit down and talk for a few minutes. Be hospitable." Anna had already pressed Stephanie once and while a lunch invitation might normally be proper, she would avoid it for Stephanie's sake. Today was not a normal day.

Stephanie opened the front door and looked at the pastor through the screen. She greeted him, "Hello, Pastor."

"Hi, Stephanie." She stared at him for a moment, hoping he might say something brief and be on his way. But he waited patiently and finally asked, "May I come in for a minute?"

The Package

Stephanie pretended to realize her rudeness. "Oh, I'm sorry . . . yes . . . please come in." She paid little attention as she reached to push the screen door at the same time the pastor pulled it open. Her fingernail caught in the door's spring, and she jumped toward the pastor to protect her finger as the door swung open. "Whoa!" she exclaimed. Surprised by her reaction, the pastor backed away from her as Stephanie began examining the nail and going back into the house.

Following Stephanie into the living room, Pastor Riddick was concerned that she had injured herself. "I'm sorry. Are you okay?"

The question drew a concerned look from both Cassie and Anna, but Stephanie eased their worry by providing her usual flourish of drama. "It's fine," she said, showing off her fingernail. "I just caught it in the screen door when I was opening it. No harm done." She resumed her filing.

"I'm so sorry to drop in like this," he said. "I hope I'm not intruding."

Anna scurried toward him and escorted him to a chair in the living room. "Not at all, Pastor. You're welcome anytime. Please sit down."

"Thank you," he said, taking a seat. "I had an urgent matter to deal with right after the service, and didn't get a chance to greet you after church, so I thought I'd stop by for a minute on my way home. I live just a few houses up the road."

"We're glad you came by," said Anna.

"I was so glad you all came to church this morning."

"It was very nice of you to come by last night and invite us," replied Anna.

"So, what did you think of the service?" he asked.

Seeing that the pastor was looking at Stephanie as he asked this question, Anna was distressed. She looked at Cassie, who gave her a puzzled look, not understanding her nervousness. Anna could feel a lump in her throat.

"It was nice!" said Stephanie enthusiastically.

Anna breathed a sigh of relief as the pastor slapped his knee in delight. "Oh, I am so glad you enjoyed it."

"It was a wonderful service, Pastor," said Anna, "and your message on suffering was right up our alley. It seems like we've had our share of it." Anna voiced the thought that had occurred to her during the service, but as she spoke the words, she realized that she might have opened a powder keg. She and Cassie had seen the indications of that on Friday evening.

"You have had your share, that's for sure," he said. "Losing your mother

Revelation

tragically like that must have been really difficult for all of you. I know it was sure hard on your dad."

"You knew Dad then?" asked Cassie.

"Cassie, I've known your dad since before your mom died. We met at the grocery store one day when you were all up here on a weekend together. We talked for awhile, and I invited him to church. He never came then, but he did come to see me right after your mom died."

While Anna shared Cassie's fascination with the pastor's trip down memory lane, she was surprised that Cassie appeared oblivious to the land mines in this conversation.

"Really?" said Cassie, inviting him to continue.

"He spent about a month up here after that; that's when I met Anna too. Your dad and I became close friends in the years that followed. We often talked about how much he struggled to make it through that time in his life. He almost didn't make it; but by the grace of God, he pressed through it, and he came through stronger than he was before. He always said that he found his faith here in those days."

Anna's concern motivated her to respond with a nonverbal look that she hoped said, "Gee, that's great. Thanks for stopping by." But Stephanie responded, rebuffing him. "What are you talking about? Dad went to church his whole life." Anna found herself biting her nails.

"Of course he did," said the pastor. "I didn't say he became a Christian here, only that this cabin was where he found his faith. Actually, I didn't say it at all. Those were his words."

Stephanie considered that to be the lamest explanation she had ever heard for anything. *Enough!* she thought. What he had said was absolute nonsense, and she was determined to hold him accountable for it, owing her resolve to the too many times that she had heard too many church people give too many pathetic answers.

"What does that mean?" she demanded. "I understand they're not your words, but what do they mean?"

"Did you ever ask your dad that?" he asked. "Surely he explained it to you."

Cassie was conscious of her own wide-eyed expression when she turned to Anna, who was gnawing at her nails. Stephanie turned away from the pastor and said, "Dad and I didn't talk much after Mom died." Until this point, her tone had been demanding and confrontational, but it had now transformed into quiet rage.

The Package

"Why is that?" he asked.

Anna was feeling Stephanie's irritation. *Wasn't this man a friend of her father's?* she thought. *What in the world did these men talk about for thirty years? Is he totally clueless?*

"You know how things are," said Stephanie, dancing around the answer. "Life gets busy. People get so distracted running here and there, trying to get everything done. It's so hard to keep up with everyone. I had stuff going on and so did Dad. It just happens." Stephanie had provided every excuse but the truth. She knew it, her sisters knew it, and Pastor Riddick knew it.

"I think your father would have made time to talk to you," he said. As Anna saw it, the pastor was senselessly needling her, and she was getting annoyed. While Stephanie could be exasperating at times, she was still her sister, and Anna wouldn't allow anyone to hurt her.

Standing to her feet in Stephanie's defense, Anna said, "Pastor, I think that's—"

"It was me," confessed Stephanie. "I just—I just didn't want to talk to him. I was angry with him." Anna melted back into her seat. Being confronted with the truth, Stephanie was unaware of Anna's intervention

"Why were you angry?" the pastor asked gently.

"I just was!" snapped Stephanie. "You wouldn't understand."

"I might not completely understand what you were feeling, but that doesn't make your anger any less real." He paused to make way for Stephanie's response, but she provided none. He continued tenderly, "Are you sure you don't want to talk about it?"

"No, I don't need to talk about it," erupted Stephanie, "to you or anyone!"

While Stephanie had tried to rattle him, the pastor was unfazed, having experienced harsh treatment numerous times in his forty years of ministry. Those years had also taught him to recognize when it was time to let go. This was one of those times.

"Okay, you don't need to," he said, trying to reassure her. He looked at his watch, then to Cassie and Anna, saying, "Perhaps I should go."

Graciously, Anna began to walk the pastor to the door. She was aware that while Stephanie had been cruel, she felt that he shared some responsibility due to his relentless agitation. "I'm sorry, Pastor. Thanks again for—"

"I had a right to be angry," said Stephanie, now sitting at the kitchen counter with her back to everyone and nearly speaking inaudibly.

Revelation

"What did you say?" asked Anna. Stephanie became visibly agitated and snapped to her feet. "I said I had a right to be angry. Dad abandoned me when Mom died; he left me there."

Anna had heard these words before, but not for a long time. "He didn't abandon you," she said in a correcting tone. Stephanie was beyond the point of reason, her rage fueled by unbridled emotion. The pastor had known when to let go, but Anna had missed it.

"He came up here with you and left me alone back in Pittsburgh to fend for myself!" shouted Stephanie. "Why couldn't he have stayed in town and gotten on with his life?"

"Stephanie, he didn't leave you alone!" shouted Anna. "He wanted you to come here with us, but you refused. You wanted to stay with the Davises. He let you do what you needed to do. I mean, I know you were going through a lot for a teenager—we all were—but you made that choice, not Dad."

"I shouldn't have had to make the choice or been allowed to make a choice!"

Deciding it was time to intervene, Cassie moved next to Stephanie opposite Anna and attempted her best peacemaker routine. "Stephanie," she said, "that was a long time ago. You have to move on."

Cassie's interference fueled Stephanie's explosive emotions. "And what do you know about it?" she shouted at Cassie. "You left me too! You got on that bus and went right back to Boston!"

"I was in college," explained Cassie. "I had classes. What was I supposed to do?"

"Everyone wants to make this big deal about family," shouted Stephanie. "Well, where was our family then? The family fell apart. You all left me!"

"Stephanie, it was a hard time for everyone!" said Anna, defending Cassie. At that moment, Anna realized that doors were opening that hadn't been exposed for years, and she decided to take a risk—or perhaps a leap of faith. Feeling uncertain yet compelled to continue, she gingerly plowed ahead. "I know he hurt you," she consoled. "What Dad did to you was wrong, but it wasn't his fault or Cassie's fault."

"Well none of you were there!" she shouted frantically. "I was alone, and you didn't have to deal with it; it didn't happen to you!"

"What are you talking about?" asked Cassie.

"What do you care what I'm talking about?" she cried. "You've never cared about anyone!"

The Package

For the first time Cassie could remember, Stephanie's criticism didn't matter. "I'm trying to understand what you're saying," said Cassie. "What happened to you?"

"Mr. Davis happened to me . . . he knew I was scared . . . vulnerable . . ."

The truth flooded Cassie's soul, washing away any doubt—but she couldn't say it aloud. "Stephanie, did he hurt you?"

"Hurt me, Cassie? No, he didn't hurt me. He molested me. Okay?"

Cassie was speechless—it was too horrible to acknowledge.

"Do you feel better?" said Stephanie mockingly. "Are you ready to help now? Well, it's a little late!"

"Molested you?" Cassie could barely utter the words. "Mr. Davis?" Stephanie stormed toward the front door as Cassie called to her. "Stephanie, I'm sorry! I had no idea!"

Before she reached the door, she turned to Cassie and seethed, "Way—late!" She then flew out the door, which made a loud crash at it slammed behind her.

Cassie crumpled into the seat behind her with her face buried in her hands. The truth had stunned her with cruelty. How could she have missed this?

Anna's gamble had not played out well, and while she felt compelled to pursue Stephanie, Cassie's state of mind left her in a quandary. "Do you think I should go to her?" she asked Cassie urgently. "Cassie, what about you? Are you okay?" Cassie didn't respond. Again, Anna asked emphatically, "Cassie, what should I do?"

Cassie understood that Anna needed an answer. There was no question in Cassie's mind that, at this moment, Stephanie needed Anna more than she needed her. Cassie surmised that Anna had to know that and was simply asking Cassie's permission. "You should go. I'll be okay," said Cassie. Anna hesitated for a moment but Cassie insisted, "Go!"

As Anna walked to the door, she again saw the pastor, having completely forgotten that he was still in the room. She was pleased that he still remained because Cassie might need some consolation. She fired a quick courtesy to him as she ran out the door. "Pastor, I'm so sorry. I need to go." As she left, the screen door slammed again, and Cassie heard Anna's voice outside, fading as she ran away from the cabin, "Stephanie, wait, please wait for me!"

Stephanie's words resonated inside Cassie's head. "And what do you know about it?" Stephanie had asked. "You left me too!" Stephanie was right—she didn't know about the molestation because she wasn't there—she *had* left her. Maybe it would never have happened if she had not gone back to Boston. All the years of pain, all the blame, all the indictments—perhaps she could have done something to prevent it. Stephanie was right, and she was wrong. Cassie's shame brought her to tears. She again hid her face in her hands and wept.

The pastor watched Cassie tumble into despair before his eyes. He sensed that this was as much of a crisis for Cassie as it was for Stephanie. Stephanie, of course, had the deepest wounds, but, in this case, time was on her side. For Cassie, this was a new revelation and a fresh wound, and he had watched Stephanie inflict it. Even with all his experience with personal trauma, dealing with it as it happened was unusual for him. He knew he would need divine guidance, so he spoke a brief prayer before he addressed her from where he stood.

"Cassie," he said gently. She was unresponsive. He sat on the sofa near her. "Cassie," he said, "it's not your fault."

"I wasn't there . . . I had no idea . . . No wonder she has been so angry all these years," said Cassie, stammering through her tears.

"Cassie," he said, "I know you don't see it right now, but this is God's time. He is working on all of us. But right now, he is performing a work in the three of you."

"No wonder she pushed God away," said Cassie. "Mr. Davis went to our church. He was one of our neighbors—one of Dad's friends. Wow! I can't even imagine what she's been through. I've criticized her for every relationship she has had with men. I've been so intolerant of her life—of her. What have I done?"

"Cassie, you need to understand the grace of God. It is his grace that has forgiven you for everywhere you've fallen short, it is his grace that will bring Stephanie home, and it is his grace that will enable you to forgive yourself. It isn't your fault. And this is his time. He is working in you what he desires . . . and he is giving you a second chance with Stephanie."

"I need a second chance for everything in my life," said Cassie. "My sister, my marriage, my relationship to God . . . I have failed at all of it."

The pastor was not nearly as naïve to their situation as the girls imagined. He had revealed to them that he was aware of the accident and how that event changed their father. He had also told them that Jim believed that God spoke to him in a special way in this cabin. But, unknown to them, the pastor had been asked to keep watch on the cabin, aware that

The Package

Cassie, Stephanie, and Anna made a promise to be here, and that the girls might need help working through the weekend. The pastor didn't know when they would come, but he believed they would come. It was simple to put it all together. Jim had asked them to come here to be healed.

"Cassie," he asked, "why are you here?"

Cassie stood and crossed the room to a waiting box of tissues as she pondered the answer. "Wow, that's a pretty difficult question. Everyone struggles with that one. I'm not sure I can answer it. To serve God?"

"Well, that's one reason," he chuckled, realizing that what she had heard was "What is the purpose of life?" He attempted to bring the more narrow interpretation into clarity. "What I meant to ask is—why are you at this place on this weekend?"

"Because Dad wanted us to come. He asked us all to come this weekend to spend one more summer weekend here together—as a family."

The pastor had given Cassie the question she needed to answer. Her response indicated she was still focused on the literal answer and not the spiritual one. He pondered how he should proceed and then decided to let the truth seek its own level. He put his hand reassuringly on her shoulder and said, "I should go now. You all have a lot to work through together." He smiled and said, "Good-bye."

As Pastor Riddick began to leave, something stirred inside Cassie. She knew there was a reason she was here—she just didn't know what it was. "Wait!" she shouted, stopping him with her urgency. He turned toward her. She looked at him intently and said, "Why did you ask me that?"

The pastor sensed the Spirit stirring inside her. She was ready for the truth. "I agree with what you said, Cassie. I know you believe you're here because your father asked you to come. But I believe the real reason you're here is because your heavenly Father brought you here. Your earthly father came to this place to find his faith. Cassie, find yours. The time is right. It's his time."

Something inside Cassie told her that his words were true. And she somehow knew that this man standing before her was given to her by God to be a voice for her father, a voice she was unwilling to hear in clarity while he was alive. At this moment, this man represented to her all that her father was; with that understanding, she threw her arms around the pastor and gave him a grateful embrace, holding onto him as she would have held her own father.

She knew that in some yet undiscovered way, this was a new beginning.

14

COUNSELING

Anna flew out the door and scanned the area surrounding the cabin looking for Stephanie, but she had vanished from sight. Without a car, Anna knew Stephanie had no way to leave the immediate area, so she commenced a search. "Stephanie? Stephanie!" she repeated as she scurried around, changing her vantage point in an attempt to catch a glimpse of her. She was becoming frantic as she searched along the creek near the edge of the property. Turning to look elsewhere, she spied Stephanie sitting on the trunk of a fallen tree tucked away near the back corner of the cabin.

Considering her own disjointed state of mind, Anna feared that she could do little to console her sister adequately. But her experience had taught her one thing well: pray always, especially when you don't know what else to do. As she ambled toward Stephanie, she prayed, *"God, please give me the words to speak to her, because I have no idea what to say."*

Stephanie was sitting with her face buried in her hands and her elbows on her knees. As Anna approached, the quiet crunch of last fall's leaves beneath her feet alerted Stephanie, and she raised her head to see who was approaching. Anna stopped a short distance away, feeling a sense of relief interlaced with trepidation. "Stephanie."

"What do *you* want?" she asked.

Anna found herself reeling, having no answer for even that simple question.

"I don't need your pity," Stephanie fumed. "Go back in the house. You and Cassie can have a pity party without me." She dismissed Anna with a nod as she dropped her face back into her hands.

Anna fought the temptation to succumb to Stephanie's attack and return to the cabin. Instead, she took the last few steps towards Stephanie and silently sat down next to her on the log. Stephanie glared as she again raised her face from her hands. "Are you deaf?" she shouted. "I said go!"

The Package

Anna withstood the rebuff. Stephanie scowled at her for a few seconds and grunted, "Gees, Anna," and stood and walked away.

"Where are you going?" asked Anna.

"Away from you! Don't you get it?" she snapped.

Anna rose to her feet, strode passed her sister, and impeded her path. "No, I don't get it!" she retorted. "I'm trying to be here for you!—to be your sister! If you don't want me to say anything to you, I won't! But I will stay with you, and I will listen to you, and I will be your sister!"

Anna's assertiveness surprised Stephanie. "Fine!" she said indignantly. "But I can't deal with Cassie right now. I'm not going back into the house right now!"

"Okay," said Anna. "Let's take a walk—a long walk."

"To where?" replied Stephanie.

"To better memories!" said Anna as she grabbed Stephanie's hand and pulled her along. "To Pinnacle Ridge!"

"What? Are you out of your mind!" she exclaimed, jerking her hand away. "What are you, mountain girl or something?"

Anna stopped, turned, and looked Stephanie in the eye. "Stephanie, what are you thinking about?" she asked.

"I don't know. Lots of stuff. I'm a little freaked out, all right?"

"You need to get your mind on something else," said Anna. "Don't let this thing consume you. Use your energy to walk."

Stephanie wasn't on the same page. Her idea of coping was a movie or the bottom of a martini. *A hike?* she thought. *Anna must be joking.*

Anna crossed her arms and glared at her. "Fine, what do you want to do?" she asked. "Sit here until Cassie comes to find you? Go back into the cabin? You want to sit in my car?"

"Sitting in the car might work—if it's *going* somewhere," said Stephanie.

Anna sighed and shook her head. She was clearly exasperated.

"Fine," said Stephanie, who began walking vigorously along the edge of the creek, which was the beginning of the trail that led to Pinnacle Ridge. She turned and walked backward for a few steps and pointed at Anna. "So help me, if you lecture me, I'll throw you off Pinnacle Ridge. Here's the deal: I'll walk if you'll shut up!" said Stephanie.

Without reply, Anna ran back toward the cabin, realizing they needed some water for a midday hike. She collided with Pastor Riddick as he was leaving. "Is Cassie okay?" she whispered, aware that Cassie was within earshot.

130

Counseling

"She'll be okay," he whispered in likewise fashion. "We had a good chat. She's got some things to mull over," he said. He looked around outside. "Where's Stephanie?"

"We're going for a hike. I have to go, Pastor. I've got to get some water. Bye," she said as she hurriedly entered the front door.

Cassie watched Anna run across the living room and secure two bottles of water from the refrigerator. As Anna rushed back toward the exit, Cassie asked, "What's happening?"

"I can't talk now, Cassie!" puffed Anna. Realizing her haste might be misconstrued, she hesitated and looked at Cassie compassionately and said, "I'm sorry, Cassie. I've got to go." She then rushed out the door shouting, "Please stay here and wait for us."

Cassie sat down in a comfortable chair and tried to relax. Her mind was racing, however, trying to untangle her conflicting emotions. For the moment, she would comply with Anna's wishes; she hoped Anna knew what she was doing.

Anna caught up with Stephanie several hundred yards down the path along the stream. "Here you go," she said, thrusting one of the two water bottles toward Stephanie, who took it without breaking stride.

"I wondered what happened to you," said Stephanie. "Thought maybe you had gone *completely* insane."

Anna matched Stephanie's gait and walked behind her quietly, doing her best to keep her promise to shut up. *If Stephanie wants me to talk*, she thought, *she'll ask me questions.*

Stephanie continued leading the way, and for a period of time no words were uttered or sounds heard except for the crunch of their footsteps on the ground. When they finished the first section of the hike and arrived at the junction with the former logging road, Stephanie seemed confused. "Where's the road?" she asked.

"You're standing on it. It's right here," said Anna.

Stephanie remembered the general direction from this point, though not the specific path, and she started walking. "This way?" she asked, looking back at Anna.

"Yes," she replied.

Again, they walked in silence along Creek Road. Occasionally, they needed to stop and climb over fallen logs by straddling them and throwing their feet over, which earned Anna several disgusted looks from Stephanie. Anna pasted on a smile to respond positively but maintained her silent posture.

The Package

At the transition to Ash Grove, Stephanie sat down for a moment to rest and drink some water. Anna was pleased to do likewise. Stephanie's nervous energy was evident—she had been walking briskly.

"Okay," said Stephanie, "so where's the road? There used to be a gravel road here."

"You're asking me to talk, right?" asked Anna.

"About the road, yes," she cautioned.

"Well, this forest was untouched for hundreds of years. Then, bull-dozers, dump trucks, and logging vehicles came in and put a large gravel-coated scar on the pristine land. But left alone, the land eventually healed itself and recovered to where you see it today—with trees and some grass. Someone looking today might miss the old road completely. But those of us who saw that scar in the forest, we remember it as it was and are aware that the scar is still there just beneath the surface."

The relevance of these words to Stephanie's circumstances didn't go unnoticed. While this connection made Stephanie uncomfortable, she realized that Anna, to her credit, had talked only about what she was asked. The symbolism in her words, though, revealed undeniable realities. *Truth is an oft-times cruel broker*, she thought as she rose to her feet and spun the top back on her water bottle. "Where to now?" she said, not remembering the way from this point.

"Through Ash Grove—this way," Anna said, finally taking the lead into the forest. As they hiked through the forest of trees, Stephanie reflected on the times they had played in the fall leaves here as children. These memories created a warm emotion on a bitter day, and the affection bubbled out of her. "Remember when we used to play in the leaves up here?" she asked.

"Every fall. I remember," replied Anna as she continued walking. Stephanie followed, reliving a few of those memories in her mind. She was taken aback when Anna suddenly stopped in her tracks and turned toward her.

"Funny thing though, isn't it?" mused Anna. "I wonder why those leaves are gone?" Then, as quickly as she stopped, she returned to the hike, not waiting for an answer.

Stephanie stood for a moment and watched her. "Because it's not fall, you ninny," she called to her, laughing. "Have you lost your mind?"

Stephanie resumed her pace and just as she caught up with her, Anna stopped again. "What's so special about fall?" asked Anna.

Counseling

"Are you nuts? The leaves die and fall off the trees in the fall. They're green in the summer, and then the days get short—you know, the photo-synthesis thing?" As she waited for a response, she realized that Anna's conversation was again leading somewhere. "Okay, smart girl, what's the point?" she asked.

"In tree jargon?" Stephanie nodded yes. "Isn't it amazing how in the life of a tree, part of it has to die so that the rest can live?" Anna smiled and again resumed her hike.

Stephanie had never made this connection—a realization that her fond childhood memories of fall were dependent on death—the death of the leaves. Though Anna had left it unstated, Stephanie sensed that Anna had some intended, obscure meaning. She stood puzzled as she watched Anna walk away, unsure whether her true meaning involved the death of her mother, her father, or possibly someone or something else. As Stephanie considered that question further, she became exceedingly curious. She sped up her pace to catch Anna to get needed clarification. "What did you mean by that?" said Stephanie.

Anna never broke stride and replied, "Only that God has a great design for the trees, don't you think?"

As they began to climb Pine Hill, Stephanie started thinking more about breathing than she did the trees, as Anna was now taking advantage of her older sister. Anna pulled ahead slightly and in the middle of some large pine trees, she paused to take a drink from her water bottle. Stephanie caught up and did the same. As they stood and rested for a moment, each one glanced alternately at the forest and each other. At one point, Stephanie looked intently at Anna, who nodded toward the ground, indi-cating something. Stephanie followed her gaze and saw nothing but two pine cones. "What?" asked Stephanie, not understanding Anna's meaning.

"They're pine cones," she replied.

"Yeah, I've seen pine cones before," said Stephanie.

"Really?" asked Anna. "When?"

"You don't remember?" said Stephanie.

"Remember what?" asked Anna.

"We used to make up wishes on Pinnacle Ridge as we threw pine cones over the edge," said Stephanie. "I think Cassie made that up, though. There is nothing to it."

Anna looked skeptically at Stephanie. "Are you sure there is nothing to it?" she asked. Anna reached down and picked up one of the two pine

The Package

cones and continued her hike. Stephanie was again unsure of Anna's point, but she picked up the second pine cone and proceeded to follow her. After a few minutes, their hike left the trees of Pine Hill and traversed the Upper Valley where Stephanie observed patches of beautiful violet wildflowers scattered about the meadow. Curious about them, she called out to Anna, who was again hiking ahead of her.

"These purple flowers! What kind of flowers are they?" she asked.

"Coneflowers," said Anna, stopping suddenly and walking back to Stephanie. "Do you know why they are called coneflowers, Stephanie?" she asked earnestly.

Stephanie suspected another life lesson was about to unfold. She considered the previous lessons and provided the most relevant answer she could imagine. "Does it have something to do with pine cones?" she asked.

"Pine cones?" she said. "Why do you think that?" Stephanie shrugged her shoulders. Anna continued, "The reason they're called coneflowers is—" Anna paused to build suspense.

"Why?" asked Stephanie.

"I have absolutely no idea why they are called coneflowers!" she said, laughing hilariously as she turned back around and resumed hiking.

Stephanie stood there shaking her head. "The girl's lost it," she said aloud to herself before she scurried to catch up with Anna. A mere four or five minutes later, Anna reached Pinnacle Ridge, where she scrambled to the top, sat down, and waited. Less than a minute later, Stephanie arrived, took another long drink of water, and sat down on the rock next to Anna. She swirled the water around in her bottle. "More than half gone," she said to Anna. "How will I ever get back?"

Anna simply smiled.

For the next few minutes, Stephanie sat silently next to Anna as they explored the vista together. "It is truly beautiful here, Anna," said Stephanie.

"Yes, it is," she replied. "I'm glad you came with me."

After another comfortable silence, Stephanie found herself gazing at her sister, conceding that Anna had no selfish intent—her single focus was Stephanie's aid. While Stephanie had the self-awareness to know that she needed help, her experience had taught her that prideful motives generally masked themselves in an appearance of charity. But Stephanie had never seen Anna be self-serving. In fact, she was the opposite—Anna was self-abasing, almost to a fault.

Counseling

"Why did you bring me here?" Stephanie asked.

"Because you needed space, you needed someone who cared, and you can find both here," said Anna. She waved her hand in front of her across the horizon. "See, plenty of space."

"And someone who cares," said Stephanie, putting her arm around Anna and pulling her close.

"I wasn't talking about just me," she confided.

"Who then?" asked Stephanie. "Cassie?" Anna didn't reply. "Oh, I get it. This is the God lecture coming."

"If you want the truth Stephanie, yes, God cares about you. If you want me to sit here and be quiet and simply be with you, then no. There is no lecture coming." Anna directed her gaze back to the horizon. After about a minute, she tossed the pine cone in her hand several feet in the air and caught it, then stood to her feet. "Ready to make that wish?" she asked. Stephanie stood up, rolling her pine cone in her fingers. Anna walked up to the edge, closed her eyes, and threw her pine cone as far as she could. The wind blew it back against the rock face, and it finally fell into the trees below. "Your turn," she said.

"What did you wish for?" Stephanie asked as she walked up next to her.

"First, you make your wish," she said, pointing back into the void below the edge.

"This is silly, you know that!" she said.

"Don't do it then," said Anna, beginning to walk away.

"Okay, wait!" said Stephanie. Anna stopped and turned back to watch. Stephanie closed her eyes and threw her pine cone over the edge into the trees below. Stephanie looked at Anna. "My wish can't come true."

"That's because nothing can change the past," said Anna. "And besides, it's only a pine cone. It's nonsense." She went back and sat down.

"How do you know what I wished for?" said Stephanie, pursuing her. "And I thought you said it wasn't nonsense?"

"Because, Stephanie, everything you think, everything you do, and everything you are is trapped in the past," said Anna. "And making wishes is nonsense, period. You can't wish it—you have to change it."

"But I don't know how," said Stephanie, sitting down next to Anna, feeling a little dejected.

"When Dad was here at the cabin after Mom's death," said Anna, "he told me something I have never forgotten. He said, 'At times like this, you

The Package

have a choice. You can be angry at God and blame him for all your pain, or you can embrace God and let him comfort you while you endure it.' You need to embrace him, Stephanie."

"It's just not that simple, Anna," said Stephanie.

They sat quietly for a few minutes, and Anna got up and looked over the edge of the cliff. "You know, Stephanie, maybe wishes aren't all nonsense," said Anna.

"What?" asked Stephanie. "What are you talking about?"

"Come here," said Anna, "I want to show you something."

Stephanie stood to her feet and joined her near the edge. Anna alluded to the remains of the Old Barn. "Do you see that pile of old planks nearly covered with grass down there in the Lower Meadow?" she asked.

"No," she replied. "Where?"

"Through the treetops, right there," she said, pointing emphatically.

"Okay, yes. Yes, I see them. What is it?" she asked.

"That's the Old Barn. Do you remember it?" asked Anna.

"Sure. We used to climb down there and play together. What about it?"

"Stephanie, the Old Barn has absolutely no hope. Everything it was is gone. All that remains is a pile of rubble. Every piece of it is rotten and useless," she said.

"Wow! Now that's an uplifting story. Should I just jump off the cliff now, or do you have more futility to share?"

Anna reached up and touched Stephanie's elbow with her hand to reassure her. "Why did you have trouble seeing it when I first pointed it out?"

"Because it was hard to see through the treetops," said Stephanie.

"What treetops?" asked Anna.

"The big tall pine trees down there. Those treetops!" she said, pointing with emphasis.

"Stephanie, do you remember those trees being there when we were kids?" asked Anna.

Stephanie gazed over the edge and compared it to her memory of this place. "No, I don't," she answered.

"That's because they weren't there. I only realized it myself on the hike up here," she replied.

"What's your point?" asked Stephanie. Tears began to well up in Anna's eyes. "What is it, Anna?"

Anna could barely speak. "Pine cones," she said. Stephanie again looked over the edge and then toward Anna. "Those trees," stammered

Counseling

Anna through her tears, "those trees are the results of our wishes, Stephanie—yours, mine, and Cassie's." Stephanie looked again and began to cry at this realization—they had personally seeded the forest below them. She embraced Anna for a moment, and they stood arm in arm admiring the beauty of their accidental handiwork.

"And, consider this," said Anna, "a carpenter could take those trees and rebuild the Old Barn, far more magnificent than the original. You see, Stephanie, the Old Barn is truly not without hope. It simply takes a carpenter and some wood that is born of the hopes and dreams of little children." They stood together in silence considering this truth.

"Your life is like the Old Barn, Stephanie. At first glance, you feel that you have no hope. But there is a carpenter who can rebuild it—Jesus—and the prayers of your family, especially Dad, are like those wishes thrown over the cliff, the fruit of which God can use to make us whole again—to make you whole again." Stephanie began to cry and Anna pulled her close. "Don't lose hope, Stephanie," said Anna as Stephanie sobbed on her shoulder. "Don't lose hope."

15

THE PRAYER

During her four hours alone, Cassie's concern for Stephanie developed into worry. She sat in a chair and continued to drink from a mug of coffee that was cold three hours ago. She longed for her sisters to return, but that longing was intertwined by with a nagging fear that, when they arrived, she wouldn't know the right thing to say. She vacillated between a feeling of hopelessness that she felt when Stephanie fled and a sense of hope embodied in the words that the pastor had spoken to her. Sitting alone for four hours amid the intense heaviness was almost unbearable. The truth revealed today overwhelmed her. And yet, for her, the truth consisted of mere words—Stephanie had actually been molested and had lived with that reality for over twenty years.

Cassie's feelings of loneliness and despair kept overpowering her reason. She shuddered, considering that Stephanie might feel this same overwhelming despair all the time, never knowing a moment's peace. Perhaps it was why she always masked her feelings. All her behaviors were simply that—her famous flourish, her blasé attitude, and her relationships with any man who would just keep her from feeling that acute sense of loneliness, even if it was for only one night.

Cassie had judged her wrongly, and she had to face her own failure. It was true, by her assessment, that many of Stephanie's behaviors were harmful to her. But Cassie also realized that she had failed to display any morsel of compassion. Examining her own life, she was confronted with a disarming revelation: she had her own set of masks. Her logical, predictable, and cold persona was a mask that faithfully obscured her true feelings from others. She had hidden her own failures by being overly critical of others, especially Stephanie. Perhaps, her over-criticism of her daughter had destroyed her marriage. She realized that while her shortcomings were not the same as Stephanie's, she suffered from the same self-deception—a

The Prayer

deception that declared a righteousness of her own making. She now understood this for the lie that it was, and seeing her own reflection in that true mirror was agonizing.

Her thoughts were interrupted by the squeak of the spring on the screen door. Stephanie entered before Anna and went to the kitchen to throw away her empty water bottle. Cassie set down her cold coffee and hurried after her.

"Stephanie! I was really getting worried. I am so glad you girls are back." Stephanie smirked in acknowledgment as she reached into the refrigerator to get another bottle of water. As she took the cap off, her eyes again met Cassie's. "Stephanie," said Cassie, "I am *so* sorry. I honestly had no idea."

Stephanie's demeanor was gentler than when she stormed away from the cabin. "Nobody did—except Anna. I've never told anyone but Anna. It's embarrassing, and I'm ashamed."

"You told Anna?" she asked. Cassie was emotionally drained, and in that state, this revelation was like a bold slap in the face.

"You weren't exactly there for me," said Stephanie in an uncharacteristic matter-of-fact tone. "You were gone. You rushed off to college and then got married—you forgot I was even there."

"That's not true," said Cassie. "We talked. I called you."

"We never talked," said Stephanie. "You lectured, and I got mad. I haven't looked it up, but I don't think that qualifies as a conversation."

Cassie knew that what Stephanie said was true, but Stephanie had missed the point. They were sisters. How could she keep something like this from her sister?

"But you told Anna? You found time to sit down and tell this to Anna, and you couldn't tell me." The discouragement was obvious in Cassie's voice as she sat in one of the living room chairs.

"Who is this about, Cassie?" asked Stephanie, becoming indignant. "This happened to me, and you're sitting there feeling sorry for yourself."

Anna had spent four hours defusing Stephanie, and she feared that Cassie was spooling her up again. "Cassie, she's right," said Anna with uncharacteristic authority. "That's hard for me to say, but this isn't about you."

"Of course I know that. I'm just hurt," said Cassie, arguing a point she knew she couldn't defend. "I'll get over it. It's my problem. But that doesn't make it hurt any less." As Cassie considered the situation, she remembered that the pastor had spoken of an ultimate purpose. She repeated his question aloud to herself, "Why am I here?"

The Package

Stephanie couldn't believe her ears. "If you want to leave, go ahead," she said. "Don't stay here on my account. No need to break the pattern."

"That's not what I meant," said Cassie. "I don't want to leave. I was just remembering something the pastor asked me."

Cassie covered her face with her hands. She was determined to say the things she had thought about saying all afternoon. She was not going to allow her own pride to beat her. Dropping her hands from her face, she looked at Stephanie across the room. Stephanie looked as vulnerable as Cassie had ever seen her. It was time. It was time for Cassie to take off her mask—time for her to be vulnerable too.

"Look, I want to be your sister," said Cassie, moving slowly across the room to Stephanie, who sat at the kitchen counter with her back to Cassie. "I want to just wave my hands and make all the pain as though it never happened. I want to be kids again, to go back to when life was simple, when we understood each other. I want to feel peace and joy again and find my way past the numbness. I want to fix my mistakes and find a way outside myself, where I can meet you, get to know you again, and love you." As Cassie finished, she gently stroked Stephanie's long hair.

While Cassie perceived that her outstretched hand would be welcomed, Stephanie's inherent vulnerability quickly threw up walls for protection. "Cassie, those are wonderful words," she answered, "but words can't change anything. They won't bring Mom back, or Dad back, or even you back—they can't change the past or make me feel anything but empty. I'm going to my room."

Stephanie disengaged and Cassie, stunned with her reply, watched her walk toward the hall. "Are you sure?" asked Cassie. "We're here. What can I do?"

Stephanie turned back toward her sisters before she left the room and addressed them with despair in her voice. "I just need to be alone. It's just too much to think about out loud." As she disappeared around the corner down the hall, a sullen Cassie sat down at the counter feeling discouraged. Only moments before, Cassie had been so hopeful. She glanced at Anna sitting on the sofa and saw that Anna looked exhausted. It had been a difficult day.

Before either Cassie or Anna spoke, Stephanie surprised them both when she returned from the hall, walked up to Cassie, and looked directly into her eyes. "Look, Cassie, I know you're trying to help. It's me . . . I just . . . I just need to think." Without another word, Stephanie turned and left the room as quickly as she came.

140

The Prayer

Cassie was beyond being overwhelmed. "Wow! That was definitely a lot to process. Do you think she's okay? I mean, do we need to do something?" During the hours that Anna spent on Pinnacle Ridge with her, she had sensed a transformation beginning inside Stephanie, and Cassie was now beginning to perceive it also. Stephanie still had no answers; but there was progress, and it was real.

"She's talking," said Anna. "She's talking about it. She's been battling this for more than twenty years, and mostly alone. She may be lashing out at you, Cassie, but she is at least telling you how she feels. If she didn't need you, she wouldn't care about how you feel, or how she feels about you."

Cassie smiled as she moved behind the couch where Anna was sitting, leaned across its back, and placed her cheek on her sister's cheek, hugging her from behind. "Where in the world have I been?" asked Cassie. "My little sister has grown up and become the wisest of us all."

"Dad was the wise one," said Anna. "I just listened to what he told me."

"Have you ever told Stephanie what Dad told you?"

"About what?" asked Anna, not making the connection.

"About pain coming and having a choice—to push God away or embrace him." Cassie had contemplated this idea numerous times today in her time alone.

"I told her today," said Anna.

"What did she say?"

"She said it's just not that simple."

"I only wish I could help her," said Cassie. "Obviously, you've been able to get through to her. I mean, she told you."

"Cassie, I've never been able to get through to Stephanie. I've just listened where you might have—*not* listened."

Cassie realized that her pride had risen up again, and Anna had called her on it. Perhaps Anna was right. She hadn't been told because she didn't listen. "Maybe that's my whole problem."

"What's that?" asked Anna.

"I don't listen very well."

"Why not ask God if that's a problem for you?" she said. But almost as soon as she spoke the words, she realized the contradiction. "Hmm, that's an interesting paradox isn't it? Asking God if you have a problem listening? How would he tell you the answer?" Anna laughed at herself.

"Is that supposed to make me think? Because I'm nearly at my thinking limit. My feelings are so pegged right now, I feel like climbing the walls. I just want to *do* something."

The Package

"Want to pray?" asked Anna, seizing the opportunity.

"Right now?"

"Sure. Why not?"

"I'm not good at it."

"Do you think that's a good thing?"

"It just feels like a cop-out," confided Cassie. "You know, everything is going wrong, so I'll toss it over this spiritual wall and not think about it anymore."

"It's really the only thing we can do," said Anna. "Like I said, I listen to Stephanie, but I can't reach her. Only God can do that. And I think he is doing it. It will simply take some time for her to embrace it. And for you—"

"To embrace it," finished Cassie.

"Yes," said Anna. "So, do you want to pray?"

Cassie still felt uneasy, but without a reason she could articulate. Fighting to set aside her discomfort, she yielded. "Okay. Me or you?" she asked.

"You. Just talk to him, Cassie. He's waiting for you."

The idea that God could be waiting for her, that somehow the Creator of the universe was interested in her affairs at this moment defied her comprehension. Pastor Riddick's words continued to resound in her mind and heart. She unconsciously repeated them aloud. "It's his time," she said.

"What?" asked Anna.

"That's what the pastor said, 'It's his time.'"

"Cassie, the Bible says that no one comes to the Father except the Spirit draws him. So if it's truly his time, it's your time and our time. Let's pray," said Anna.

Cassie was sitting on one of the stools at the counter, and Anna sat on another one behind her. Cassie closed her eyes to pray and felt Anna place her hand upon her shoulder. She struggled for the right words to say, but finally spoke to God as a friend who was patiently waiting to hear from her. "Dear God, I haven't talked to you for some time. I'm sorry I've been . . . selfish. I'm sorry I went on with my life and left you behind. I guess I did the same thing with Stephanie." As Cassie spoke her name, Stephanie walked into the room, and hearing it, she eased back into the hall to listen unnoticed. "God," continued Cassie, "please help Stephanie find her way, and please help me know how to love her and how to love you more. Speak to me, Lord. I will try to listen to your voice. I'm not too good at that, but I want to be. Please help Stephanie to . . . to . . ." She looked back toward Anna. "I don't know what to say."

The Prayer

"You're doing fine," said Anna, rubbing her shoulder in encouragement.

"God," stammered Cassie, "please help Stephanie right now. . . please touch her and give her peace. . . I don't even know what to ask for, God . . ." Cassie began to cry.

"Thank you, God," prayed Anna, "that you are able to do exceedingly abundantly above all we can ask or think, and we put Stephanie in your hands right now. Amen."

"Amen," said Cassie.

Anna hugged her from behind as Stephanie watched from the hallway. Stephanie lingered a moment and entered the room again, acting as though she had just arrived. "Hey, I just need a bottled water." She opened the fridge, picked up a bottle, and closed the door as she turned back to her sisters. "Sorry to interrupt."

Anna smiled and said, "You're not interrupting anything."

Stephanie was moved by Cassie's sincerity, and while she didn't feel that she could reveal her deliberate eavesdropping, she wished she could acknowledge Cassie's kindness. She lingered at the counter as she contemplated her options. Finally, she elected to let it be. "Good night," she said as she again headed for the bedroom.

"You're going to bed for the night?" asked Anna. "It's only seven."

"I just might fall asleep, and I don't want to be rude," she answered gently as she left the room. "Good night."

After Stephanie exited, Cassie gave Anna a worried look. "Do you think she heard us?" she asked. "What if she did?"

"What does it matter?" asked Anna.

"I don't want her to feel that I think I'm better than her, because I was, you know, praying for her."

Anna sensed that Cassie's concern for Stephanie was genuine and thought it a blessed change, having seen it lacking as recently as Friday morning. "You were praying for you too," she said, smiling. "Don't worry." This eased Cassie's mind a little, but she still looked worried, so Anna completely changed the subject.

"So," said Anna, "what do you think is in the package from Dad?"

"I have no idea," said Cassie. "Yesterday, I couldn't believe we had to wait until Monday to find out. Today, so much has happened that I almost forgot about it."

"And what do you think?" said Anna.

"I can't even venture a guess."

143

The Package

"Me neither," said Anna. "But one thing I am fairly certain of is that Dad prayed about us coming here, and he asked God to do something special."

"How do you know that?" said Cassie.

"Well, I can't say for certain that Dad prayed about us coming here, but I do know God is doing something special. I sense it. And I'd bet what God's doing has something to do with that package."

"What time does the post office open?"

"At 8:30," said Anna.

"How do you know?"

Anna laughed and said, "Believe me, I checked."

"Tomorrow could be an interesting day," said Cassie. As the day's events had caused Cassie to rethink some things she thought unchangeable, she reconsidered her earlier criticism of Anna. "Maybe God really does have a plan," she admitted.

"Not just good fortune?" quipped Anna. Cassie sported a sheepish grin and shook her head no. Anna's excitement about what God was doing made her think about it all from his perspective. She looked directly at Cassie, smiled, and said, "I'll bet God can't wait."

16

THE POST OFFICE

It was 8:30 on Monday morning, July 7th. The postmaster, Sadie Wilson, slid a ring of keys from the service counter into her hand and walked to the front door. Searching through them, she identified the right key and placed it into the lock. Before she turned it, she jumped backwards, being surprised by three women standing just on the other side of the glass door. They were bouncing around impatiently in a light drizzle with a single yellow raincoat stretched over their three heads. The one in the front smiled and held up a peach-colored notice, which Sadie recognized as a "Sorry We Missed You" Form 3849 —as if that should somehow explain their bizarre behavior.

Sadie stepped back to the door, unlocked it, pulled it open, and watched as the girls piled inside past her. She smirked as she watched them lower the raincoat and wipe the moisture from their clothes as best they could. Sadie suspected that they were the intended recipients of the mysterious package that had arrived at their post on Saturday. Sadie and her office mate, Mary, had talked about the package all day that day. It was rare that a package, or even a single letter, arrived that was addressed to strangers. They knew most everyone in the zip code.

This package, however, was truly an enigma. First, the delivery address was a place they recognized—Jim Mullins' cabin. But the recipient's names were unfamiliar. Conversely, the return address listed the familiar name of Jim Mullins as the sender, but with an unfamiliar Pittsburgh address. As if these anomalies alone didn't arouse enough suspicion, Jim Mullins had died a few months ago. The whole situation was very odd.

"What in the world are you three ladies doing standing out in the rain?" Sadie asked.

"We're here to pick up a package," said Cassie excitedly. "This note was left at our cabin on Saturday." She tried to hand it to Sadie.

The Package

Being compliant employees of the US Post Office, Sadie and Mary had garnered years of experience at downplaying their nosiness about other people's mail. She answered Cassie in a raspy, shrill tone. "Now, hold your horses there, young lady. At least wait till I get behind the counter."

"Okay," said Cassie, embarrassed.

Sadie stepped through the door leading to the area behind the counter and closed it. Unseen by the girls, she stood behind it for a moment to heighten the suspense. In these parts, she and Mary were renowned for their good humor, and Sadie was simply living up to her reputation. But they were also responsible for upholding the public trust, never forgetting that they worked for the government of the United States. As such, they ran a tight ship and did business with the utmost respect and order. She smiled in knowing that, today, they would be ornery but upright officers of the US government.

The girls stood at the counter three abreast, impatiently waiting for Sadie to appear. Finally, she appeared around the corner and ambled up to the counter. Cassie slid the note across to her and said, "We got this note."

Sadie's glasses hung on a chain around her neck. She pulled them up to her eyes and examined the note. Then she returned it back to the counter, slid it across to Cassie, looked over her glasses, and asked, "You got a number?"

Stephanie shook her head in disbelief and uttered, "What?"

"A number," said Sadie. "You gotta have a number." Without looking away from them, she pointed at the "Now Serving" electronic sign on the wall.

"It isn't working," said Stephanie.

Sadie looked surprised and shifted her gaze to the unlit sign. "Oops," she said. "Sorry." She walked along the counter to the sign and flipped it on with a switch on its side. It lit up and proudly displayed the number one. Sadie walked back to them, looked Cassie straight in the eyes, and with great dignity and ceremony she loudly yelled, "One!"

The formerly giddy girls were now subdued. Stephanie finally spoke up. "You're kidding, right?" Sadie gave a puzzled look, looked at the sign, took her glasses off, and then leaned toward Stephanie and confidentially said, "What number do you see?"

Stephanie was stunned; she was speechless. Anna stepped back and scanned the area and saw, on the right side of the counter, a set of hanging plastic tags, the front one having a bright red number one emblazoned on

The Post Office

it. She snatched it and excitedly passed it to Sadie, shouting as though she had just won a prize, "Here's number one!"

Sadie calmly took the tag and placed it behind the counter in its place. Looking at Anna, she politely asked, "Can I help you?"

"Finally," said Cassie, sliding the note toward her again. "This was left on our door on Saturday saying we have a package here; we've come to pick it up." Sadie stared at her with disdain. "If we can," pleaded Cassie.

Sadie gently slid Cassie's hand holding the note back across the counter. "I'm sorry," she said. "I'll be with you in a minute. I'm helping another customer right now." She looked back at Anna and smiled.

"She's with me," said Anna.

Sadie pretended to have a revelation. "Oh. I see. You're all here together!" she noted as she waved her hands playfully about her silliness in not realizing it.

"Yes," said Anna. "These are my sisters."

"Okay, I understand," said Sadie. She looked back at Cassie with a sly smile. "Why don't you let me see that again?" Cassie again slid the note across the counter. Sadie looked at Cassie over her glasses as she picked it up. "So, a parcel was delivered to your house, and you weren't home?" she asked suspiciously.

"Yes," answered Cassie.

"On Saturday?"

"Yes," said Cassie. Sadie again looked at her with misgiving. "I mean," said Cassie, "it was actually delivered to our father's cabin. But, see here, it's addressed to us. I'm Cassie, and these are my sisters, Stephanie and Anna." Sadie again examined the note and successively glared at each of them. Attempting to lighten her grumpiness with humor, Cassie pointed at Anna and said, "Anna, here—she's number one."

"I see," said Sadie. "Well, this is a Form 3849."

"A Form 38—what?" stammered Cassie, missing the point.

"I can't help you. A Form 3849," she said, pointing to it. "See here, it's sort of like a missed delivery notice."

"That's right. That's what I've been saying," said Cassie.

"Well, missed deliveries are handled by Mary. Excuse me for a minute while I see if she is available." Sadie walked away from the counter toward a back room and called out, "Mary! Counter!"

Mary Evans, a plump but kind looking woman, scurried into the room. "You're needed at the counter," said Sadie.

The Package

Sadie stood and watched as Mary walked up to the counter. There was silence for a moment. When Cassie was about to speak, Mary looked at the illuminated sign and called out with a resonant voice. "One!"

Cassie pointed at Anna, and declared impatiently, "She already gave her number one!"

"That right, Sadie?" asked Mary.

"That's right," she replied.

"I'm sorry," said Mary to Cassie. "My mistake."

"No problem," she said. "Now, about this note—"

"Two!" shouted Mary.

"Wait," said Cassie. "I'm 'one!' I need help!"

"Now, dear," said Mary, "you told me yourself that she was 'one.' Isn't that true?"

"She is 'one,' but we're together," said Cassie.

"I'm sorry, I wish you had explained that better," said Mary. "But we're on 'two' now. I afraid you'll have to wait until your number is called." The girls all looked at each other in disbelief as Mary waited patiently. "Two!" she shouted. "Anyone?"

Finally, she leaned across the counter and whispered to Cassie. "If you want help, you'll need to take another number."

Cassie pushed past Anna, grabbed the placard marked 'two,' and slapped it on the counter in front of Mary. "I'm 'two,' okay?"

"Yes, I see. Number two." She rewound to the beginning and smiled politely. "Can I help you?"

Cassie started very slowly and sped up as she went. "We . . . have . . . come . . . to pick up a package . . . that was delivered to our cabin . . . when we weren't at home . . . Saturday!"

"Was there a Form 3849? Taylor always leaves a 3849 when folks aren't home, doesn't he, Sadie?" Sadie nodded in the affirmative. Taylor Franks was the rural post deliveryman.

Cassie held the note up in front of her face and sputtered, "You mean, this—form—3849!"

Mary cleared her throat in disapproval and took the form. "Yes, this is the form I was looking for." She fully examined it. "I see here that a package was delivered on Saturday to Jim Mullins' cabin, and no one was home." Mary looked up. "Which one of you is Cassie Carlisle?"

"Me," replied Cassie.

"Okay, you're first on the list, so you'll need to sign for it. It was sent certified mail. Got to get a signature!" she said, nearly singing her words.

The Post Office

"Fine, where do I sign," replied Cassie. Sadie walked up and stood next to Mary. She looked at Cassie suspiciously and then whispered something in Mary's ear. Mary turned her attention back to Cassie. "You wouldn't have some ID, would you?"

"Okay, ladies!" shouted Stephanie, finally reaching her limit. "I don't know what insane asylum you two escaped from, but we'll show you our ID when you show us our package!"

Anna gave Stephanie an I-wish-you-hadn't-done-that look.

"Oh," said Mary. "So you want to play it that way, do you?" She looked over at Sadie, and Sadie nodded her head in understanding and agreement. Mary glanced down behind the counter twice to get her bearings, reached behind the counter with deliberation, and with the snap of her wrists pulled out a large parcel wrapped in plain brown paper. She glared at them as she set it on the counter. Cassie reached up to turn the package so she could read the address label. Before she touched it, Mary interjected, "Ah, ah, ah—ID," and warned her off with a wag of her finger.

Cassie rolled her eyes and pulled her wallet from her purse. She removed her driver's license from its slot and set it on top of the package for Mary to read. "Cassie Carlisle," she cried, tapping on the license. "Okay? See the picture? It's me, right?"

"California?" said Mary, looking to Sadie for approval. "She's from California! Is that okay?"

Sadie examined the license and compared it to the address label. "Yep, looks like it's her."

"Well, thank you," Cassie said indignantly.

Sadie initiated an investigation. "The address on this label is Jim Mullins' place. You staying there?" she asked.

The girls were all surprised that Sadie recognized their father's address, but it was a small town. "Jim Mullins was our father," said Cassie. "We're here for the weekend."

Sadie touched Cassie's hand on the counter. "We heard your dad passed away, and we were pretty sad about it. We liked him a lot. Everyone around here did."

"He came over and fixed my hot water heater when it went out," said Mary. "Remember that?"

"Yep," said Sadie, "He helped out nearly everyone in these parts at one time or another."

"Your dad was a good man, girls," said Mary.

The Package

"Yep," said Sadie, "A good man."

Cassie smiled at them. Somehow, the warm feelings these two women felt for her father erased the frustration that had surrounded the last few minutes.

"This package is from your dad?" asked Mary.

Cassie couldn't resist the opening. She put on her glasses, looked over the top of them with one raised eyebrow, repeatedly tapped her index finger on the label, and asked, "What does it say?"

Sadie looked at Mary and said, "She's got you there."

"Okay," said Mary. "It says it's from Jim. Postmarked in Siler City on Thursday. Care to explain that one?"

Cassie shrugged her shoulders. "Honestly, we don't know how it came to be here, what's in it, or why Dad sent it—or if he actually did. But we would like to take it now—if that's okay—and take it home and find out what this is all about."

"Sure, take it," said Sadie. "Hope it's something you want."

"Thanks," said Cassie. Cassie picked up the package and followed her two sisters out the door. Fortunately, the light rain had stopped and the cloud cover was breaking. Before they reached the car, Sadie and Mary walked out, stood near the door, and waved good-bye.

"Sorry we teased you, girls," shouted Sadie. "But, trust me, you father would have laughed himself silly."

The girls looked at each other, realizing they had been snookered. Cassie and Anna laughed while Stephanie rolled her eyes for a moment and then joined them. After they entered the car, Anna looked through her car window at Sadie and Mary. She thought she detected sadness in their eyes. Trying to put herself in their place, she envisioned that perhaps seeing Jim's daughters drive away was the closest they would ever come to saying good-bye to their friend.

"Wait!" shouted Anna. Cassie stopped the car as Anna popped open the door and ran to where the women stood. She hugged each one of them successively, stepped back, looked at them both for a brief moment, and smiled. "Thanks. From all four of us," she said with a knowing wink.

Sadie's eyes filled with tears as Anna ran back to the car. Mary looked over at her. "You crying, Sadie?" she asked. "You bet," she said as she turned to follow Mary back through the doorway. She stopped and watched through the window as the car drove out of sight and repeated to herself, "You bet."

17

THE PACKAGE

Almost as soon as Cassie put the car in gear to leave the post office, Anna picked the package up from the seat behind Cassie and shook it gently. "Want me to open it?" she asked.

"No," said Stephanie, as she looked at Anna over her shoulder in the back seat. "Put it down."

Anna returned the package to its place on the back seat. As they began to drive the five miles down the road back to the cabin, Anna began to snicker repeatedly and finally laughed out loud.

"Cassie, you should have seen your face when Sadie yelled 'One!' I thought you were going to go ballistic."

"Me!" said Cassie. "How about the whole insane asylum bit that Stephanie did? Now that was precious."

"I was wrong," said Stephanie. "I admit it. They didn't escape from an insane asylum. They both work there." They all laughed together as they shook their heads in agreement.

After the laughter subsided, Anna asked again, "Are you sure you don't want me to open it and find out what it is?"

"No, we agreed we would take it home and open it together," said Cassie. "Get with the plan, Anna."

"Okay," she replied in a tone suiting only a little sister.

A few miles from the cabin, they turned off the main highway. Folks called it the main highway because it was paved. As the girls individually contemplated the contents of the package, the gravel on the road popped and crackled beneath the tires. Cassie stayed focused on the winding road ahead, and Stephanie stared out the passenger window at the passing brush and trees. The package had again found its way onto Anna's lap. Her fingers tapped nervously on it, and the hollow drumming sound was making Stephanie edgy.

The Package

"Anna, could you please put that down?" asked Stephanie. "You're about to drive me crazy."

"I'm anxious," said Anna, returning the box to the seat. "Sorry."

"This is all very strange," said Cassie. "How could we be getting a package from Dad? I thought maybe it was some kind of mistake."

Anna leaned over to examine the address label again. "There's no question about it, Cassie. That's his handwriting. Are you sure you don't want me to open it up?" she asked.

"No!" her sisters shouted in unison. This time Anna got the message.

The car remained quiet as they traveled the last mile. Cassie turned the car into the driveway of the cabin, stopped it, and turned off the ignition. "Here we are," she said. Cassie got out of the car and opened the back door to retrieve the package. But Anna grabbed it the same time as Cassie. "I have it," insisted Cassie. Anna let go, climbed out, and shut the car door. Cassie was still the older sister.

They stepped onto the porch, and Anna entered through the screen door. It was already a very warm day, and they had left the front door open to get some ventilation. Stephanie held the door for Cassie and entered close behind her. Cassie entered the living room and placed the package on the coffee table in the middle of the room. Cassie sat down in a nearby chair while Anna and Stephanie sat down on the sofa behind the table.

Stephanie stroked a tuft of her long hair alternately with both hands as they all sat staring at the package. Eventually, she looked toward Anna, then Cassie, and then again toward Anna. "So, shall we open it," said Stephanie, "or shall we just sit here and admire it for a while longer?"

"I'm being a little reflective," said Cassie. "There's something special about this moment. I mean, here is a package addressed to us by Dad in his own handwriting. It's the last time we'll ever hear from him."

"I am a little conflicted," said Anna. "Like you, I want to know what is inside, but the idea of saying good-bye all over again—I'm not sure I want to do it."

Stephanie gave them a look of disbelief as she stood to her feet. "Reflective? Conflicted? You girls are starting to creep me out here. He didn't send this to us from somewhere beyond; it came in the mail!"

"Well, obviously, that's true," said Anna. "None of us believes in that sort of nonsense. But Dad put some thought into this. I don't want to lose the moment."

They all three stared at it for another four or five seconds. Then Cassie

The Package

erupted. "Okay, enough! Let's open it!" Cassie pulled the coffee table toward her as Stephanie returned to her seat for a closer look. Cassie and Anna together removed the twine that wrapped the package in both directions. Cassie turned it over and opened it from the bottom so she could preserve the mailing and return address labels intact. Once the outer wrapping was removed, Cassie lifted the lid from the remaining box to reveal it contents. Stephanie leaned closer to see what was inside.

"What is it, Cassie?" she asked.

Cassie pulled out an additional, smaller box. "The mystery continues," she said. As she inspected it, she read a small label attached to the outside. She said, "Stephanie, it looks like this one is for you." Cassie passed the box to Anna, who then gave it to Stephanie. Stephanie stood up and walked to the kitchen counter with it and sat down on one of the stools. Cassie withdrew a second box, and after examining its label said, "This one is for me." Reading the label on the remaining box, she said, "And this one, Anna, is for you."

They sat a moment before Anna asked, "Who's going to go first?"

"I think we should do it together," said Cassie. "Stephanie?"

"I agree," she replied.

Cassie looked at Anna. "Fine by me," said Anna.

"Okay!" said Cassie, signaling them to begin.

Stephanie managed to open her box first. On top of the tissue paper inside was a letter with her name on the envelope. "There's a letter here," she said.

"Mine too," said Anna.

"Same here," said Cassie.

Anna had anticipated a gift but not a letter. "This is going to be hard," she said.

"Like Dad said, embrace it, right?" Cassie encouraged Anna with her own words.

"Right," said Anna, "embrace it."

Anna, Cassie, and Stephanie each opened their respective letters simultaneously, and each one displayed a curious fascination as they began to read.

Anna hesitated before reading her letter and pushed aside the tissue paper shrouding the box's contents. Inside, she saw a green hardback book with maroon binding and a small wooden box. She returned her attention to the letter in her hand and began to read.

My dearest Anna,

I am writing this letter to tell you how much I love you and how much I appreciate the love you have given me throughout my life. You will never know the strength your love has given me or the joy that has welled in my heart as I have watched you grow in your love for Jesus. When your mother died, I nearly died with her, but you were there with me, caring for me and giving to me when you were hurting too. Because of your strength, I lived, and because of the strength that I found in him during that time, I became more alive than I ever was before.

In this box are two gifts for you. The first is my journal. It is my journal from that month after your mother's death. In it, you will find that what I have told you is true. You will find that my struggle brought me to a place of rest, and that God used you to rescue me and carry me to safety. Anna, you are a lifeboat for all who are drowning around you. God has filled you with compassion. May he use you for his glory.

The second gift is my harmonica. On that harmonica, I played hymns to God—hymns of both praise and agony. I remember the evenings when I would play, and you would sing with me. Your voice raised to God was a blessing to me, and so I leave you this gift as a reminder of those times when we praised God together.

Be at peace, my loving daughter, for we will be reunited soon, never to be parted again.

I love you more than you can possibly imagine,
Dad

Anna pulled out her father's journal and flipped through it, reading a few select words on several pages. She closed it and held it close to her chest with one hand. With her other hand, she reached in and removed the small wooden case and opened it with her index finger. The harmonica shined as though it had been washed in sunshine.

These gifts flooded Anna's memory with times they had shared alone together, both good and bad. Closing her eyes, she pictured her father sitting on the porch with his harmonica. She said, "Oh, Daddy. Thank you, thank you, thank you. I love you ~~so much.~~"

The Package

Cassie chose to read her letter before she examined the rest of her package's contents.

My darling Cassidy,

I am writing this letter to express my deep love for you and to encourage you in many ways. Cassie, you have always been so strong, always leading the way. You were the first to give your life to Christ. You were the first in many generations of our family to graduate from college. I so wish your mom could have seen that. You raised my first grandchildren, and they are strong—like you. You have so much to be proud of.

I know the pain you feel having lost your husband. I know the loneliness and that sense of not knowing what to do next. God is tearing down the strong walls you have built, Cassie, so he may come in and touch you. I know you think you have failed God; and certainly, we all have. You must know, though, that God looks upon you with compassion and desires that you become soft before him and love him with all the passion you can muster. Find your relationship with him, for it is in relationship with him that you will find true joy.

Inside this box are two gifts for you. The first is my wedding ring.

Cassie paused from her reading and looked inside the box. Indeed, there in the bottom, wrapped in tissue paper, was her father's ring. She placed it on her left thumb and spun it around with her index finger as she resumed reading.

This ring is the most precious earthly possession I own, for it is truly not a possession but a promise from your mother. While I know you are living with broken promises, I give you this ring as a symbol of kept promises, for your mother loved me all the days of her life. Cassie, God will keep his promises. Trust him, and he will never fail you.

The second gift is your mother's music box. It is scratched, and the lid is broken. But if you open it carefully, it still plays the same beautiful music it did when it was new. Cassie, open the box and set the music free.

Cassie again paused from her reading and removed the tissue paper that wrapped the music box. True to his words, it had a large scratch on its cover. She heeded her father's advice and opened it carefully, and it began to play a beautiful tune she remembered hearing when she was a child. She sat back in her chair and listened to it until it wound down. Then she

The Package

opened her eyes and resumed reading.

Cassie, God knows your life is scratched and broken, but the beautiful Cassidy inside you still has the ability to play the beautiful music that your creator intended.
With much love and the promise of tomorrow,
Dad

Cassie cried, seeing the truth in his words. For the first time, Cassie began to perceive the depth to which her father understood her and the trials she endured. *How sad*, she thought, *that I never understood this before he died; and how wonderful that he found a way to tell me now.* She whispered aloud, "Daddy, it's beautiful. Thank you."

Stephanie opened her letter with hesitation. She had learned much about herself these past few days, and she didn't like most of what she had seen. Her father couldn't possibly understand her, because she couldn't even comprehend herself. What if this letter incensed her? How could she ever resolve it? "Embrace it," she had heard her sisters say. She convinced herself, *I can do this!* as she opened her letter and began to read.

My little lost lamb, my sweet Stephanie,
I am writing this letter to you to make one last attempt to correct the years of mistakes I have made with you, and in spite of my many failings and shortcomings, to tell you I love you with a deep love—a love that groans in agony with each pain you feel, each failure you suffer, and each heartache you face. I know you have questioned my love for you from the moment your mother died, and while I have never understood the breadth of your pain, I have sensed it; and I have prayed for you daily that you might find peace.
Of all my children, I fear I have failed you the most, because I have not found a way to reach you or a way to lead you to the place you seek. There is no place to find peace other than in Jesus, and while I have not left a tree of life within you, I pray that I have left a seed; and that God will, in his time, water it and nurture it so that it grows inside of you, causing you to become the woman that God desires you to be.
Stephanie, I am leaving you with two gifts. The first is my key to this cabin. I know this is not a place where you long to be, but this is the place where God spoke to me, where he met me, and where I found my way through the pain. I

The Package

will pray until my last day on this earth that you will find what I found, that you will embrace it, and that you will finally find rest.

The second of my gifts to you is my Bible. Stephanie, this Bible is also a type of key. It is the key that unlocks eternity for you. It is the key to how to live your life today. It is also the key that will bring us together again, the key that will bring you to where I am. No matter what you choose today, Stephanie, don't lose these keys. They are most precious, and I am entrusting them to you.

I know I will likely leave this earth without knowing if I will see you again. But I have been praying; and I believe that God will speak to you, and that you will do the right thing. Read at the bookmark in the Bible.

I love you, I love you, I love you,
Dad

Stephanie was in tears by the time she opened her father's Bible. She opened the Bible to the bookmark that he had carefully placed at a passage he had marked. She had to wipe the tears from her eyes so she could read it. She read it slowly and carefully, considering every word.

In my Father's house, there are many rooms; if it were not so, I would have told you. I am going to prepare a place for you. And if I go and pre-pare a place for you, I will come back and take you to be with me that you also may be where I am.

Stephanie stared long and hard at the last phrase.

As everyone finished reading and examining their gifts, Cassie finally broke the silence. "Wow!" she said. "I'm speechless."

"This letter," said Anna, "what a gift. I can't believe it."

"This is why he wanted us to come," said Cassie.

"Remember," said Anna, "when I told you how he wrote every day in his journal that month after mom died?" Anna held up the journal for Cassie to see. "He gave it to me—the whole thing. It's the journey he took—every step . . . every prayer. He gave it to me. He told me it would show me how much I helped him, and how God desires to use me to help others."

"And Dad was right about that one," said Cassie, smiling. "You are the most selfless person I know." Suddenly realizing that Stephanie hadn't said a word, she asked, "Isn't she, Stephanie?"

The Package

Stephanie glanced toward them and smiled through her obvious tears. "She's very special," she replied.

Anna continued, "And look at this! It's his harmonica. Remember how Dad used to play this thing." Anna blew in and out of it a couple of times making a familiar dissonant train-like sound, then stopped and laughed. "He would play it almost every time we came here. He almost never played it back home. I can hardly believe it." She realized she was focusing on herself. "What about you, Cassie, what did you get?" she asked.

"Dad gave me his wedding ring," said Cassie.

Anna answered, "Really?"

"I feel so bad," said Cassie. "I gave that funeral director such a hard time because they lost his ring, and all the time he had taken it off to give to me." Anna giggled as Cassie continued saying, "He gave it to me to remind me of kept promises."

"Was that Mom's old music box I heard?" asked Stephanie.

"Yes, it was," Cassie replied, "and I will treasure it forever. He gave this to me to remind me that even though my life is scratched and broken, God can still play beautiful music through me. Wow! What an incredible moment. I simply want it to last forever."

Anna looked at Cassie, who was indeed trying to treasure the moment by closing her eyes. She then turned to Stephanie and said, "What about you Steph? What did you get?"

Stephanie sat silently, staring into the box where she had returned her father's keys and Bible. When she heard no answer, Cassie opened her eyes and insisted, "Stephanie! What'd you get?"

Stephanie continued to gaze at her package for a moment and looked at her sisters, saying, "Dad gave me hope." She began to cry, and through her tears, she stammered, "My package was full of hope."

18

THE KEYS

Monday afternoon had arrived, signaling the end of the girls' weekend together. Anna and Cassie's suitcases were packed and sitting by the front door. Cassie and Stephanie were finishing up changing their bed sheets and straightening their rooms while Anna cleaned the kitchen. Anna had nearly finished when they heard a knock on the door.

Anna called out down the hall, "I'll get it."

As Anna went to answer the door, Cassie entered the room with a renegade sock she had found and placed it into her suitcase. Through the screen door, Anna saw what had become a familiar face—it was Pastor Riddick. "Hi, Pastor," she said. "Please come in."

"Thank you," he said as he entered the room.

"Hello, Pastor," said Cassie. "I now see why you do what you do. You have a lot of courage to come back here after yesterday."

Anna gestured for him to take a seat on the chair as she sat down on the sofa next to him. "Well, yesterday was kind of a rough day for everyone," he said as he sat down. "So I thought I'd stop by and make sure you were all okay."

"Yeah, I'd say we're good," said Cassie, sitting on the arm of the sofa next to where Anna was seated. "What do you think, Anna?"

"Really good," said Anna. "Yeah, I'd say really good."

"Well," said the pastor, "I must say I'm a little surprised. I mean, yesterday was—"

"Not good," said Cassie. "I'd say not good. Anna?"

"Definitely a loser day," she said.

"How's Stephanie?" he asked. "Is she still here?"

"Oh, yeah, she's doing . . ." said Cassie, searching for the right word.

"Good!" said Anna. "I mean, I wouldn't say excellent—"

"No," said Cassie. "Definitely not excellent. But good."

The Package

"Yeah, good," said Anna.

"Good is a good word for it," finished Cassie. They both shook their heads in agreement.

"Well," he said, "you two are certainly . . ." He struggled for the right word, but then finally picked the obvious one. "Good!" he exclaimed as they all laughed together.

"It's time," said Cassie, "for us all to head back to the realities from whence we came."

"Whence—very good," said Anna. It reminded her of a game they played as children speaking King James English. "Dost thou desire liquid sustenance whilest we wait for Stephanie?" she said, playing along.

"No," said Cassie, "for then I will have to stop at the place whither thou goest? If you catch my drift." Anna laughed loudly and then Cassie joined in.

"Okay," said the pastor, shaking his head, "I can't keep up, I admit it. Where are you off to, Cassie?"

"Sacramento, California. I have a 7:00 p.m. flight out of Pittsburgh," she said, looking at her watch. "Which by the way I will miss if we don't get going." She moved toward the hall and yelled, "Stephanie! We need to go!" She addressed the pastor saying, "She's riding to the airport with me."

Stephanie entered the room.

"And you, Anna?" he asked. "Heading back to Pittsburgh?"

"Yep, headed home," she replied.

The pastor rose from his seat and said, "Listen, I don't want to hold you up, but did you girls get the package today? You know, the one you told me about on Saturday? From your father?"

"We picked it up at the post office this morning," said Cassie. "Why do you ask?"

"I just wanted to make sure you received it before you all left town."

Cassie found his questioning suspicious and said, "Pastor, I sense you know a bit more about this than you're telling."

"Well," he said, hedging, "it's possible I might have an inkling about it. But this weekend was your dad's doing. It was between him and God, and if you don't mind, I'd like to leave it at that."

"I understand," said Cassie.

"However," he continued, "if you'd be so kind as to forgive my curiosity, would you mind telling me what was actually in the package? I have been just as curious as a tomcat."

The Keys

"You honestly don't know?" asked Cassie. The pastor shook his head no. Cassie smiled and said, "He sent each of us a letter and gave each of us two very special gifts."

"He gave me his harmonica," said Anna, "and the journal he used when he was here, you know, after Mom died. He had some very nice things to say about you in there. I'll share it with you sometime."

"I'd like that," he said.

"He gave me his wedding ring," said Cassie, "and a music box that belonged to my mother. I don't know if you know this, but I recently went through a divorce from my husband. It was a very meaningful gift."

The pastor walked over to Stephanie, who was standing behind the kitchen counter with her package in front of her. "How about you, Stephanie?" he asked. "What did your father give you?"

Avoiding the question, Stephanie picked up on Cassie's assumptions and pressed him further. "Pastor, you had to have mailed this package for Dad. There's no other explanation."

The pastor smiled and said, "There are always possibilities."

"Dad must have really trusted you to give you these things," said Stephanie.

"Yes, I suppose he did."

"You knew him well, didn't you?"

"I did," he answered, smiling reflectively. "I knew him well."

Stephanie opened her box and showed him each of her two gifts successively. "He gave me the key to this place and his Bible," she said. "He told me they were both keys and that his Bible was the key to the place where he is now."

"Indeed!" he affirmed.

"Look, Stephanie, we need to get going," said Cassie anxiously. "I have a plane to catch. What time is your flight?"

Stephanie walked around the counter and stood near Cassie. "I'm not going to the airport with you," she said.

"Why?" asked Cassie. "Are you upset with me? What did I do?"

"Relax, Cassie. I'm not going to the airport with you because . . . because I am staying here."

"What do you mean, you're staying here?" asked Anna.

"I know," she said. "It's crazy. But I'm going to try to do what Dad asked me to do. I'm going to stay here and do who-knows-what until I find what Dad found." She pointed to her box on the counter. "I've got the keys."

The Package

"And I thought yesterday was a big day!" exclaimed Cassie.

"I hardly know where to start," said Stephanie as she turned toward the pastor. "But if Dad trusted you, maybe I can too. It's been so long. I have a hard time, you know, trusting people."

"I will do anything I can to help you," he said.

"Do you think I could spend some time talking with you over the next few weeks?" she asked. "I have a lot of questions. It's all pretty confusing."

"I would be happy to do that," he replied. He looked successively at each of them, smiled warmly, and said, "Your dad would be very proud of all of you."

"Thanks, Pastor, but I really have to go," said Cassie. She looked directly into Stephanie's eyes and said, "I love you, Stephie." Cassie embraced her.

Stephanie heard her words—the words that often paralyzed her. But she also heard something noteworthy. She looked at Cassie and said, "You haven't called me Stephie in twenty years."

Cassie affectionately ran her fingers along Stephanie's hair down the side of her face. "I haven't done a lot of things for twenty years, but with God's help, we're going to change that." Cassie turned to Anna and said, "Anna, I love you too." They shared a hug and a kiss on the cheek.

"Here, Cassie," said Pastor Riddick, "let me take your bags out to the car." He picked up Cassie's bags and looked back toward Anna and Stephanie. Since his hands were full, he waved with a head nod as he headed for the front door, and said, "Good-bye girls. I'll see you soon, Stephanie."

"Okay," she said.

"Thanks, Pastor," said Cassie as he walked out. One last time, she looked back at her sisters and said with regret, "Got to go!" She blew them a kiss as she backed out the door.

Through the window, Anna watched Cassie get into her car and leave, and she walked back to Stephanie, placed a hand on each of her shoulders, and looked at her intently. "Wow!" she said, "so you're staying." She embraced her and then stepped back to arm's length. "I think that's great. I love you."

Stephanie looked away from Anna's face and began to tear up. Shrugging Anna's hands from her shoulders, she walked away, fell into a chair, and hid her face in her hands. Anna watched her and then moved to sit down next to her. "What's wrong?" she asked.

The Keys

Stephanie raised her eyes slowly and revealed her tears. "I couldn't tell Cassie I loved her." Anna was moved with compassion. Stephanie stood to her feet and moved away, nearly across the room, but then turned back to Anna. "Why is that so hard for me?" she asked. "I wanted to tell her, I just . . . I just couldn't."

Anna walked to her and said, "God is working on you; the words will come."

"I just haven't been a very good sister."

"That's who you *were*."

"Okay," said Stephanie, glancing away from Anna's gaze and then back again. "I just wish I'd said it."

"Trust me; she knows," said Anna. "You going to be okay here?"

"Yes," she replied. "You'd better go. Your family is expecting you."

"Yes, they are. But don't forget, you're my family too!" She moved to the door to gather her bags as Stephanie followed. Anna turned to her at the door and said, "I love you, Steph."

"I know you do," she replied. Then Stephanie gathered herself and said, "And I love you, Anna." Anna smiled knowingly and gave her one final embrace.

"You know how to get hold of me. Call me if you need me. It's not that far." She hesitated at the door before leaving, looked back, and once more said, "I love you!" Anna pushed the screen door open and started her trip for home.

Stephanie ran to the window and watched Anna get into her car and drive away. Looking around the cabin, she felt a sense of loneliness and wondered how she would make it through the myriad emotional—and perhaps spiritual—roadblocks ahead. Contemplating this, she walked to the shelves, picked up the portrait of her father, sat on the sofa, and took her first step down that road. She looked intently into her father's eyes. "Dad, I'm sorry I have blamed you all these years for abandoning me. Please forgive me." She closed her eyes and imagined his reply. "Thank you, Daddy," she said, "thank you."

As she stood to return the portrait to its place, she saw something curious sitting on the chair near the sofa. As she moved closer, she saw that it was the case for Cassie's glasses. Opening the case quickly, she saw that the glasses were indeed inside. Thinking she might catch her, she called out "Anna!" But it was only a brief moment before she realized that Anna was long gone. She thought for a moment about what she should do and sud-

The Package

denly had an unusual idea. She decided to follow her father's lead and stepped to the counter where the box containing her gifts from her father sat. She emptied it of its contents, put the glasses inside it, and said, "Oh well, it looks like I'll have to take them to the post office tomorrow and mail them." She ducked behind the kitchen counter, searching for some tape to seal the box for mailing. She considered that she could get some at the post office when she went to mail it. "The post office," she snickered. "This time, I'll get a number first thing!"

The number thought drifted to phone numbers, and that sparked a reminder that she needed to change her travel plans. She picked up the phone and called the familiar number of the travel agency she always used. "Hello? Is this O'Bannon Travel agency? Sorry, I didn't hear you. Yes, my name is Stephanie Mullins. I was supposed to travel from Pittsburgh to New York tonight, and I need to reschedule that flight." Stephanie exchanged information with the agent and put her flight on hold. She was wrapping up the call and had just said good-bye when she glanced at the box containing Cassie's glasses and had a sudden epiphany. "Wait! Hello? Are you still there? Yes, I'm sorry. You know, there is something else you can do for me. I need a round-trip ticket for this weekend, departing Pittsburgh Friday afternoon and returning Monday morning. Sacramento, California. That's right, Sacramento," she said with a warm smile.

"I have a package to deliver."

19

QUESTIONS ANSWERED

The morning breeze blew the window curtains about, and the relentless tapping of the drawstring on the woodwork woke Stephanie from a sound sleep. Accustomed to waking to the sounds the city, the chorus of birds welcoming the beginning of the day was disorienting at first. Within a few seconds, however, she managed to get her mind wrapped around where she was and why she was here.

It had been two days since the package arrived and her sisters left for home. Stephanie had spent the previous day reading random chapters of her father's Bible, broken by brief periods of prayer—or at least what she understood prayer to be. The whole notion was still disconcerting. Something inside her felt different from the day she had first arrived at the cabin, but she couldn't rationalize what the difference was and even found herself questioning her ability to assess her own feelings.

Maybe this day would provide some answers. True to his word, Pastor Riddick had called the cabin on Monday evening after her sisters left for home. About an hour or so after arriving home, he realized that Stephanie was at the cabin without transportation. Having two vehicles of his own, he took one to Stephanie that evening so that she could run necessary errands, the most important of which was a trip to the grocery store. Stephanie thanked him—such neighborly kindness was uncommon in her life—and offered to drive him home, but Pastor Riddick insisted that the evening air was quite comfortable and that a brisk walk home would provide some needed exercise. But before he left, he invited Stephanie to have breakfast with him and his wife, Evelyn, on Wednesday, and afterwards, he would spend the morning with her in an attempt to answer some of her questions. She had accepted the invitation, and the appointed morning had arrived.

As she showered and dressed that morning, she considered the oddity of a breakfast invitation to someone's house. Such an invitation would

The Package

never be extended in New York. With the exception of employment, all the activities that Stephanie and her friends engaged in fell into one encompassing category—partying. In the city, it was all about gathering after work for happy hour at the local pub or going out on the town for a big evening. *A breakfast engagement?* she mused. No, breakfast was for filling up on coffee, overcoming the hangover from the night before, or concocting excuses to evict someone you slept with. A breakfast social was indeed a bizarre idea. Maybe everything in this part of the country was backwards.

Taking one last look in the mirror, she fluffed her hair with her hands and checked her make-up. It was her normal routine, that last minute appearance inspection before beginning her day. Today, though, Stephanie hesitated before she left, gazing at her own reflection. Who was she, really? It was almost as though her reversed image in the mirror provided a provoking observation. *Maybe you're the one who is backwards.*

Pastor Riddick lived in a two-story house about a mile north of the cabin on Cabot Road. It was a simple house, which seemed appropriate for what Stephanie perceived as a man with simple needs. She felt trepidation as she pulled into the driveway, wondering if Pastor Riddick was really someone she should trust. She reasoned that his long friendship with her father should give her some assurance, but then again, she had been beaten by that deception before. In her mind, she determined that she would remain cautious but suddenly reversed her resolve, knowing that honesty was required to obtain the answers she sought. Her inability to settle her own mind left her perplexed. *No question, is there?* she thought. *I am most certainly confused.*

For an instant, standing at the front door, she felt the urge to flee. But she quickly rang the doorbell and waited. The door opened, and the woman who answered it said, "Hello, dear. You must be Stephanie. I am so pleased to meet you. My name is Evelyn."

"Nice to meet you, Evelyn," said Stephanie.

"Please come in," she said. "Rodney is on the phone at the moment, but he'll be right out. Would you like some coffee or tea?"

"Normally, I drink coffee, but a cup of tea sounds great this morning."

"Okay. Please have a seat on the divan, and I'll bring your tea in a moment. Is there anything else I can bring you?"

"No," said Stephanie as she took her seat. "Thank you." As Evelyn glided out of the room, Stephanie considered that Evelyn was not at all as she had imagined her. She had expected her to be somewhat backwoods

166

and frumpy. Instead, she was tall, thin, elegant, and had a style that graced the room with her presence. Stephanie considered her charm to be as comfortable as a warm wool sweater. She found herself relaxing.

As she reviewed her short conversation with Evelyn, she chuckled as she realized that she had never even considered the fact that Pastor Riddick had a first name. *That should have been obvious*, she thought. However, in the few days that she had known him, she and her sisters had simply referred to him as Pastor Riddick. "Rodney," she whispered. *No wonder he calls himself a pastor*, she thought. The alternative alliteration made her giggle as she whispered it to herself, "Reverend Rodney Riddick." Then she started thinking, *What if he was righteous; he would then be—*

"Hi Stephanie, it's great to see you again," said Pastor Riddick as he entered the room and offered his hand to her.

She rose to her feet, shook his hand, and said, "Reverend—I mean—Pastor Riddick. Good morning! How are you?" She had nearly slipped on her own banana peel.

"I am quite well. Please sit down. Can I get you anything?"

"Your wife is bringing me some tea, thank you. And really, Pastor, she is quite elegant, and she seems very kind. Very pretty too."

"God works in mysterious ways, doesn't he?" Seeing Stephanie's confused look, he continued, "By that I mean, I am blessed that one so lovely should grace the life of one as lowly as I."

Evelyn sashayed back into the room with a cup of tea and set it on the coffee table in front of her. "There you are, my dear," she said.

"Thanks, Mrs. Riddick," said Stephanie.

"Please call me Evelyn."

"Evelyn, then," said Stephanie. "This smells wonderful."

"Do you need sugar or cream?" asked Evelyn.

"No, thank you again," said Stephanie. "I wouldn't dare spoil it."

Evelyn smiled. "You were right, Rodney, a delightful young woman. Delightful, indeed! Please excuse me. I must return to the kitchen to finish breakfast. Do you have everything you need?"

"Yes, I am fine, thank you," answered Stephanie. Evelyn nodded politely and walked out the room.

"Pastor, again, she is a treasure. Not what I expected at all."

"Me, neither," he said, smiling. "And yes, she is a treasure." He changed the subject. "So, how have you been the last few days? You had an eventful weekend."

The Package

"Yes, I certainly did. I mean, we did." Stephanie again found herself fighting back the uneasiness.

"So what have you been up to since your sisters left?"

"Nothing much, really. Made a few trips to the store, took a drive, and I've done a little reading—mostly in Dad's Bible. I didn't really know what part to read, so I have just been reading it here and there. When I was a child in Sunday school, I read it often; but it reads differently now. I'm trying to figure it out."

"Good for you. That's how it begins with everyone God calls. They find they are hungry, and they start searching for food—spiritually speaking, of course."

"Everyone he calls?" asked Stephanie, surprised at his choice of words. "Don't you mean everyone who finds him?"

"It's a fine line, Stephanie, but an important one. You will soon come to understand that you are where you are because God has called you to be here. You are asking the questions you are asking because he has placed them in you, and you are now hungry because you are becoming spiritually alive."

Evelyn had entered the room a few seconds before he finished and waited to speak. "Speaking of being hungry, breakfast is ready. Would you two like to join me in the kitchen?"

"I hope you brought your appetite, Stephanie," said Pastor Riddick. "Evelyn here is quite the cook."

"I am looking forward to it," she replied.

"Shall we?" urged Evelyn, escorting them into the kitchen with a gentle wave of her hand.

The trio entered the kitchen, sat down together, and enjoyed a lovely breakfast. Evelyn had proved her husband right—she was indeed an excellent cook. While they ate, Pastor Riddick and Evelyn asked Stephanie about her life in New York and extolled the virtues of life in this sleepy place—although it didn't seem quite so sleepy when they talked about it. People lived their lives, raised families, laughed, struggled, provided aid, fought to survive, suffered, and healed here. It was exactly the same as New York—yet completely different.

They each spoke of their families, and Stephanie learned that her father had eaten many meals at this same table with the pastor and Evelyn. As they reminisced about those times, Stephanie felt a connection to her father she had never felt before, seeing him through the eyes of others who loved him. Their love for him was not based on a sense of obligation, as with a family member, or because of status, power, or fame. No, it was clear that the people in this community loved him for his honesty, integrity, his transparency in revealing his innermost feelings, and his faith in God.

Listening to them speak of her father's character made her realize that she had loved those things about him too, and yet she always felt such a sense of separation from him. Why was their relationship so strained? What was it that made her feel the way she did? Why was she unable to see his true value while he was yet alive? She hoped that the man sitting across the table from her would be able to help her find answers to these questions.

After breakfast, their conversation dwindled. Once Evelyn began to slide her chair away from the table, Stephanie responded likewise in order to help her clean up the dishes. "Please relax, Stephanie," said Evelyn. "Thank you, but I'll clean up. Would you like some more tea?"

"No, thank you. I'm fine," replied Stephanie. "It was an excellent meal. Thank you very much. Are you sure you wouldn't like me to help?"

"Why don't you and I let Evelyn do what she wants in the kitchen?" suggested Pastor Riddick. "We can go to the study and talk." He leaned toward her confidentially. "Believe me, it's the way she likes it."

"Is that okay with you?" Stephanie asked Evelyn, not wanting to impose on her kindness.

"Yes," she said. "I know you two have much to discuss."

"Thank you again," said Stephanie. "This was lovely."

"See, I told you," he said.

Stephanie had brought her father's Bible with her to the house but had left it in the living room before breakfast. She excused herself to retrieve it, and when she returned, Pastor Riddick escorted her into his study. He began to close the door behind them but then remembered Stephanie's confession from the prior weekend and decided that, for Stephanie, the security of an open door trumped the privacy of a closed one.

Stephanie took a seat at a chair sitting in front of his desk, and Pastor Riddick took his place behind it. He smiled reassuringly to Stephanie and asked, "So where would you like to start, Stephanie? You told me on Monday that you had a lot of questions."

"There is a lot I am confused about. I hope you don't get upset with me," said Stephanie, who was genuinely concerned that Pastor Riddick might not be kind when he heard her questions. Cassie didn't have the pa-

The Package

tience to answer them, and if Pastor Riddick reacted in similar fashion, this discussion wasn't going to go well.

"Let's start with a few simple ground rules," he suggested. "I will commit to listen to you carefully and promise to tell you the truth without accusing you of anything. Does that sound fair?"

"Yes, I guess so," answered Stephanie, who couldn't help but be suspicious. It had become second nature to her.

He continued. "And I'd like you to commit to do two things."

Ah, the catch, she thought. *There's always a catch.*

"I'd like you to commit to have an open heart and an open Bible."

That doesn't sound unreasonable, she thought. She feared that she might be missing the catch, so she sought clarification. "I'm not exactly sure what you mean," she said.

"Stephanie, the heart of man is simply not good. All of us have collections of junk in our own hearts that we cherish; we cling to them like treasure."

"You?" she asked.

"Yes, Stephanie. Everyone struggles with his or her own heart. Some people harbor anger or bitterness inside. Others build up resentment and unforgiveness. Many of us hold in great esteem our own ideas that are often, frankly, wrong—we simply deceive ourselves."

"If that's true, what hope is there?" asked Stephanie. "How can we ever know the truth?"

"As I said, Stephanie, in order to receive what God has to give, you must keep your heart open. First, so he can mend that which is broken inside you; and second, so he can begin to align your desires with his. So, in order for me to help you find your answers, you must have an open heart. Does that make sense to you?"

Stephanie had to admit that his logic did make sense, and that assessment surprised her. She knew that she would have dismissed this entire line of reasoning as recently as last week, but today, for some unknown reason, it seemed perfectly rational. She wondered why yet cautiously answered, "Yes, I guess that makes sense."

"And, as I said, you need to have an open Bible. Do you know why I say that?"

"Because it's important that I read it?" she answered.

"That's right. As you search for the truth, Stephanie, and God is dealing with your heart, you'll need to make sure that what anyone is

170

Questions Answered

telling you, *even what I tell you*, is consistent with the Bible. Once you give your trust to him, he will begin to take the things out of your heart that are false and replace them with things that are true. You will need to use your Bible as a guide so you will know you are on the right path. Do you understand?"

"Yes. But how do I know everything in the Bible is true? Why should I trust it? I mean, why is it any different than any other book?" This had always been a sticking point with Stephanie.

"Okay, let's begin there. Those are pretty big questions on their own. Stephanie, the Bible describes itself as the infallible, unimpeachable, and eternal word of God. It is his message to us; it tells us how to live our lives in personal wholeness, how to live and interact with others around us, and how to commune with and serve the God of the universe."

"But the Bible has changed over time," she argued. "It has been passed down through generations and translated and retranslated. What if people simply added stuff they wanted it to say? You have to admit that's possible."

"I agree, Stephanie, that with the corrupt nature of man, this certainly could be possible. But the New Testament is the most reliable of ancient texts on the face of the earth," he said. "The existing manuscripts are closer to their original sources than any other ancient book. The Bible we have today is indeed accurate; it's what was written."

"So you don't think it has changed?" asked Stephanie.

"The evidence says that it hasn't—it's not just what I think."

Stephanie stopped for a moment to evaluate what she had just heard. She found herself thumbing mindlessly through the pages of her Bible. "I didn't know all that," she responded. "You know a lot of detailed information." Her disengaged demeanor suggested that she had not yet arrived at her most pressing question. Pastor Riddick hesitated in the conversation long enough that the silence spurred Stephanie to reengage. He had counseled many people in this study who had something they needed to say yet avoided saying it.

"Thank you for the compliment, Stephanie," he said. "But somehow, I don't think these questions are really what you came here to ask me."

Stephanie reacted with surprise, unaware that she could be read that easily. His statement seemed a little presumptuous, and that made her uncomfortable. *He has no right to tell me what I need to talk about*, she thought. Catching sight of the door, she thought she might simply excuse herself and return home.

The Package

"Stephanie," he said. "I can see I've upset you. I'm sorry."

Amid her own internal clamoring, Stephanie found a way to trust his sincerity, confirmed by an inner voice declaring his words to be truth. "Ask the question you came to ask," it said. Stephanie found herself conflicted within her own swirl of emotions. When Pastor Riddick asked his question, it made her withdraw and want to run. And yet, when this internal voice spoke, it seemed to bring a sense of security. She could not reconcile it, but she decided to relent to the voice and surrender her will. She looked at the pastor, her eyes welled up, and she struggled to form her words.

"All I ever hear is that God is love. *God is love?* How can a loving God allow suffering? How can he allow bad things to happen to good people?" she asked.

Pastor Riddick stood from his chair and walked around his desk to sit in the chair next to Stephanie. He looked at her reassuringly and spoke gently to her. "Now this question comes from the open heart I asked you to have." He paused for a moment to allow her to gather her thoughts. "Go on," he said.

"My mother was committed to God, and he allowed her to die—and for what? So we could be left alone? So that Dad might find him? So that I could be . . . I could be . . ." Stephanie choked on her words. After a brief moment, she continued with a biting tone. "And God expects me to love him when he has stolen everything from me?"

"Stephanie, I hear you saying that you have suffered a lot of pain in your life and because of that, it's hard to understand how you can ever love God, or how it could be possible that he loves you. Is that right?"

"It does make it hard to believe, don't you think?" asked Stephanie.

"Yes, I do," he replied.

Stephanie was surprised at this response. It eased her mind to know that her feelings were not so unusual or out of touch. Even the pastor concurred that her doubt was reasonable.

"If you will promise to keep your heart open for a short while and trust me," he said, "I will lead you to the answer to this question. Will you trust me?"

Stephanie nodded in agreement but said nothing.

"What you are asking is a question that we have all wrestled with. But the truth is," he said, "it's the wrong question."

"Well, that's just great!" she snapped, rapidly becoming agitated. "I thought you said you'd answer my question, and now you tell me it's the wrong question! What kind of help is that?"

Questions Answered

"You said you'd trust me," he replied, "and that you would keep your heart open. I *will* answer your question—I promise. But let's explore a slightly different question before we tackle yours."

Stephanie could not hide her dissatisfaction with this approach, but she allowed him some latitude, at least for the moment. Her voice only modestly evidenced that. "Fine," she said. "Go ahead."

"Here's my question for you, Stephanie. It's not really much different from your question—it's just asked in a little different way. So, here it is. Why does God allow *good* things to happen to *bad* people?"

"That's the *right* question?" she shouted. "How's that the *right* question? That's the ultimate injustice! It's worse than the question I asked."

"Open heart, Stephanie," he said. "Stay with me here. We're going somewhere with this." Stephanie's stern look did not contain even a hint of patience. "Can we look through some Scriptures together?" Stephanie let out a deep sigh. "How about we start at Romans 3:23 and look that up together." He helped Stephanie find the book of Romans in her Bible and asked her to read what it said.

She felt a bit like a small child being led around by the hand. She didn't like it but obliged him anyway. "For all have sinned and fall short of the glory of God," she read. "So everyone sins," she said, rolling her eyes. "So what! Good people make mistakes. Everyone makes mistakes."

"You're right!" he said in agreement. "Everyone makes mistakes. Everyone sins. It also says in chapter three that there is no one righteous, not even one . . . there is no one who does good, not even one. So, Stephanie, how many good people are there in the world?"

"I guess it says there aren't very many," she replied.

He looked at her patiently, waiting for her finally to admit the truth to herself.

"None," she stammered, "but—but—but that just doesn't make sense. There are some really good people out there. Many of them aren't even Christians. They feed the poor and work in homeless shelters. It just doesn't make sense."

"Sin entered the world through Adam, and death through sin," he said. "That's in chapter five. You see, Stephanie, when Adam and Eve were in the garden, they had a perfect relationship with God. But once they sinned, they became alienated from God. Because of their sin, and ours, we are all separated from God in a similar way. None of us is good. There is an impassible void between us and God, putting a relationship with him out of our reach."

The Package

"So you've argued against yourself," she replied. "If what you have just said is true, and no one can do anything good, and God is out of our reach, then it's hopeless. And, as I said, it doesn't make sense. There are a lot of good people out there."

"There are many who accomplish good deeds," he explained. "God does influence us in this way. If God were uninvolved and allowed all the evil in the hearts of men to be unrestrained, mankind would destroy itself. Through his intervention, he has preserved for himself a group of people that the Bible terms 'called out ones.'"

"Those who are good. See!" she asserted.

"In his greatest act," he said, continuing, "God reached across the chasm to us through the sacrifice of Jesus on the cross. It is a great mystery how the death of Jesus can be payment for our sin. But that one single act allows God to restore once again our relationship with him. We can be delivered not only from an eternal hell, but from the emptiness and pain we feel in our lives today—by entering into relationship with him."

"We can be delivered? I don't understand. I mean, if we can do nothing good, why would God *want* to have a relationship with us? " she asked. Pastor Riddick sat for a few thoughtful moments and simply smiled at her. "What?" she asked. "Why are you smiling?"

"Because you just asked me the same question I asked you," he answered. "You essentially asked me, 'If all men are bad, how can good things happen to them?'"

Stephanie was surprised to realize that the same question she had found irritating only a few moments ago now peaked her curiosity. She laughed at herself a little, realizing that she had come full circle to join the pastor in asking the "right" question.

Pastor Riddick directed Stephanie to the book of Ephesians in her Bible, pointed to a verse, and again asked her to read it. Stephanie complied with ease this time and read, "For it is by grace you have been saved through faith—and this not of yourselves, it is the gift of God—not by works, so that no one can boast."

"In this verse," he said, "think of the word *saved* as meaning, having a broken relationship with God restored. So, looking at that verse, how is that relationship restored? By our being good enough?"

"It says through faith," she answered. "But what does that mean? Faith in what?"

"Faith," he explained, "is our ability to believe in and trust in God. And this verse has something very interesting to say about that. If you accept

Questions Answered

what it says, can you find faith within yourself? An ability to believe in and trust in God?"

"It says that faith is not of yourselves," she answered. "It says that it is a gift—a gift of God. So I guess that means no." Stephanie pondered what this meant for a moment. "Are you saying that I can only believe in God because he gives me the ability to do so?"

"That is exactly what I am saying," he answered. "It is a gift that he gives to you. So, with that in mind, can you regain a lost relationship with God by being good, by feeding the poor, or working in homeless shelters? Is there anything that you can do on your own to earn it back?"

"If it's a gift," she said reluctantly, "I guess that means no. Does the Bible say we shouldn't do good things?"

"No," he said, "in fact, the Bible teaches that faith by itself, if it is not accompanied by action, is dead."

"I don't understand then," she replied. "Does God reward us for doing good? For being good?"

"It depends upon our motives, Stephanie," he explained. "If we do good works as a result of our relationship with him and at his urging, those works are good, and he promises to reward us. But to do good works without being in relationship with him, that accomplishes nothing eternal for us. It is a godly principle to treat your neighbor well, and God may very well bless you for it in this life. But without his gift of a restored relationship, an eternity without him is the ultimate reward we all face."

"I guess that makes sense," she said. "Anyone can do a good deed, but the reward depends on our relationship to him. Right?"

"That's right. Now," he said, "let's answer my question, and then we'll circle back to yours. Why do good things happen to bad people? If there is no one who does good, not even one, how many bad people are there?"

"If you accept what the Bible says," said Stephanie, "I guess everyone is bad, if, to you, bad means not good."

"And what is the just reward," he asked, "for being 'not good' as you say? What do we deserve?"

"I guess God owes us nothing. He leaves us alone, without a relationship with him. Is that right?"

"Yes," he said cautiously. "So, when God gives a person who is not good a free gift of faith, and that faith has the benefit of restoring a relationship with him, do they get what they truly deserve?"

Stephanie struggled a little with this answer. "I don't know, Pastor," she said. "Maybe not." She liked the concept of accountability, and she liked

The Package

making sure that people were held responsible for their actions. This concept of not getting what you deserved just didn't sit right with her.

"The answer is no," he said. "They do not get what they deserve. They deserve alienation from God, and they are given fellowship. They deserve death and are instead given life. A good thing happens to a bad person. Right?"

"I guess so," she said, aware that she had no basis for argument.

"Earlier," he said, "you called that injustice."

"Well, if a judge gave mercy to someone who didn't deserve it," she answered, "I would think that was wrong; that is injustice. But when God is the judge, and he shows mercy to people—to me—I don't know."

Pastor Riddick waited, hoping she would think this concept through a little further.

"I guess I was wrong," she admitted. "It's not injustice. It's kindness that isn't earned."

"The Bible calls that mercy," he explained. "God gives us unmerited favor. Stephanie, you compared God to a judge, but you need to know that he is also a Father who seeks relationship with his children. His mercy makes him a righteous judge; his love makes him a compassionate Father."

"It's hard for me to see God as a father," said Stephanie. "I only feel his judgment."

Pastor Riddick carefully considered what he was about to say next. He waited to feel a peace in his spirit before he pressed forward. He understood the risks—and the need. "Stephanie, I knew your father for many years, and he confided in me and sought advice from me about many things in his life. He mourned the fact that the two of you had a strained relationship, and he never knew why. I believe that I now understand that you felt that he failed you, and that you may have felt judgment from him for living a life that he found ungodly. Do you sense truth in any of that?"

This question created angst in Stephanie that was evidenced by an actual physical discomfort in her chest. Despite that feeling, she knew that she could not honestly deny the reality that the pastor had described. She had felt accusation from her father, though she had never thought of him as a judge. But in a turnabout, she realized that she had become his judge as well. Her heart had already convicted him for being guilty of failure and sentenced him to isolation. His reaching out to her through the package had appealed that verdict. How could she even hear an appeal on his case? Then again, how could she not? "What you are asking of me is very hard, Pastor."

Questions Answered

"I know, Stephanie. But, if you sense the truth in what I said, it is important that you face it head-on. Because, if you don't, you will likely view God in the same way you view your father. You will see him as a judge who can only fail you. Do you understand why this is so important?"

Stephanie went through a mental evaluation of her image of God and how it compared to her image of her father. There were striking similarities that created a sense of awe at how something so obvious could go unseen for so long. The pastor had asked her to have an open heart so that she could face what was truly inside, but she had no idea that she would find this lurking interconnection of God with her father. Then suddenly, her comparative examination revealed another, more disturbing, reality. Not only had she seen both God and her father as judges, but in her own pride and injustice, she had also rendered a verdict on God and sentenced him to isolation—isolation from her. *Perhaps,* she thought, *the problem isn't with God. Perhaps I am the one who has been his judge.* "You may be right, Pastor," she admitted with difficulty. "But I can't talk about that right now. It's too much to sort out."

"Admitting that it might be the truth is a bold step, Stephanie," he said. "We don't have to talk about that further right now. But it is something you can think about and pray about. Okay?"

Stephanie nodded in agreement.

"Well, I want to keep my promise, so let's go back to answer your original question." He repeated it again. "How can a loving God allow bad things to happen to good people? That's your question, right?"

"Yes," she answered.

"Again, according to the Bible, how many good people are there?"

There was only one possible answer. "None," she said.

"That's right," he answered, "and what is the penalty for not being good?"

"I don't know," she replied.

"Well," he said," the Bible says that the wages of sin is death. So the appropriate and just penalty is death, or as I have described it, separation from God."

Stephanie nodded that she understood.

"Now with an open Bible and an open mind," he asked, "can you answer your own question?"

"I don't know," she said. Stephanie rose from her chair, walked to a bookcase in a corner of the study, and aimlessly ran her fingers across a set of books. If death were separation from God, had she brought about her

The Package

own death by her banishment of God from her life? How could she face these truths? Her mother deserved no mercy? Her father, no condemnation above anyone else? And as for her pain, did she have no right to own it and hold it a debt, even though it could never be repaid?

She turned back toward the pastor, who was patiently waiting for her in his chair. As she struggled to sort out her emotions, she pinched her lips together and gently clenched her lower lip between her teeth. She looked toward her feet, then back to the pastor and asked, "What does God want from me? I obviously cannot be good enough. I can't undo what's been done. I get it. I deserve nothing. What can I do? Why is this happening to me?" She hesitated for a moment and again asked him, "What does he want from me?"

"Stephanie, this is happening because God is calling you to relationship with him. He is handing you a free gift of faith, and you are seeking how to trust and believe in him. Are you familiar with the Lord's Prayer?" he asked.

"Yes."

"Do you know the part where it says to forgive us our debts, as we forgive our debtors?"

"Yes."

"Here is what God wants from you. He wants you to ask for forgiveness for your sins—'forgive us our debts.' And he wants you to forgive those who have wronged you or failed you in any way—'as we forgive our debtors.' He wants you to let go of the past, turn away from your wrongdoing, and enter into relationship with him. That's what God ultimately wants from you. He wants a relationship with you."

Stephanie again turned back toward the bookshelf, placed her hand upon a shelf, and rested her forehead against it. While letting go of the past might be what she needed to do, she had no idea how to do it.

"Stephanie?" The pastor spoke so gently that he had nearly whispered her name.

She slowly turned and saw him patting his hand on the arm of the chair that she had vacated, encouraging her to return.

"Can I pray with you?" he asked.

While she had not prayed with anyone in a long time, her feelings swept her to the moment when she stood in the hallway and listened to Cassie praying for her. Recalling Cassie's sincerity at that moment made her smile weakly and provided the needed motivation to return to her chair. "Okay," she answered, "if you want to."

Questions Answered

The pastor bowed his head, and prayed sincerely. "Jesus, I ask you right now to give Stephanie the courage she needs to see your truth. Help her to untangle the confusion in her own heart, and I pray that you would ease her grasp on the doubt and fear within her, and give her the ability to speak your truth from her own lips. In your name, Lord Jesus, amen."

"Amen," she repeated.

The pastor looked at her, but Stephanie continued to look down at her hands folded on her lap. "Stephanie," he said again gently, "back to your question: why do bad things happen to good people? Can you answer it?"

Stephanie struggled to state what was now obvious. She didn't want to believe it, but she was at a decision point. Her mother had died at an early age in a terrible car accident; her father had died from a horrible disease; Cassie's husband cheated on her; and she was molested. These were injustices. She was certain of it. How could Pastor Riddick ask her to accept and forgive these situations? They were clearly wrong.

"Stephanie?" he said gently.

Yet, her father had found peace with God after his wife's death. Anna too. She wasn't bitter or angry. And Stephanie had seen Cassie change just last weekend. Something had happened to her. Had they also forgiven God? Could it really be this simple? Perhaps it was. Perhaps God was indeed seeking a relationship with her. Maybe she really *could* let go—maybe she *could* forgive.

"Stephanie?"

"Yes," she said as she broke down and cried. "I understand. Yes, I can answer it."

Pastor Riddick again prayed with Stephanie, and a mere two days after Jim Mullins' package had arrived at the cabin, another one of the miracles he had prayed for had occurred. God revealed himself to Stephanie, and he had given her the faith to receive Christ as her Lord and Savior.

Pastor Riddick had seen enough in his ministry and was sensitive enough to the Holy Spirit to know that God had begun a healing in Stephanie. He knew it would not be instantaneous; but, in fact, God had revealed his truth to her. It wasn't something she had done or even could do on her own. It was a free gift of God, exactly as they had discussed.

As the pastor had told Cassie during the previous weekend, this was God's time for Stephanie and her sisters. He smiled as he thought about God's free gift.

It was still early July in Pennsylvania. But for Stephanie, Christ had

The Package

just arrived in her heart. It was a season for pine cone wishes, packages with presents, family gatherings, and wise men bearing gifts; namely, her father and Pastor Riddick.

In Pennsylvania, it was the ninth of July. For Stephanie, it was Christmas.

20

THE VISIT

It was late Friday afternoon, July 11th, when Stephanie's plane was about to land at the Sacramento airport. She nervously diddled with Cassie's eyeglass case in her hand. As the wheels touched down, she remembered the call she had received from Cassie earlier in the week. In fact, the phone rang only a matter of hours after she had left for the airport. Stephanie answered the phone, suspecting that Cassie was the caller. *Who else would be calling?* she thought. "Hello," she answered.

"Hi, Stephanie. This is Cassie."

"Hi. Calling so soon? Miss me already?" she said jokingly.

"Sure," she said flatly. "I mean, of course I do. I had a great weekend with you, Stephanie. I think we were all surprised." Cassie was stumbling over herself, and she knew it. "I mean, you know, surprised by how well things went. Weren't you surprised?"

"You're still breathing, aren't you?" said Stephanie. Cassie was caught flatfooted, considering how to respond. "At least we didn't kill each other, right?" asked Stephanie. Still silence. "Cassie, you are breathing, aren't you?"

"Of course I'm breathing, silly. Listen, I'm a little pressed for time here."

"Okay. What's up?" asked Stephanie.

"I'm at the Pittsburgh airport," she said, "and I reached into my purse to get my glasses to read my boarding pass, and they aren't there. The last time I remember having them was sitting on the chair reading the letter from Dad. Have you seen them?"

"Let me check," said Stephanie. She put her hand over the receiver for about ten seconds, pretending to be searching for them. "Yes," said Stephanie, "I found them. Right where you said they were. You have a very good memory. I could never have remembered that."

"Well," said Cassie, "without my glasses I'm going to have to remember

The Package

a lot of things. I certainly can't write anything down or read anything either."

"Do you want me to send them to you?" she asked.

"Could you please?" replied Cassie. "That would be great. I would very much appreciate it."

"Not a problem. I can send them this week. Can you give me your address? I don't have it here." This much was true, and Stephanie was counting on this call to get Cassie's address, which she provided.

"Okay," said Stephanie, "I'll get them to you. How far is your place from the airport?"

"The airport?" asked Cassie.

Stephanie realized her blunder. "In case I send it . . . air mail?" stammered Stephanie.

"Air mail?" said Cassie. "And what century do you live in?"

"Never mind," said Stephanie. "I'll send them."

"Thanks. Listen, my flight's boarding. I need to go."

"Okay," said Stephanie. "See you soon."

"Okay. Thanks again. Bye."

"Good-bye."

It was a short conversation, but Stephanie had obtained the information she needed for her surprise delivery.

After she gathered her bags at the airport baggage claim, Stephanie went outside and motioned for the next cab in line. She handed Cassie's address to the cabby as he loaded her baggage in the trunk of the cab. Compared to Stephanie's usual entourage of baggage, she was traveling light. She carried only one small suitcase and a shoulder bag on this trip.

"How far is that address?" she asked.

"About twenty-five minutes," he said.

Stephanie got into the cab and examined the eyeglass case in her hand. Everything had gone so well the previous weekend, and that confidence caused her to plan this trip impulsively. While she knew it was an impetuous decision, she hoped it was not a stupid one. *What if I'm wrong?* she thought.

The cabby, who looked to be in his sixties, struck up a conversation. "Do you live here, or are you visiting someone?" he asked.

"Visiting," she replied.

"First time in the city?"

"As a matter of fact, yes. I'm visiting my sister."

The Visit

"She new in town?" he asked.

"No, she's lived here for nearly twenty years."

"And this is your first time here?" he said, surprised.

"Yeah. It's complicated."

"Yeah, I guess it must be," he replied. He waited for her to explain, but she never did.

Stephanie looked at his credentials on the dashboard. His name was Arnie. "Arnie, you have a family?"

"Yep. Got a wife, two grown kids, a grandson, and a mortgage. The whole nine yards," he replied.

"Brothers and sisters?"

"One brother and one sister," he answered.

"Are you close?" she asked.

Arnie had been a cab driver for a long time, and he had seen and heard a lot. He was exceptionally wise. "Having problems with your sister?" he asked.

"I'm paying her a surprise visit. You're right, though. I've never been here, and it's pretty scary." She stopped to think about what she was doing. "Maybe this was a mistake," she said.

She repeated that over and over in her mind during the last few minutes before the cab reached its destination. Arnie stopped the cab, placed the gear in park, put his right arm along the top of the driver's seat, and looked at her in his rear view mirror.

"House is right there across the street." He hesitated before saying, "Listen, ma'am, it's never wrong to love somebody. And if that's why you're here, then it'll work out. Give your sister a hug, and tell her you love her. It'll work out."

"Thanks, Arnie. I hope you're right."

"Trust me," he said. "I've been around the block a time or two, so to speak." Then he said, "The fare is twenty dollars." Stephanie handed him forty. She didn't really have the extra money. In fact, it was all the cash she had. But he seemed like someone who deserved a break, so she gave him one. Perhaps, subconsciously, she hoped that Cassie would reciprocate with her.

Arnie got out of the car, unloaded Stephanie's bags, set them on the ground, and opened the passenger-side door against the curb. Stephanie seemed reluctant to get out of the car.

"You want me to wait?" he asked.

The Package

Stephanie's apprehension was growing by the minute. She leaned down and looked at Cassie's house through the opposite window, wondering if Cassie were inside. "Yes, if you don't mind," she said. "I would appreciate it." Stephanie removed her cell phone from her purse and dialed Cassie's number while Arnie waited patiently outside her open car door. The phone provided a safer way to announce her arrival. She was extremely nervous as Cassie answered the phone.

"Hello."

"Cassie? Is that you?"

"Yes."

There was silence for a few seconds. "Cassie, this is Stephanie."

"Stephie, how are you?" Cassie said warmly.

"Good," said Stephanie.

"It's great to hear from you," said Cassie. "By the way, did you get my glasses mailed? I need them, and they haven't come yet."

"Well, Cassie," Stephanie said with apprehension, "as a matter of fact, at this moment there's someone outside your door who has them."

"What?"

"Outside your door, Cassie. Across the street."

Cassie thought this was about as confusing as a phone call could get. "Across the street? What are you talking about?" she replied. Cassie opened her front door and looked across the street, seeing a yellow cab with a cabby standing next to it. He politely nodded and tipped his hat. She was fascinated. And while Cassie watched, a woman with flowing blond hair talking on a cell phone got out of the cab, turned toward her, and held her glasses in the air. "Here they are—your glasses," the voice on the phone said.

Without her glasses, Cassie was not positive she was seeing what she thought she was seeing. "Stephanie? Stephanie, is that you?" asked Cassie, still speaking into the phone.

"Yes, it's me," said Stephanie. "I've come for a visit."

"This can't be happening," said Cassie.

"Oh, I assure you it is," said Stephanie. "If you promise to resist hitting me, I'll bring you your glasses so you can see for yourself."

"I'll come get them," said Cassie as she hung up her phone and broke the connection.

"Uh oh," she said to Arnie. "Here she comes."

Cassie set her phone inside the front door and started walking slowly

The Visit

down her front steps and moving toward the street. As she grew closer, her pace quickened until she was nearly running when she arrived. She stopped in front of Stephanie and put her hands on her shoulders, staring at her in disbelief. "What are you doing here?" she asked, nearly shaking her shoulders.

"She wanted to come and see you," said Arnie. "She's never been here before." Cassie glared at him with disdain. "Stephanie's a little nervous," he explained.

"Cassie, this is Arnie," said Stephanie. "Arnie, this is my sister, Cassie."

"Pleased to make your acquaintance, ma'am," he said, again tipping his cap.

Cassie, still puzzled, refocused on Stephanie. "Why?" she asked. Stephanie held up the case and jiggled it to hear the glasses inside. Cassie continued, "You could have mailed them. What are you doing here?"

"I'm trying to . . . I want to . . .," she stammered. "Do you want me to go?"

"No, she doesn't want you to go," said Arnie. Cassie jerked her head toward him with an irate, intolerant stare. "Why don't you go ahead?" he suggested to Cassie. Then he leaned over to Stephanie and whispered, "I see now why you were worried."

"Excuse me?" Cassie shouted.

"It's okay, Arnie," said Stephanie. "She's usually not like this; she's just surprised. Right, Cassie?"

Cassie was indignant, but Stephanie gave her a knowing wink. Cassie rolled her eyes but made an effort to respond positively. "Right. I'm just surprised—extremely surprised."

"Look," said Stephanie, "I came to stay with you until Monday. You know, spend the weekend together." She hesitated, expecting a response from Cassie but receiving none. "But I can get on a plane and head back home if you want. That's why Arnie here is waiting for me. Just tell me what you want me to do."

"Stay, of course," she said, interlocking her fingers behind her head. "This is amazing!"

"Do you want me to carry your bags to the house, ma'am?" asked Arnie.

"No, Arnie, I think we've got it from here."

"You're sure?" he asked, looking suspiciously at Cassie.

"She's actually harmless," replied Stephanie.

The Package

"Okay, if you're sure," he said as he walked around the front of the cab, opened his door, got in, and prepared to leave. Cassie picked up the suitcase, and Stephanie retrieved the shoulder bag. Stephanie started across the street but broke her stride and returned back to the cab. She walked to the driver's side window and tapped on the glass, and Arnie rolled down his window thinking she had a question.

"Thanks for taking care of me, Arnie," she said, smiling. "I'll bet you're a great dad."

"Ah, get outta here. Hey, do you want me to pick you up on Monday?" he asked.

"No, thanks." She leaned closer, pointed to Cassie and whispered, "I'll have ol' sourpuss over here take me to the airport."

"Tell her you love her. She looks like she needs to hear it." He laughed as he rolled up the window and waved good-bye.

Stephanie backed away a few steps to make way, leaving her standing in the middle of the street. As she watched Arnie drive away, Stephanie realized that this fellow had shown pretty keen insight. Then, strangely, as if she were reminded, she recalled something she had read that week in her Dad's Bible. It had described something about angels, and how we sometimes entertain them unaware. She pondered that as she watched the cab drive down the street until it turned a corner and disappeared.

"Are you coming, or are you going to continue to stand in the middle of the street?" Cassie asked jokingly.

Stephanie turned toward her but stood motionless.

"I have something I need to tell you," she cried. "I tried to do it at the cabin, but I couldn't. I came here . . . I came here to tell you something."

Cassie dropped the suitcase on the sidewalk and scrambled into the street, took Stephanie's arm, and gently led her to the sidewalk. "Okay, so you have something important to say. But let's not get run over saying it, okay?"

Stephanie drummed up her resolve. "Cassie, I have lived in fear my whole life. I almost don't know how to be anything but fearful."

"I understand," said Cassie, starting to pick up Stephanie's suitcase. "Let's go in and we'll talk about it." Cassie wasn't sure what crisis was coming next and even wondered if she had the capacity to deal with another one.

"Wait," said Stephanie. "I can't go in yet. I have to say what I came here to say."

The Visit

Cassie set down the suitcase again and walked up to her, deciding to accept whatever confession or criticism Stephanie needed to get off her chest. "Stephanie, whatever you need to say, just say it. You've come a long way. You deserve that at least."

Stephanie began to cry.

Cassie felt an unusual wave of compassion come over her. She moved even closer. "What's wrong, Stephanie?"

Stephanie stood with her arms wrapped around herself and said, "I just want to tell you . . . I need to tell you that I . . . that I love you, Cassie. I really love you."

Cassie broke into tears and stammered, "You flew all the way across the country to tell me . . . to tell me you love me?"

"Yes. But also, to tell you that I need you. I need you too."

Cassie embraced her, and Stephanie responded likewise.

"I love you too, Stephie," said Cassie as she held her tightly. "I love you too."

Any unwitting bystander might have found the sight a little strange: two adult women standing on the sidewalk, surrounded by baggage, crying and embracing each other for more than five minutes. But, unbeknownst to either of them, a cab stopped at the end of the street, a mere three houses away. The driver watched them with delight. At that moment, God had begun dealing with the baggage—not the luggage sitting on the sidewalk, but the heavy weight that had been held inside their hearts.

Later that evening, Cassie and Stephanie decided they needed some ice cream. "Sometimes," said Cassie, "you simply have to take care of basic human needs." They drove to the local ice creamery and stood in line to place their orders. Stephanie had offered to buy but was embarrassed when she remembered that she had no money after giving it all to Arnie. Rather than admit her mistake, she elected to search her wallet to see if she had any forgotten money tucked away somewhere. As she opened her wallet to search, her eyes began to well up.

"It's okay," said Cassie. "It's just ice cream. I can cover it. You don't need to get upset about it."

Wiping the tears from her eyes, Stephanie was shocked to see that the new, crisp twenty-dollar bills she had given to Arnie had mysteriously returned to her wallet. Showing them to Cassie, she broke into tears again as she realized the truth; Arnie was more than a cab driver. Somehow, she already knew that.

The Package

"Wow!" said Cassie. "Forty bucks?"

"Uh-huh," stammered Stephanie, nearly speechless.

"You, sister, have some very serious feelings about ice cream," said Cassie. "I mean, if you feel so strongly about it that you're crying and willing to throw in that kind of cash, I am willing to be sympathetic. For you, I will sacrifice!"

Cassie looked across the counter at the lady waiting for her order and quipped, "I'm in for a triple dip sundae!" Stephanie could do nothing but nod her head and smirk as Cassie flinched her eyebrows up and down in a playful way and leaned across the counter to finish her order. "A triple dip with lots of hot fudge and anything else you got to stack on it," she said, laughing hysterically. "At least twenty dollars worth!"

21

THE NEXT SPRING

While Stephanie could continue to operate much of her event planning business over the phone, it was not practical to stay at the cabin full-time and still give her job the attention it deserved. Stephanie felt she needed a month away from her normal routine in New York—that's what Dad needed—so she asked Becky if she could hold down the fort for a month without her. There was significant discussion of the "whats" and "whys," but Stephanie was evasive and persistent. So Becky, as the result of much arm twisting, seeing that she really had little choice, relented. They agreed to a plan to hire a temp, using a portion of Stephanie's salary. He or she would assist Becky with the office work and pre-event staging activities. Becky would be required to do the on-site legwork with clients, and she would push as much of the phone work to Stephanie as she could.

Becky certainly could not comprehend the transformation that was happening to Stephanie. As a friend, she was worried about her, but she also fretted about what impact Stephanie's new and strange attitude would have on the business they had built together. When Becky tried to discuss it, Stephanie simply answered that this was something she "just needed to do."

How could Becky possibly understand it? thought Stephanie. *I can't even fully explain it to myself.*

The month at the cabin passed quickly though, and in mid-August, Stephanie returned to work. Becky was glad things were now getting back to normal, so much so that she took a few weeks off shortly after Stephanie returned to recover from dealing with the pressures of working the clients alone. A few weeks after Becky returned from her time away, she and Stephanie found themselves sitting in the office in one of the intermittent lulls that sprinkled into their day, and Becky's curiosity finally overcame her.

The Package

"So, what's up with you?" asked Becky.

"What do you mean?"

"You haven't actually been here since you got back."

"You don't think I'm holding up my end?"

"I didn't say that," Becky answered. "It just seems like your mind is somewhere else."

"Honestly, Becky, I feel like I have been working harder since I got back."

"You have," agreed Becky.

"Then what's the issue?"

"Never mind, Stephanie. I shouldn't have brought it up." She refocused on a stack of papers on her desk. "I need to call the Pallinis. We couldn't get the Fender House for their fiftieth anniversary party." She picked up the phone and started to dial.

"Becky, please give me some time. Something happened to me at the cabin last month. I am still working through it, though, and I still can't explain it to you. I will. I promise. Just give me some time."

Becky returned the receiver to the cradle. "What happened, did you find Jesus or something?" asked Becky.

"Something like that," said Stephanie.

"Well, I hope you get it figured out soon," said Becky. "And when you do, would you please go back to wherever it is you came from and send Stephanie back?"

"That might not be possible," said Stephanie. Becky rolled her eyes and picked the phone up again. "Just give it some time," insisted Stephanie. "Please!"

"Fine," said Becky. "Whatever."

Stephanie looked at her watch and motioned to Becky that she needed to meet a client. She pulled out a drawer, grabbed her purse, and stood to leave. Becky, who was already engaged in her telephone consultation, waved at her as she left.

A few blocks away, Stephanie walked into her favorite coffee shop, ordered a cappuccino, and slid into a corner booth with windows to the outside world all around. As she observed the hustle and bustle of hundreds of scurrying people appearing to sense nothing more important than their next appointment, she became anxious, contemplating how she could proceed with life as normal. In her time away at the cabin, she had realized that her life needed to change—that she needed to change. The Stephanie

The Next Spring

that Becky knew and loved was no longer who she desired to be. God had visited her and changed her life. She had seen an angel. *How can I explain that to Becky?* she thought. *She'll think I'm out of my mind!*

In that time, shared with a hundred nameless faces and a cappuccino, Stephanie came to understand what her father had dealt with for years. He could have chosen to drone on and on about this spiritual idea or that Scripture, and Stephanie would have rejected every last bit of it as psychobabble. Instead, he chose to wait patiently for God to do his work. He had waited for what Pastor Riddick had called "his time." For Dad, this was the month after the accident. For her, "his time" followed the Fourth of July. Stephanie realized that she would have to show the same patience with Becky that her father had shown with her. God would show her when the time was right—his time for Becky.

Over the fall months, when Stephanie could find a breather in her work, she would hop into her car and drive the six hours to the cabin to stay for a few days. She would always call Pastor Riddick and visit with him and Evelyn, and they would study the Bible together. On a trip near Christmas that year, Stephanie realized that Pastor Riddick had become more than a friend—he had become a surrogate father. He was teaching her and loving her, and his love had a breadth that was beyond his own experience. Pastor Riddick felt a passion for her that her own father had birthed within him, and that passion was personified by the pastor's nurturing spirit. It was a gift that God had given her—a chance finally to have a relationship with her dad. God had given her a surrogate father who, inside, carried her father's heart.

As the winter months brought fierce weather to Pennsylvania, Stephanie stayed in the city more and focused on her work. In her time away from work, however, when she was alone with God, her spirit was learning to discern his voice. While at the office, she would often find herself looking across the room at Becky and considering that she should possibly come clean. At those times, Stephanie would stop to pray and seek God's guidance. Each time, upon hearing it, she knew that the time was not yet right.

Every week, Stephanie called the pastor to stay in touch, and occasionally to ask a question about a particular issue or Scripture she was studying. As the winter dragged on, the calls became less frequent, and by the time April arrived, it had been nearly a month since they had talked.

The arrival of spring meant the opportunity to return to the cabin for a

The Package

visit. Easter Sunday was a little more than a week away, and in that Stephanie did not yet regularly attend a church in New York, she decided to travel to the mountains to join the church in Spring Valley, where in the fall she had become a regular visitor. Stephanie picked up the phone on a Saturday morning and called Pastor Riddick, anxious to tell him about her plans. For Stephanie, going to the cabin was like going home for Easter. In fact, it was the first time in her life that Easter really had meaning for her.

"Hello," said the voice on the phone.

"Evelyn?"

"Yes, may I ask who is calling?"

"It's Stephanie. How are you?"

"Hello, dear. I'm fine."

"I'm glad to hear it."

"I'm getting a little weary of the travel, though."

"All the travel?" asked Stephanie. "What are you talking about?"

"To the hospital in Pittsburgh," explained Evelyn. "Since they moved him, I have been going there most every day."

"The hospital? Evelyn, who is in the hospital?"

"Oh my!" she exclaimed. "I am so sorry. I thought someone had called you. Rodney is in the hospital in Pittsburgh. They moved him there last week. He has cancer."

"Cancer!" said Stephanie. "Is he going to be all right?"

"He started chemotherapy about three weeks ago," she explained, "and because of his depressed immune system, he contracted pneumonia and is struggling to breathe. They may have to put him on a respirator."

"Evelyn, how are you?" asked Stephanie. "Are you okay?"

"These things happen at our age," she answered. "It's part of life."

"Can I come?" asked Stephanie. "What if I came to the cabin for a while to help you out?"

"You sweet girl," she answered. "You have your own life to live there in New York. We'll be fine. People from the church have been a real blessing."

"My life is not my own," said Stephanie. "And I *have* no life in New York. I have a *job* here. And your church is my church, and you and Pastor are like my own family."

"You have come a long way, my dear," said Evelyn, "from the frightened woman I met here last summer."

"I have to come," said Stephanie. "It feels like the right thing to do. I'll come tonight."

The Next Spring

"Tonight?" said Evelyn. "So soon?"

"Yes. I'll be there tonight."

"My dear, I'll be at the hospital tonight. Perhaps I'll see you at church in the morning."

"How will you get there?" asked Stephanie.

"Sadie is taking me today," she replied. "We're leaving at noon."

"I'll be at the hospital by six o'clock. Tell Sadie she should feel free to go back to her home. I'll drive you home. Is that okay?"

"I'm sure Sadie would appreciate that," said Evelyn. "Are you sure? I don't want to inconvenience you."

"I'll see you there in about eight hours. Good-bye, Evelyn."

"Good-bye, Stephanie."

"And Evelyn—I'll be praying."

"Thank you, dear. Good-bye."

As she hung up, Stephanie thought of how she admired Evelyn's class. Even in her own personal tragedy, she handled herself with dignity and decorum.

Stephanie dialed Becky. "Listen, Becky, I know you're not going to understand this, but I need to go to the cabin for about a week or so."

"Not this again," Becky answered.

"Look, it's important. A close friend of mine is in the hospital, and I need to go there to help out."

"Who is it?" asked Becky.

"It's the pastor of my church there," she replied.

"Wait a minute," said Becky. "The pastor of the church is a good friend of yours? Are you like, having an affair with him or something? Is that what this is about?"

"Don't be ridiculous," said Stephanie. "Get your mind out of the gutter."

"Hey, I've seen you do worse than that!" retorted Becky. Stephanie had to admit that Becky was correct. But that was before, and this was now.

"This pastor, along with his lovely wife, Evelyn, helped me get my life back together," said Stephanie. "After that weekend with my sisters last July, I was a total mess. But God did something inside of me. This pastor and his wife have been like parents to me since then."

"Wow, you really did find Jesus, didn't you?" asked Becky.

"Yes, Becky, I did. And that's why I'm different. That's why I don't go to parties with you anymore. It's why I make so many trips back to the cabin. It's real, it's important, and I need to go."

193

The Package

"Okay, go!" said Becky. "I can cover for a week. But we need to talk about this. I can't be covering for you every time you get a whim to leave town."

"I understand," said Stephanie. "Maybe we need to discuss some other arrangement. But later, please!"

"Okay," she replied. "And maybe we need to talk about this Jesus thing later too."

"In his time, we'll do that," she answered.

"In what time? What are you talking about?"

"Do you pray, Becky?"

"Sometimes," she answered.

"Well, I have a dear friend in the hospital, and he needs our prayers. Please pray for him. And when I get back, if you want to know more, I'll talk to you about it." Becky didn't answer. "Are you still there Becky?" she asked.

"Yes, I'm here. I've never seen you like this, Stephanie."

"You've never seen me like this because I've never been like this, Becky. When I get back, I'll share the reason why."

"Okay, fair," said Becky. "Be careful. See you when you get back."

"Good-bye," said Stephanie as she hung up the phone.

Stephanie quickly stuffed clothes into her bags and hurried to her car. She considered how this crisis had opened the door for her to discuss Christ with Becky, similar to the way a crisis had opened her to the truth and likewise for her Dad. She realized how God often uses crises to draw people to him. She wondered how God would use this crisis, the one happening right now in Pittsburgh. Would he use it to help a son, a daughter, a neighbor, a church member? Her discussion with Becky popped into her mind and her spirit declared the truth.

God has already begun.

22

FINAL NOTES

Stephanie and Becky worked out a leave of absence for Stephanie beginning in early May. They together decided to cut the number of events they bid on, Stephanie gave up most of her salary, and they rehired the temporary. Stephanie continued to work the phones from the cabin part-time, but she had promised to return to full-time work in New York in the fall. Thanks to her father's trust, the cabin's expenses were covered. So, for this one last summer, Stephanie decided to stay at the cabin, knowing that she needed the time with God and desiring to be near the pastor and Evelyn.

Pastor Riddick survived his April hospital stay and returned home, but as the month of May waned, his condition began weakening. Most every day, Stephanie spent time at their house helping Evelyn cook, clean, and take care of the pastor. On one memorable day, she found herself outside with a hammer and nails trying to reattach a shutter that had come loose. She laughed as she imagined how the sight might look to a camera; certainly, no one in New York would believe it.

Throughout this time, Stephanie kept in touch with her sisters and advised them as the pastor's condition progressed. In mid-June, Pastor Riddick took a severe turn for the worse, and early in the morning on the 20th of June, he went home to be with the Lord.

For Stephanie, the pain and remorse that accompanied the pastor's death exceeded that of her own father. Not because she loved the pastor more, but because of his link to her father and the transformation she had experienced in her own life. Stephanie's spirit was now alive, and she experienced the reality of her father's love through this man. He had enabled her to seek the forgiveness that had nearly escaped her grasp, as though her father had encapsulated his forgiveness inside the pastor so that, like a needed medicine, it could be administered to ease her pain.

It was Stephanie's belief that Pastor Riddick had been entrusted with

The Package

the package they received on that Fourth of July weekend. While she had never managed to pry the truth from him, he was never able to deny it. Knowing he was bound by his honesty, she drew her inevitable conclusion. As such, she surmised, he would be forever linked to her—and her family.

Stephanie phoned her sisters and told them about the planned memorial service. Cassie and Anna had both observed the change in Stephanie since their time together at the cabin, and they understood the role that the pastor had played in that transformation. Therefore, when she asked them to come to be with her, to come to the service, and to spend another weekend together at the cabin, they both gladly complied. Stephanie was not surprised, because their relationships with each other had changed as their individual relationships with God had changed. It was as though everything was new.

The night before the memorial service, Cassie and Anna arrived and spent the evening with Stephanie at the cabin, and they told each other of their experiences over the last year. They each talked of the package and how it had changed their lives for the better. When they received their gifts and letters, each of them realized how much their father truly loved them. But they had each independently discovered its true significance—it pointed them toward the only true answer for their lives, a relationship with Jesus Christ.

The entire mood of the evening differed from that of the previous year. Cassie was dating a doctor she met at a new church she was attending. Their relationship was based on faith, and Cassie had changed in ways Stephanie couldn't have imagined possible. She was compassionate and kind, and the biting tone that had been characteristic of the prior visit was absent. Occasionally, Stephanie would catch her unnecessarily apologizing for something or the other. It was residue of the foundation upon which she had built years of guilt and failure. But the guilt was waning, and Stephanie could discern the change in Cassie's spirit.

Even though Anna was already close to God, she was growing too. Much of her growth came from learning to let God be God. Most of her life, she had attempted to protect everyone from everything. The control she exhibited sometimes stood in God's way, hampering God from accomplishing what he intended. Anna was learning to let go, and Stephanie could see that she was feeling more relaxed on this outing than the last, enjoying her sisters without needing to be a referee. God had a plan of his own, and this time, it involved peace and reconciliation.

Final Notes

The next afternoon, they attended the memorial service together, and at one point in the service, to Cassie and Anna's great surprise, Stephanie stood and walked to the podium to speak. During the last few months, Evelyn and Stephanie had become very close, and Evelyn had asked Stephanie if she wanted to say a few words at the service—and she did.

"My name is Stephanie Mullins. I am here today to share with you the impact that Pastor Riddick had on my life. He was my friend, but more importantly, he was a friend of my father's.

"Twenty-five years ago, my sisters and I lost our mother in a horrible car accident. That accident, while it killed my mother, nearly destroyed four more lives. My strong father became weak. My sister Cassie allowed guilt and shame to creep into her life. As a consequence of circumstances following the accident, I was angry and unforgiving. And my sister Anna was suffering from trying to make everything be fine for everyone, even when it wasn't.

"God used Pastor Riddick to save my father. After the accident, my father spent many hours with him seeking answers to his questions. In that chaos, Pastor Riddick helped my father to find a relationship with Christ that overcame his intense grief and helped him find peace. Through this kind pastor's words, my father found his faith during that time in his life— a time when his relationship with Christ became deep and real, far beyond a name on the wall of a church he attended.

"My father died last year. But before he died, he made my sisters and I promise to come to his cabin, which is near here, to spend a weekend together. Our relationships with each other were strained, and our relationships with God were, at least in my case, nonexistent. To this day, I believe that my father told Pastor Riddick we would be there, because he watched over the three of us and helped us through the weekend as God gave him the wisdom and guidance to do it.

"He spoke with Cassie, and told her she needed to understand God's grace and leave her guilt at the cross. He told her it was time for her to find her faith as my father did. He said that those days at the cabin were 'his time,' the time God had chosen to speak into our lives. And Cassie has not been the same since. It was 'his time.'

"Then came the true miracle—at least for me. God used Pastor Riddick to save me. A year ago, I came to Dad's cabin with no need for God. By the time I left a month later, Pastor Riddick had shown me the

The Package

greatest gift I now possess. He led me to Christ. He taught me how to have a relationship with God, how to forgive others, and how to understand difficult questions like why bad things happen to good people.

"Since I first met Pastor Riddick and Evelyn last year, they have become as parents to me. Pastor Riddick listened to the heart of my father and understood his love for his daughters. That enabled him to exhibit the love of my father to me every time I spoke to him. He had the heart of God for everyone who was suffering; but for me, he also had the heart of my father.

"There were many things I was not able to say to my father; many things I regretted not saying. I needed forgiveness to move forward, and I could no longer ask him for it. But Pastor Riddick, having my father's heart, was able to hear my regret, cry with me, and provide the forgiveness I so desperately needed.

"If he were here today, he would tell you no one is good, not one of us. It is only by the grace of God we can even do anything good. He would tell you we all deserve punishment for our sins, and each breath of life we are given is a gift from a loving, benevolent God. He would tell you his disease might be the result of our sinful nature, but that God would turn its tragedy into His glory.

"However, this day is not about my father, my sisters, or the trials we have suffered. You did not come to this place to celebrate the new life that has blossomed in my family. We are here to celebrate the life of one who has left us. I relate this story as a representative of many. I speak on behalf of many of you:

Those who have shared together in his benevolence;
Those who felt elation because of his joyfulness;
Those who found a gentle strength in his meekness;
Those in conflict who discovered his tranquility;
Those who struggled, his perseverance;
Those who were broken, his encouragement;
Those needing truth, his sincerity;
Those seeking character, his restraint;
Those who were guilty, his forgiveness;
And, most importantly, those who needed Christ,
for his personal introduction.

"'The fruit of the Spirit,' says Galatians 5:22 and 23, 'is love, joy, peace, patience, kindness, goodness, faithfulness, gentleness, and self-control.' Verse 25 says that since we live by the Spirit, let us keep in step with the Spirit.'

"To God be the glory, now and forevermore, and for his servants, who by their very lives perform his service. We are forever grateful. Amen."

Stephanie returned to her pew next to her sisters. If Cassie and Anna had any residual doubt about the change in Stephanie, that doubt had now been eradicated. Stephanie was indeed a new person, a new creation, for God had performed a miracle inside of her.

The service ended, and Evelyn invited them all to join the family at her house for a dinner provided by the church; they decided to accept. At the dinner, Evelyn was being the perfect hostess—Stephanie had learned to expect no less. As she and her sisters were beginning to discuss returning to the cabin, Evelyn took a short break from her activity to visit with them for a few minutes.

"Stephanie," said Evelyn, "your words were positively beautiful, and they were delivered with such poise and grace. Bless you for your kindness."

"Evelyn," replied Stephanie, "it is so easy to speak the truth and to ascribe beauty to one who has exhibited it."

"You have become such a beautiful woman, Stephanie. God has uncovered your inner beauty."

"Thank you, Evelyn," she replied. "You are too kind."

"Will you all be at the cabin in the morning?" asked Evelyn.

"Yes, we will. Why?"

"I have something to give you," said Evelyn. "I'll come by about nine if that's okay."

"How will you get there?" asked Stephanie. "Should we come here instead?"

"No, I can still drive the car a short distance," she insisted, "and I will look forward to seeing each of you in the morning." Evelyn gave them a gracious nod of her head and gently backed away and moved to greet other guests.

As they watched her walk away, Cassie leaned over to Stephanie and asked, "What do you suppose that's all about?"

"I don't know," answered Stephanie. "She loves to bake. Perhaps she made us some cookies or a pie or something."

The Package

"I guess we'll find out tomorrow," said Cassie. "Ready to leave?"

"I'm ready," said Stephanie. "Anna?"

"Yep, ready," she replied.

The girls walked to the car and took the short ride back to the cabin.

The next morning, Stephanie and her sisters completed breakfast, cleaned up, and were sitting in the cabin's living room chatting and waiting for Evelyn's arrival. Several minutes before nine, a car rolled up into the driveway. Stephanie looked out the window to verify her arrival and saw that one of Evelyn's family members had driven her to the cabin. Evelyn got out of the car and walked to the door, carrying nothing but her purse, and Cassie met her and invited her in. Evelyn entered the room, looked around, and smiled.

"I haven't been here for several years," she said. "It's good to be here again. I have many fond memories of this place."

Everyone stood motionless for a few moments and Stephanie, realizing that Evelyn's sense of etiquette would not allow her to sit without an invitation, quickly obliged and corrected her blunder.

"Would you like to sit down, Evelyn?" asked Stephanie.

"Thank you," she answered as she moved toward the sofa. "I am much obliged."

As Evelyn took her seat, each of the girls did likewise. "I see you are all here," she said. "All three of you."

"Yes, we are," said Cassie. "And you and your husband have done so much for our family. How can we ever thank you?"

"You have no need to thank me, sweetheart," said Evelyn. "But I am glad you are all here together."

"Why do you keep saying that?" asked Stephanie. "Why do you keep talking about us all being here?"

"Because I have something for the three of you," said Evelyn, smiling. She reached into her purse and pulled out an envelope, which she ceremoniously placed on the coffee table in front of her, brushed it off, and straightened it. "This is for you," she said. "It's for the three of you." Without further adieu, Evelyn closed her purse and stood up, saying, "I have accomplished my task here. I should go."

"You don't need to leave, Evelyn," said Stephanie. "Would you like some coffee?"

"My brother is waiting for me in the car" she said. "Enjoy, ladies," she said, smiling. Cassie, Stephanie, and Anna walked onto the porch and successively gave Evelyn a hug and said good-bye. Again, she smiled and gently said, "Enjoy," and walked back to her car and was soon on her way. The girls all waved as she left.

As they walked back into the cabin, the discussion turned to the envelope that Evelyn had set on the table.

"What do you suppose that was all about?" asked Anna.

"She probably bought Stephanie a gift certificate or something for speaking at the funeral," said Cassie.

They all returned to their seats, and Stephanie picked up the envelope.

"It has all our names on it," said Stephanie. "It's for all of us."

"Well, open it up," said Anna.

Stephanie tore open the envelope. Inside it was a card, and another sealed envelope that simply said "To My Daughters." Stephanie handed the unopened envelope to Cassie saying, "Look at this."

"What's the card say?" asked Anna.

"It's from Pastor Riddick," said Stephanie, glancing inside.

"Read it out loud," said Anna. Stephanie again opened up the card and began reading:

Dear Stephanie, Anna, and Cassie,

Before your father died, he made each of you promise to come to this cabin for one last weekend together. What you have all suspected, but I had promised to conceal until today, is that he indeed gave me the package that he prepared for you and asked me to mail it when you arrived. I kept each of those promises.

But, beneath your suspicion, I also made another promise to your father. He told me that he believed that you would each fulfill your promise to come to the cabin that first weekend. Here was the third promise he asked of me. He said, "If all three of them, of their own volition, return to the cabin together again, please give them the enclosed letter." Since it is clear that my illness will keep me from delivering it personally in that circumstance, I have given this note and similar instructions to Evelyn so I may dispatch my final promise to your father.

May it be a blessing to your souls!
Your pastor and friend,
Rodney

"You have got to be kidding me," said Cassie, examining the envelope in her hand.

"Dad really thought this out, didn't he?" asked Anna.

The Package

"You have an uncanny knack for understatement," said Cassie.

"Go ahead, Cassie," said Stephanie. "Open it."

At her urging, Cassie began to open it but then hesitated and said, "If it weren't for you, Stephanie, we probably wouldn't be here to read this. You brought us here. You made all this happen. You should open it."

"Cassie, I didn't make anything happen," said Stephanie. "Don't you see? This is God's plan. And I think he is taking delight in watching us walk through it."

Cassie stretched her hand toward Stephanie to pass her the envelope. "Okay," she replied. "I understand what you're saying—this envelope belongs to all of us. But you've earned the privilege of opening it and reading it. Please."

Stephanie smiled and took the envelope from Cassie, opened it, and removed a card from inside. She unfolded it and began reading. Cassie and Anna both sat back in their chairs with their eyes closed.

Dear Cassie, Stephanie, and Anna,

If you are reading this, then you are again sitting together at the cabin. I believe in my heart you will read it, because I believe God will speak to you on your first visit here, and that hearing his voice will cause you to return here again. I have prayed that he would speak to you, and I believe he will.

Your mother taught me a great lesson—patience. She waited for four years to marry me while I was in the service. What if she had not waited? Secondly, she secretly saved for five years to fulfill my dream of a cabin in the woods—this cabin. I could, of course, loathe that decision because it led to my greatest personal tragedy, for it was here that your mother left us. However, after that tragedy, as is so often the case, God used this very same place to provide an opportunity for me to find my faith.

Having learned that lesson, I put it to practice when I sent you the package on your first visit. I prayed over each gift and each word I wrote to you. It is my hope and prayer that, by my patience, you were moved toward Christ. Without that outcome, my patience would have resulted in nothing more than an interesting but pointless story.

As you are reading this note, each of you has returned to this place once again. I recognize that this unity would not be possible apart from a transformation in your hearts, and I know that only Christ could be the source of these kinds of changes. Therefore, as your presence here demonstrates, and as was the case with your mother, patience has prevailed. God, in his time, has caused each of you to

202

Final Notes

seek him; and within each of you, he has indeed been found.

Rest in the assurance of his love, nurture the love you have discovered for one another, and finally, continue to find his peace in your own hearts.

Strive toward perfection in Christ. Overcome your guilt, overcome your anger, and overcome your will with his love.

I love you all, and I go before you in peace,
Dad

For the rest of the day, Cassie, Stephanie, and Anna talked and laughed together. When they received the package last summer, it was to ease the pain of their wounds. The letter they received today was a blessing. This final note helped them further understand their father. It told them how the package came to be and why he sent it. It set forth his desires for their lives and encouraged them to persist in the journey they had each begun. With the package, he sent three individual messages of hope; with this final note, he collectively sealed it inside them.

That evening, Stephanie suggested they should sell the cabin in the fall. The trust was running out, and Dad had accomplished what was intended. Stephanie had grown to love the place, but it was time to move on—time to find her own cabin—and time to establish her own legacy.

With that in mind, Stephanie shared with her sisters an intention to write a book documenting the story of their family, the trials they faced, and how God, in his time and in this place provided grace. Their father had left them hope wrapped in a brown package. Stephanie wanted this story to be known by anyone who needed to hear its message. She proposed to write it down. Cassie and Anna were excited about the idea and enthusiastically agreed to help fill in any personal details that were outside Stephanie's experience.

With the decision to sell the cabin behind them, they knew the fall would bring an end to this unique phase of their lives. Instead of a sad ending, though, it felt like a joyous beginning for each of them, both as individuals and sisters. Each promised the other to keep their relationships alive and vital; and also that in each year, on the Fourth of July, they would gather together again at some place or another, to celebrate and remember—remember their past without regret and celebrate their future with hope.

EPILOGUE

The deed to the Mullins' cabin had been transferred, and Stephanie's departure day had arrived. Still sitting on the front porch of the cabin in her favorite rocker, wrapped snugly in her blanket, Stephanie again opened her eyes, put her pen to paper, and continued to write. The celebration of the creation that surrounded her, the promise of the day, and the miracle of her changed life provided inspiration, and she quickly finished the letter she was writing with surprising ease. She set her pen down on the table and read the letter aloud to make sure it said what she wanted to say. Stephanie then placed it in an envelope and penned the name of its recipients on the outside. Again picking up her coffee mug, she took a sip, only to find it had cooled considerably. With that, she downed it quickly with one long swallow and then grimaced at the taste. It simply wasn't the same when it was cold.

She stood up, picked up and placed the blanket over the arm holding her coffee cup, gathering her books and stationery in the other hand. Fortunately, since her hands were occupied, she had left the door ajar. This allowed her to push it with her elbow and pop it open. While she enjoyed her morning visit outside on the porch, the warmth inside the cabin shocked her cool skin and made her shiver. Setting her books and stationery on the counter and placing her coffee mug in the sink, she headed for a hot shower.

A few short minutes later, Stephanie emerged from her bedroom with a backpack. Once in the kitchen, she slid it from her shoulder and set it on the counter. From the refrigerator, she successively retrieved and packed away two sandwiches she had prepared, some string cheese, a diet soda, and several bottles of water. To finish her pack, she added a camera, some binoculars, a comfortable cotton blanket, and some potato chips in a plastic bag.

Stephanie sat down on the sofa and pulled on her hiking shoes. As she laced them up, she chuckled, visualizing the reaction of her New York friends seeing her in these shoes. It simply did not fit her persona—at least as she was before. But, she reasoned, that person no longer existed.

Epilogue

As she stood up and threw the pack over her shoulder and walked towards the door, she stopped abruptly and turned back toward the counter, realizing she had forgotten one key item she needed for this trek. Her hand reached out, hooked her fingers on the binding of the new book, and slid it off into her other hand as she walked away. She slid the backpack off her shoulder to the floor near the door, placed the book inside, and zipped it closed with a flip of her wrist. With that, she threw it back onto her shoulder and exited out the door.

Stephanie had taken this same hike repeatedly over the last year, but today in particular, she recalled the time she had walked it with Anna on that life changing weekend, the weekend they had received the package. Much had happened that day. It was the day she finally admitted her shame, the day she acknowledged her anger, and the day Anna helped her begin to work through it.

Yes, Anna had walked with her on this same path. Considering the length of the walk that day, much more could have been said. But Anna possessed the wisdom to listen, making the words she spoke resound with meaning and purpose. In the midst of the excruciating clamor and chaos of that day, something had emerged in retrospect; with truth now revealed, it was actually a good day.

Stephanie followed the path down Creek Road into Ash Grove and finally across Pine Hill. When she arrived at the edge of the Upper Meadow about an hour later, she searched about the ground and found, as she hoped, a pine cone. As she picked it up, she heard a thunk-thunk-thunk sound in the trees above her head, and looking up, saw a red-bellied woodpecker rapping his bill on a dead ash tree. Little joys like this had escaped Stephanie's notice for most of her life, but everything in nature had come alive for Stephanie. As she looked at the pine cone in her hand, a smile crossed her face. Creation itself spoke to her of the glory of her God.

When she arrived at Pinnacle Ridge, she set her pack down about ten feet from the drop-off and eased forward to gaze over the edge at the large pine trees at the bottom. The evidence of things wished for still stood grandly like sentinels at their duty. And, like protectors of all things noble, they displayed hope within the tops of their boughs—in an array of pine cones.

Backing away from the edge, she closed her eyes and hurled her pine cone into the void beyond the edge. She popped her eyes open and rushed to the edge to watch it waft on the wind and vanish into the trees below.

The Package

No wish was necessary for this toss, however. Stephanie had learned that faith is not rooted in our own wishes and desires, but if it were, she already been given more than she could have wished for.

Unzipping her backpack, she withdrew the blanket, and with the whip of her hands unfurled it across a portion of the rock. She pulled the sides of her pack open and removed her water bottle and the book. She sat down on her blanket with the book in her hand, opened the bottle, took a drink, and spun the lid back onto it.

Stephanie then examined the book she held in her hands, skimming her fingers across its cover with pride considering her accomplishment. "The Package," she read aloud, "by Stephanie Mullins." She smiled with satisfaction as she laid the book on her crossed legs, opened its cover, and turned to the dedication page. It read:

To my mother,
Whom God longed for and called home;
To my sister Cassie,
A precious jewel I nearly lost;
To my sister Anna,
Who believes wishes can come true;
To my Father,
Whose love and hope for me was the inspiration for this book;
And to My Lord and Savior Jesus Christ,
without whom there could be no hope.

As if with purpose, a gust flipped several pages leaving the first page of chapter one before her. She began reading, but had only read a few pages when she heard a whip-o-will in the distant trees of Pine Hill behind her. *All creation!* she thought.

For most of the day, Stephanie read her novel, pausing here and there to have lunch, listen to a singing bird, watch a soaring eagle through her binoculars, or simply take a drink of water. As the afternoon waned, Stephanie finished reading the last page of her first book. She closed it gently and looked out across the expansive valley in front of her with tears in her eyes. *Today is the day*, she thought, meaning the day she would put her past behind her. Not that the pain would be forgotten. In fact, that was why she had written it down. It was never to be forgotten.

Last night's storm had left Stephanie in total peace for the first time

Epilogue

since her mother died. There had been a change inside her spirit. The walls that were her life were not simply covered over with a fresh coat of paint. No, painting over it would simply leave behind a wall that was, itself, unchanged. In fact, in a radical reconstruction, God had torn down the walls inside her and replaced them with new ones. She was a new creation.

In that one summer weekend with her sisters, Stephanie had begun a journey—a long journey—that takes an entire lifetime. But this day was a milestone on that journey. Over time, with God's help, she had unlocked the doors and exorcized the pain imprisoned inside her, and in doing so, set her free. By writing her story down, she intended to leave behind a milestone marker for others who would follow. To her, this monument would serve as a reminder of the grace of God. To others, it would be a guidepost on the journey to hope. Like her father's gift to Anna, she prayed that her journal might provide direction to someone who was lost—that somehow that person might find assurance on a path that others had walked before.

Yes, the pain was now behind her. And before her? Stephanie smiled, tapped her finger on the cover of the book, and looked heavenward. "Hope lies ahead," she said.

Indeed, the storm *was* finally over.

The deadbolt lock slid open with a thud, and the door opened to a new era. Aaron and Deanna Carter and their two children, Alex and Maria, were arriving for their first weekend at their new cabin. Alex, who was six, settled in quickly by chasing his two-year-old sister Maria down the hall toward the bedrooms. After driving for more than an hour to get there, Aaron and Deanna took a short break on the sofa before unloading the car.

As they rested, Aaron glanced over at his wife and smiled. This was a big day for her. She had practically begged him to buy this place. While Aaron was a successful stockbroker, this purchase was possible because of a sum of money willed to him by a rather wealthy aunt. Initially, he had considered doing some investing or perhaps buying a rental property. However, Deanna had come to this cabin with a friend who was in the market, and she immediately fell in love. It was several weeks before her friend told her that she had decided to pass on buying it, and several minutes before Deanna called her husband at work to tell him the news.

"Aaron, Cindy isn't going to buy the cabin after all. Can we go look at it this weekend? I am sure you'll love it as much as I do. It's a gorgeous place!" While Aaron complied, he was not really enamored by the cabin. He was, however, most certainly enamored by Deanna, and that was beauty enough. So with that, the Carter's had become the new owners of the cabin. Aaron reached across the sofa to take his wife's hand.

"So," he asked, "are you happy?"

She leapt toward him and pressed her lips against his, giving him a very long kiss while she tickled him and giggled. They were both unaware that Alex had walked back into the room.

"Yuck," said Alex. "Cut it out. Gees."

Deanna backed away from Aaron and they had a sheepish laugh together. Aaron grabbed his son and sat him on his lap.

"How about you, tiger? You like it here?"

"Uh-huh," he said as he laid his head back on his father's chest. His father's lap was a very comfortable place to be.

Deanna stood up from the sofa to check on Maria. A short moment before she rounded the corner, down the hall she heard the rapid thump-thump-thump of little two-year-old feet rumbling toward her. As Maria flew around the corner, Deanna swept her up in her arms. "Gotcha," she said as Maria giggled and laughed with delight and begged her to do it again. As Deanna was playfully kissing all over her daughter's cheek, she noticed something sitting on the kitchen counter. She secured Maria in her arms and walked toward it. As she moved closer, she looked back at Aaron and said, "It looks like someone left us a gift."

Aaron stood and joined his wife at the counter. Upon it was a small present wrapped in brown paper with a card attached. The handwriting on the card simply read "The Carters." Deanna picked up the note to open it, with Maria still in her arms. Alex climbed up on one of the counter stools and saw the present.

"Can I open it?" he asked excitedly.

"You sure can," said Dad. "Go for it!"

Alex tore the paper away to reveal a book. Aaron took the book from his son and turned it over. The title read, *The Package*. Deanna finished opening the card, and since she was engaged in wrestling with a fidgety Maria, she handed it to Aaron to read. He read the note aloud.

Dear Mr. and Mrs. Carter,

Welcome to your new cabin. There is something, however, that you should know—miracles happen here. Not just water-into-wine type miracles, but those that are indeed the most miraculous of all. God speaks to people here and that

Epilogue

changes their lives forever. You see, he transforms them into new creations. My family has experienced many such miracles in this place, and the book I am leaving you is my family's story of our experiences in this cabin. I am giving you the first published copy.

I pray this book will show you that owning a little piece of heaven is about far more than possessing the deed to a secluded place in a beautiful earthly setting. It is truly about owning a piece of heaven itself, with the mortgage bought and paid for by the blood of our blessed Lord and Savior Jesus Christ.

If you do not understand these words, then I pray you will read this book and listen for his voice. I believe he will speak to you.

Yes, miracles do happen here. I know. I am one.

In His Love,

Stephanie Mullins

Darren and Deanna looked at each other and at the book. Alex, who had heard only the part about the miracles, became wide-eyed, considering the possibilities.

"Wow! he cried. "How cool is that!"

At that very moment, Stephanie was driving toward Pittsburgh in her open convertible with her long hair blowing in the wind. She had decided to take the long way home—a path that would take her along Route 8— past the point of heartache and on to the place of hope. It would take her through Hope, Pennsylvania.

"Hope lies ahead," shouted Stephanie heavenward, smiling in acknowledgment of the deep meaning of those words. Again, she whispered to herself, "Hope lies ahead."

Resources

If you have been touched by the message of hope offered by this story, it is our prayer that you will share this experience with others, and consider sending the book as a gift to fathers, sisters, pastors, mentors, and friends.

If this story has caused you to evaluate issues in your own life, whether they relate to your relationship with God, your family, or you have been emotionally or sexually abused and need to seek help, the author recommends the following resources:

Recommended Reading
God's Crippled Children, by Lana Bateman.
Door of Hope: Recognizing and Resolving the Pains of Your Past, by Jan Frank.
Love Me Never Leave Me, by Marilyn Meberg.
Staying Together When an Affair Pulls You Apart, by Dr. Stephen Judah.

Phillipian Ministries (www.phillipian.org)
1002 Weeson, Forney, TX 75126, 972-552-1097

The main goal of this ministry is to lead each of those sent to them by our Lord to a time of intercessory prayer. This prayer is designed to break the chains of the past, with the debilitating hurts and memories, and open the door to the emotional stability and freedom which has been promised by God to each of his children.

CrossTV (www.crosstv.com)
370 West Camino Gardens Blvd. Suite 300, Boca Raton, FL 33432, 877-CROSSTV

CrossTV is a Christian television production ministry that creates a unique programming series called Word Pictures. These programs are designed to address the most vital, life-changing, soul-shaking biblical subjects in a compelling video format.

Note from the author: This web site contains an excellent compilation of recommend reading and the "Word Pictures" series of videos is highly recommended.

The Package Web Site

If you would like to review additional resources,
then please visit www.thepackagebook.com.

At this site, you can also get additional information about the story, read a biography of the author, or contact him. You may also share your feelings about *The Package,* and read what others are saying about how the story has spoken to them.

The story of *The Package* began as a play and, at the time of publishing, is still being performed by Christian Art Players near Cincinnati, OH. Christian Art Players is a traveling troupe, and takes the production to churches and community venues in and around the Cincinnati area. Information on performance schedules and booking information can be found at www.christianartplayers.org.

At some point in the future, the script for the play will be made available at www.thepackagebook.com for production by other companies and church groups across the country. For specific information regarding the availability of this script, contact the author directly through the website.

ABOUT THE AUTHOR

Glenn Crabtree and his wife, Jenny, live near Cincinnati, Ohio, and have six children and nine grandchildren. In 1993, he co-founded the Christian Art Players, a faith-based community theater company where he has been a Producer, Director, Technical Director, and Actor in more than twenty different productions.

Glenn is also a singer/songwriter, has worked in Christian radio as a producer and announcer, and held leadership positions in local churches including Drama Director and Worship Leader. An aerospace engineer by trade, his unique combination of practical and artistic skills provide theater productions that are technical, artistic, and thought provoking.

Printed in the United States
127591LV00002B/1-132/P